In Too Deep

Bea Davenport

Legend Press Ltd, 107-111 Fleet Street, London, EC4A 2AB
info@legend-paperbooks.co.uk | www.legendpress.co.uk

Contents © Bea Davenport 2013
The right of the above author to be identified as the author of this work has
been asserted in accordance with the Copyright, Designs and Patents Act
1988. British Library Cataloguing in Publication Data available.

Print ISBN 978-1-78719806-7
Ebook ISBN 978-1-78719805-0
Set in Times. Printing managed by Jellyfish Solutions Ltd
Cover design by Anna Green | www.siulendesign.com

First published in 2013 by Legend Press

Bea Davenport is the writing name of former newspaper and BBC journalist Barbara Henderson. Shortlisted for a Luke Bitmead Award, *In Too Deep* was her first novel, first published in 2013 by Legend Press. It was followed in 2014 with another adult crime novel, *This Little Piggy*.

Bea also writes for children and teens. Her children's novel *The Serpent House* was written as part of her Creative Writing PhD. It was shortlisted for a *Times*/Chicken House award before being published by Curious Fox in 2014. Her other novels for younger readers are *My Cousin Faustina* (2015) and *The Misper* (2018). Bea teaches journalism and creative writing. She lives in Berwick upon Tweed with her partner and family.

For Mark, Naomi, Patrick and Mary

Chapter One

Two paramedics are lifting the body of a young woman out of a large, wooden tank of water and carrying her, quickly and with surprising smoothness, across the market square to their ambulance. I am watching them through the dusty window of the office, my hand across my mouth in case I vomit, my back to the wall and my head turned to the side. The window is so small I can't see what happens next. But what I do know is that Kim is dead. And I know this, too, that I helped to kill her. Kim, my lovely, only, best friend.

This memory is five years old. So is the photo of Kim in today's newspaper. I am staring fixedly at the page. I have, as they say, seen a ghost. The newspaper's computer has touched up Kim's face so she has unnaturally dark eyebrows and outlined lips. But, as Kim might have said, not bad for five years dead. When the photo was taken, she was just twenty-seven years old and beautiful. And I was Maura.

I say I was Maura, because I haven't answered to that name for a long time. After her death, I ran away and became another person. It worked. Or I thought it did. I convinced myself I'd become invisible. I should've known it wasn't really possible. I thought I'd done a pretty good disappearing act. It's surprisingly easy to do the thin-air thing, if you really want to. Five years ago I was Maura Wood. A bit plain, a bit non-descript. I'm still ordinary; my hair is mousy blonde, not mousy brown. I wear glasses in public, glasses I don't really need. And of course I use a different name. But you'd never spot me in a crowd.

So how has Kim found me and managed to haunt me, after all this? The newspaper says there are plans to revive Dowerby Fair. It was cancelled after Kim's death. A respectable five-year period has elapsed, or I guess that's how they're looking at it. After a little time, it no longer seems callous to celebrate an event where, once, someone tragically died.

It's easy to find Dowerby, and lots of tourists do, every summer. Dowerby, like every other little market town in England, has its castle, its haunted pub and its gift shops. It seemed to me that everyone I ever met had been there at some point in their lives, usually as a child. They would say: 'There used to be a tea shop on the corner – oh, but I'm talking about fifteen or twenty years ago.' And I would reply: 'It's still there.' 'And a clock tower, with a funny sounding chime?' 'Still there, still sounding tinny.' And they'd be delighted and launch into misty-eyed stories about their childhood holidays. When Kim died, the place was full of reporters and photographers from London, Manchester, even one from America. It was amazing how many of them found they'd been there before.

To get to Dowerby, you come off the trunk road they still call the new road, and it's very well signposted for such a little place. When you've driven in a straight line for miles, probably stuck behind a tractor or two, it's very tempting to turn off, following the big brown road sign with its storybook pictures of the castle, the bed and the teacup.

But I'm telling you, up close, Dowerby is a huge disappointment. The service in the tea rooms is always sullen and the cakes are always dry. The ghost in the haunted pub hasn't actually been seen since 1862. The castle is remarkably well-preserved, but that's because it's still lived in, so you have to pay £9.50 for a ticket only to come across a large TV squatting in the grand Regency lounge. Everyone laughs at that.

When I first went to live in Dowerby, I was always being taken for a tourist. And in a way, I was, because you don't qualify as local here until you're about fourth or fifth generation. I wasn't very good at making small talk and getting to know people. It was my husband, Nick, who was the talker. Nick brought us to live there, because it was where he'd grown up, although his parents had since moved abroad. Some old friend of Nick's dad had got him a job at the local pharmaceuticals factory, and it seemed that within a few weeks of moving in, Nick was a member of the rotary club and on every social committee. He sort of forced people to make us welcome. If it had been left to me, Nick complained, we would never speak to anyone for years. I'm just like that. Closed. It's been a useful trait, recently.

Funny, looking back, that Nick and I ever got it together in the first place. We were so very different. But it made sense at the time and I was really happy, at first. Totally in love. We had a little girl, Rosie, who was just a year old when we first came to Dowerby. She was a naturally undemanding, good child and I spent my days decorating the cottagey house we'd bought, reading, walking, listening to the radio, feeling blissful. Nick made me laugh and we made love every week. Ordinary, you see.

I didn't really want anything else, not even friends of my own. I thought I didn't need any. It was quite enough for me when, eventually, people started to nod at me in the street. I didn't even mind not working, which seems strange to me now, even though I've only reached the dizzy heights of bar and waitressing jobs. It still means I don't have to ask anyone else for money. And there's only me to spend it on. Not exactly Businesswoman of the Year, but good enough for me. It's so hard to remember that once, I lived off Nick's wages and it didn't feel old-fashioned or demeaning. It would now. The new me.

We'd lived there for about two years when Kim arrived. She was the new district reporter for the regional evening paper. Nick knew all about her before she came. He'd joined the Dowerby Fair committee, where there'd been mutterings that there was no local reporter to get them a bit of publicity. The post had been vacant for a few months after the last reporter retired. Nick took it upon himself to write to the editor of the *Evening News* and complain they weren't covering the area properly. It worked. The editor phoned Nick personally to say they were sending one of their brightest young reporters to cover the patch. And Nick promised to make her welcome.

Around ten-ish on a March Monday morning, Kim Carter ca.ne to Dowerby. I happened to see her arrive. I was sitting with Rosie in the café in the market square, right opposite the ne\'spaper office. I had a window seat with a very good view. Fii `t, the newspaper's little car pulled up, with its logo emblazone\' across the bonnet in yellow and black. The driver parke\' it, inconsiderately, at the end of a row of cars, making it diffi\ult for delivery vans to get past to the shops. The car door ope.\ed and Kim swung her silky legs out of the driver's side door.

I watched as she fumbled with the keys to the dingy news-paper office, and disappeared up the stairs. Minutes later, she emerged and headed towards the café. She was quite stunning to look at, with dark long hair, a girlish face. All the café's customers and its dour owner, Jim, watched her quite openly. I was a bit embarrassed to be honest, about the way they were staring. I swear one old woman even had her mouth open. It's a northern habit, staring straight at pcoplc likc that. Some people think it's open and direct. Personally, I've always found it rude. They don't do it in London, in fact they famously go to the extreme opposite and it's as if you're not there at all. I much prefer that.

Anyway, Kim didn't seem at all fazed by this. I guess when you look like that, you get used to people's eyes popping. She just marched up to the counter and asked for some milk to take out. Jim served her without a word. Kim remarked that it was chilly outside. Jim said, "Yes. It's March, you know," and clattered her change down on the counter top. Kim raised her eyebrows and left. I glanced around the café at the Biblical quotations Jim had painted on the walls, to see if there was one about being bad-mannered to your customers, but there wasn't.

Kim must have felt the cold. She was dressed in quite a short skirt and jacket, sheer black tights and heels. Way too smart for Dowerby. The clothes looked like some I'd seen in last month's *Elle* (I had a weakness for glossy magazines). I'd also noticed she had small, clean hands and pointed, very white nails. I've often wondered if other women notice as much about each other as I do. I can't help it, taking in details. I enjoy it. But I didn't like to ask anyone if this was normal, just in case it wasn't.

I was watching Kim cross the market square when Sally, who works in Dowerby's little Co-op in the afternoons, joined me. Sally had also given Kim an undisguised stare, even turning her head as she passed by. She sat opposite me and leaned over to chuck Rosie under the chin. "So that's the new ace reporter," she said.

"Nick didn't tell me she was a supermodel." She grinned. "Bet he didn't tell you, either."

I shrugged. "Well, I don't think Nick will be having that much to do with her."

"Hah!" Sally gave me a bit of a leer. "She'll be beating the men off with a stick."

Sally made me wince, but Nick seemed to think she was a laugh. She managed to get a coffee brought to her at the table just by nodding at Jim from the other side of the café. "So," she said, leaning back and smiling at me. "Busy day?" It was only later I realised she was probably being sarcastic.

Kim didn't have a good first morning. A van driver and the flower shop owner had sworn at her for the way she'd parked her car. She was thrown out of the café for doing what she said was a 'vox pop', which involved asking customers' opinions on some local story. I knew Kim had asked permission from a young assistant, who'd just shrugged, but when Jim came in from the kitchen he sent her out as if she was a naughty schoolgirl.

I told all this to Nick when he called home at lunchtime. He shook his head and laughed. "Do me a favour, Maura," he said. "There's a big envelope by the phone with a load of details about Dowerby Fair in it. Will you drop it off at the newspaper office for me? Give you a chance to apologise to Ace Reporter for the local yokels and their bad manners."

And so I did. I planned to drop it through the office letter box, but the envelope was too big so I rang the doorbell. Nothing happened so I pushed open the door, hoisted Rosie onto my hip and climbed the staircase, with its shabby, brown carpet and its musty smell. I tapped on the door at the top of the stairs and Kim put her head round it. "Hi?" she said, with caution in her voice.

"Hi. I'm sorry to bother you. Your bell isn't working. I've got this to give you."

Kim gave me a small smile. "Is it explosive?"

I smiled back. "No, it's very dull. It's stuff about Dowerby Fair. Have you had a tough day?"

"Tough? I feel like I've stumbled onto the set of The Wicker Man." She held out her hand. "I'm Kim."

"Maura. Hi, again."

"Nice to see a friendly face. I've just made some tea, will you join me?" I hung back. Kim held her arms out. "Please?" So I sat down on a huge, black chair with a torn, fake leather cover. Rosie sat on the floor and Kim made a bit of a fuss of her, giving her a biscuit. "What did you say this was?"

"It's about Dowerby Fair."

"Right." Kim looked blank.

"Well, my husband, Nick, he's on the fair committee and he wants to get some publicity for it. Umm, if you would, that is. I don't know how these things work. Getting stuff in the papers, I mean. This fair happens every summer and it's quite a big thing for Dowerby. People dress up in medieval costume and there are stalls in the market place. The big thing is a sort of re-enactment of history. It's like a court where they put women on the ducking stool or in the stocks, that sort of thing, like they would've done, a few centuries ago."

"You mean they don't do that all the time here anyway?" said Kim, wrinkling her nose.

I grinned. "Don't think they'd get away with it. But it's a bit of a crowd-pleaser, so Nick says it's a good thing to do. It always brings the TV cameras in. And he says the women queue up for it, they love it. Apparently."

She looked at me quizzically and it suddenly seemed hilarious. We both burst out laughing.

Later, I told Nick all about her. "She had a really grim day. No-one helping her, everyone treating her like she'd just landed. Awful. I felt ashamed."

He was bouncing Rosie on his knee. "She'll soon settle in."

"Well, Nick, I've asked her round for supper on Thursday. Is that okay?"

He stared at me. "Sure. Of course. Bloody hell, Maura, that's not like you."

"What isn't?"

"Being social. Letting someone in the house without me forcing you to."

I frowned, "God, Nick. I'm not that bad."

People came from all parts of the country to live in Dowerby, even though the joke is that everyone there is inter-bred. There is actually an RAF base, the factory where Nick worked, and of course the district council, all attracting lots of professional men with wives in tow - although rarely, for some reason, professional women with husbands in tow. I was never sure if this was because the employers in Dowerby didn't tend to take on women or whether career women just don't move around and expect their families to follow them, the way that men do. Or maybe most women just had more sense than to come here.

The first thing these newcomers remark on is the weather. It's so cold! It was March when Kim arrived to take up her new job, but in spite of the shocks of garish daffodils splashed along every patch of grass, there was little sign of spring in the temperature. The very sight of a daffodil still makes me shiver, because spring in the north of England is always so bitter. It's as if there is a different sun, one that blinds you with its light and makes your eyes smart, but offers no heat whatsoever. A sunny spring day in London warms you up.

Kim, I remember, didn't bow to the climate much. She wore jackets rather than jumpers and very short skirts. She said that people kept staring at her legs, women just as often as men. "I don't know what you expect," I said. "I think you like it, really."

"I tell you," she complained one day, "this woman looked at me this morning, like I was some sort of alien. She was wearing maroon tights – big thick ones – and green shoes. I mean, how can you go round looking like that? And if you do, how can you judge other people?"

But it wasn't all hostility. Kim was actually a good reporter. It was very hard to dislike her, even if you wanted to. She was very pleasant to talk to. She smiled a lot, and had a sweet, trustworthy sort of face. Her editor was pleased with her. People in Dowerby grudgingly said the town was getting some good coverage in the *Evening News*.

Kim came for supper. It was a funny sort of evening. I was used to having Nick's friends round for drinks or a simple meal, but I worried about how to impress Kim. I'd cleaned the house from top to bottom, until Nick said it was like a hospital. I lost confidence in my own taste and put some of my carefully collected pots and ornaments away in a cupboard.

Kim arrived as Rosie went to bed, distracting her a little and making her cross about being put upstairs. But Kim found an easy way to my heart by telling me how beautiful my child was. (A tip: it works on almost any parent, any time). Kim admired the little low-ceilinged living room, with its pink-mushroom coloured walls, its wooden dresser and the remaining pots and plates. I was secretly very pleased.

Looking back now, I don't expect she really liked any of it. She was just practised at that sort of thing. She did it in almost every house she went into. But at the time, what she said made me feel good. She followed me into the kitchen and offered to help. When I turned down the offer with a smile, she sat on the chintzy chair opposite Nick, who of course didn't offer to help, and started to chat. "Rosie is a really lovely little girl. Is she good?"

"Oh, great," said Nick. "Sometimes we wonder if it's just us. You know, are we just being starry-eyed parents when really she's a little sod? But we get so many compliments about her, I think she really is special. We can take her anywhere. We took her on holiday to a hotel last year. My parents booked it and it turned out to be full of OAPs and they all just loved her. Showered her with sweets and money. It got a bit embarrassing. We're very lucky."

Kim just nodded and smiled.

"I'm quite keen on discipline, though," Nick went on. "I can't be bothered with these stupid people who let their kids run riot. And I'm not one of these fathers who doesn't get involved with their kids at all. I love playing with Rosie, it's just the best thing. These men who don't get involved are missing so much. I do a lot of cooking too, you know. Maura's doing it tonight because, well, it's fancy stuff, you know, she likes doing that kind of thing, but I do a good spag bol, and a chilli and things like boeuf bourguignon. That sort of thing. I'm not a bad cook, am I, Maura?"

"A rare man," said Kim, smiling.

I bit my lip as I listened from the kitchen. You'd think Nick did the cooking regularly. I couldn't remember the last time he'd cooked for me. It struck me that the New Man act was all for Kim's benefit. If it had been his own mates, he'd never have boasted about his cooking skills. Supposed cooking skills.

"What did you do before you had Rosie, Maura?" Kim asked, next.

"Oh, I just, I worked for a charity. Helping old people. Not very interesting."

"Oh? What sort of charity?"

"We visited old folks' homes and talked to them, you know, about the past. Reminiscence work, it's called, you know. Really boring, honestly."

"I've heard a bit about that," said Kim. "Isn't it supposed to do a lot of good? Getting people to remember the past?"

"Well, yes," I said, motioning her to the table and sitting down. "It's supposed to help people with dementia, that sort of thing."

"Bet you heard some fascinating stories, too?" Kim asked.

"It was a crappy place to work though, wasn't it?" said Nick.

"Yes, it was really," I said. I think I blushed a little bit.

"So's the factory, in lots of ways," Nick continued. "But at least they've got money to spend and we get a few perks. That outfit you worked for was just a bunch of amateurs. Hopeless. You were glad to get out, weren't you?"

Nick was glad when I got out, I remembered that. He liked to know where I was and who I was with. And I went along with it all.

"So did you go and talk to the old people yourself or did you organise the volunteers?"

Kim asked me lots of questions. During the course of the evening I ended up telling her all about my school days, what I did all day with Rosie, even a bit about how childbirth felt. I remember we giggled about men a little. I suppose that can't have been very interesting for Nick. Usually, when people came round, it was me who sat on the edge of the conversation. But Kim hadn't asked him about the factory and every time he offered his views on fatherhood, Kim turned back to me for my opinions.

"You know, I do a lot for Rose," Nick interrupted, eventually. "I've always helped a lot. I never minded changing nappies and getting up in the night when she was younger. I didn't, did I, Maura? But I never get any credit for it. Even my own mother keeps saying how wonderful Maura is for producing such a lovely daughter. No credit to me at all." He paused. Kim was looking at him with a half-smile. "It's bloody sexist," he ventured.

"I suppose so," said Kim. She had a placatory kind of a voice. "But then you get all the perks too. Going out to work all day instead of being stuck in the house with a toddler for company, that sort of thing. Not getting the blame when Rosie's not so well-behaved."

"I would have stayed at home," said Nick. "I don't think it should automatically be down to the woman. But Maura and I thought Rosie should have at least one of us there. And I earned more than Maura, so my giving up work wasn't really an option."

"But I suppose most men earn more than their partners," said Kim.

"Yes, exactly," I said, probably a little excitedly. "So it's very convenient for them. And it'll never change."

"But you were glad to leave work," said Nick. He gave me a look that said he wasn't pleased with me. "I'm quite a feminist, you know. But I still end up getting the blame for everything." He got up and began to clear the dishes away, proving his point. Kim and I looked at each other and smirked.

After Kim left, Nick was quiet.

"She was really nice," I said. "Really good fun. I liked her much more than I thought I would."

"I just hope she wasn't bored. You spent a lot of time talking about yourself, you know. I kept trying to change the subject and you just wouldn't have it. Was it the wine or something?"

"She asked me questions," I said. I felt my face flush. "I thought she wanted to know."

"She's a reporter, it's her way of being polite. She asks questions for a living," sighed Nick.

"She talked about herself too."

"Well, that really was interesting. She has a job worth talking about, she's done all sorts of things. You just showed yourself up."

I sat in front of the mirror taking off my make-up. My cheeks were very pink – something I hated about my face – perhaps I had drank too much and talked too much.

"She's really pretty, isn't she?" I asked him, knowing I shouldn't.

"She's gorgeous. Really sexy, and not even stupid with it, like most attractive women. She's brainy and witty. I can't believe she hasn't got a boyfriend," he said, still with his back to me.

I was silent. I'd asked hoping for reassurance, not honesty.

I got into bed and put my arm around Nick's smooth back, stroking him gently. Nick didn't respond, which was unusual. We both liked to make love most nights, and not always in the same ways. We were lucky to be so compatible; Nick was always saying our bodies fitted together well. Men he knew complained about not getting sex very often and that's why, he told me, they ended up having affairs at work that everyone knew about and always ended in embarrassment and tears. That's why there is a pile of tattered girlie magazines in the men's toilets at the factory, and why no-one thinks anything of it. I found all that a bit shocking. Even if I sometimes felt a little too tired for sex, or would rather have read, I never let Nick know.

But tonight he was sulking. I was usually good at getting him out of a sulk. I'd always rather make peace than have a row. I knew if I persisted in stroking him, kissing his back, or slipping my hand down between his legs, I could make him turn towards me easily enough. He would make love to me silently, and afterwards everything would be alright. But I didn't and Nick didn't. So we both went to sleep, thinking separate thoughts.

When we started seeing each other, we were both in our

first year at college and back then he told me he couldn't believe his luck. But after Nick ditched his thick-framed glasses for contact lenses and cut his wiry black hair short, he discovered that lots of women found him attractive and they said so. And he always made a point of telling me when women made a play for him. It kept me on my toes, I suppose, looking back. By then, though, Nick was with me and he told me he'd never been unfaithful, in spite of some of the chances that came along. He had a good sex life already, he said. Sometimes, I suppose, I wondered if I could keep on being enough.

The next day I was delighted to receive a little card from Kim through the door, thanking us for a lovely evening. I noticed it had been addressed to me, so I hid it in my bedroom drawer. I can't really explain why. I thought Kim was lovely. I'd have liked to ask her around again, in fact. But I knew I probably wouldn't.

It's funny how my memories of that time in Dowerby seem so much clearer now. The time before Kim arrived isn't quite so vivid. Does it seem crazy to feel hatred for a place? Or do you really just hate what happened there? I think I really hate Dowerby, as much as if it was a person. For its smallness, its unwelcoming feeling, its inability to change. I'm grateful to London, though, for allowing me and those like me, to blend into its people-wallpaper, totally unseen. People go on about how great it is to live in the countryside, but it seems to me that it has all sorts of disadvantages. Although you can be isolated, although you can walk for miles and never see a single soul, you are always conspicuous and someone, at least, will know where you are, who you are with and how long you should take. You imagine yourself alone, for example, walking just a few minutes outside of Dowerby, when you're surrounded by nothing but purple-brown moorland and the odd shaggy grey sheep, but in fact you're sticking out like a neon light. Kim once said to me, "The bloody countryside. You think you're on your own but someone's always peeping up your knickers." And that is Dowerby summed up, if you ask me.

In London, as anyone will tell you, no-one will really see you unless you want them to. And I have chosen to live the most invisible of lives. No-one here, not one person, knows my former name. I don't have a bank account and I pay my weekly rent in cash, from the used notes and coins I pick up from my two casual jobs. I do waitressing during the day and bar work at night, in a pub just minutes away from my flat. I know only a handful of people here: the people I work with and my landlady, Mrs Yeadon, who lives below me and owns hers and my apartment in this building. Apart from Mrs Yeadon, no-one comes inside this flat, three floors up from the grubby south-east London street. It is tiny, clean, pale-walled. Part sanctuary, part cage. I have an eventless and loveless life, but it is safe. That is the most I can ask for. And after what I did to Kim, probably more than I deserve. So then as I just get out the shower and the door buzzer sounds, I catch my breath. No-one ever comes to see me, and I don't receive post unless it's junk mail. When a man's voice asks for Maura Wood, I feel a grip on my heart, clenching like a fist. I am frozen with fear.

Chapter Two

I shiver involuntarily, goose bumps covering my body like guilty fingers. I haven't heard that name for almost five years. I pull my towel tighter around me. "No, sorry. There's no-one here of that name."

But the voice has picked up on my pause. "I was told Maura Wood lives here. Is that not you, Maura?"

"No, I'm not Maura. I've told you. Who is that?"

"I'm from the *Daily Jet*. I'm Paul Hollings, Mrs. Wood. I just need a quick word with you."

"I'm not Mrs. Wood. How many times? You've got the wrong address, I'm sorry. Goodbye."

I take my finger off the intercom button and walk back into the bathroom. For a few moments, I am slightly stunned. I start slowly drying my legs and back, and then the buzzer sounds again. I let it ring a few times before I go back and answer it, my fingers trembling as I reach for the button.

"Hello? It's Paul Hollings from the *Jet* again. I'm really sorry to pester you like this. Do you think I could just come up and have a quick word?"

I give a heavy sigh to show him that I'm getting fed up. "I don't know who told you I was this, this Wood woman, but they were wrong. Please just leave now."

"Yes, well, you see, I really did have it on very good information that Maura Wood was living in your flat. Can

I ask how long you've been there yourself? Perhaps she's moved on, you see."

"I've been here for f – for a few years. The man who lived here before was called Edwards and he died." The second part is true and comes out with genuine authority.

"Do you know where I might be able to find Maura Wood? Is she in any of the other flats? Can I ask your name?"

"No, no and no," I say. "I'm sorry I can't help you. I've never heard of this woman. Please go away, I'm very busy. I have to go to work."

"Okay, sure. Sorry to have bothered you, Miss… er… ?"

"Okay. Goodbye." I hear his footsteps walking away and then it goes quiet. I sit down and run through the conversation again in my mind. Stupid to have told him I was on my way to work. He might wait outside to get a look at me. I can't take this risk.

I sit wrapped in my towel for almost an hour, getting colder and colder and trembling slightly. I'm twisting and tugging at the end of a piece of my hair, something I haven't done for a long time.

How has he found me? I can't work it out. Or worse, why has he found me? Eventually, I make a mug of tea, force myself to take deep breaths and try to think straight. This is when I decide not to go to work.

I pad downstairs to Mrs Yeadon's flat, wrapped in my dressing gown, and tap on her door. As soon as she opens it she cries, "Oh, my dear, you look terrible!" Which is just what I want her to say.

"Mrs Yeadon. I'm so sorry. I think I'm getting the flu. I feel dreadful," I snuffle. "Would you mind ringing the café for me and telling them I can't come in?"

She agrees and clucks around me for a few minutes, before promising to come up later and bring me some soup.

I go back to bed, tucking myself up like a child in my old pyjamas, wrapped around with warm blankets. I can only think of one reason why a reporter would want me. It has to be something to do with the revival of Dowerby Fair. And if that is the case, I had better leave the flat now and try to do another disappearing act, because if Paul Hollings knows where I am, the chances are certain other people will soon get to know, and surviving the past five years will have been for nothing.

The thought of going through it all again is overwhelming. Finding a new anonymous home, finding a new job where the boss won't ask too many questions, remembering to answer to a new, made-up name. I don't even know if I have the strength to pull it off a second time, and anyway, how many more times would it take? The first time I thought it was worth it. The surety of my own life was worth it. But a life that consists of permanent hiding away? Maybe it's too high a cost.

Looking back, I never really took to life in the countryside, although I don't remember seriously hating it. I thought I wasn't used to it, that was all. Nick convinced me that living somewhere like Dowerby was better for Rosie. And once you've lived somewhere like that for a while, so quiet, conservative and sheltered, it's easy to become quite terrified of the cities. They begin to sound like other planets. As I've said, I have quite a talent for blending into the background, and I did it as much as was possible in Dowerby. But that was a talent Kim didn't possess, not at all.

Mine and Kim's daily life were polar opposites. Although I got up early to see Nick off to work and give Rosie her breakfast, I often sat around in a dressing gown until late morning, taking things very easily. Later, I would take Rosie out for a walk, I would shop without rushing, I could sit and read or take time to bake or finger paint with my daughter. Life was slow and it centred around what time Nick came back from work, waiting for him to come in and talk to me. I didn't mind that, but I sometimes minded the people Nick spent his time with instead of me, his workmates, including lots of women, and recently, the wretched Dowerby Fair committee. I didn't complain, though, of course. Not then.

Kim's day, however, seemed to be frantic. It involved finding a certain quota of stories for the newspaper or else she'd be in trouble. She did a lot of driving around, she tapped her feet and fidgeted in shop queues for coffee or sandwiches. She always looked in a hurry. I wondered what it was like to be that way. I thought it might be quite nice, feeling important.

One day, a couple of weeks after she'd come for dinner, I saw her walking down the main street beside the clock tower, and she stopped to chat. The tinny old clock chimed in the middle of her greeting and Kim raised her eyes, laughing.

"What is that supposed to be? What a pathetic apology for a bell. It makes the Avon Lady sound dramatic, doesn't it?"

I grinned. It was a typical Dowerby bell, quiet, flat and rusty.

Kim said she had a bit of time to kill waiting for someone to come and see her, so we went into Jim's café for a coffee. Jim's wife made a great deal of smiling directly at me and saying hello, how are you, in the way people do to make a point of ignoring someone else. I winced. Kim just smiled, her lips perfect and pink lipsticked, as if rudeness just bounced off her. I found I couldn't stop staring as we chatted, trying to take her all in. "I don't suppose you get much of a break, in your job. It must be really interesting."

"Oh, that's what everyone says. It must be so *interesting*."

(I cringed again. That was what everyone said).

Kim went on, "I suppose that's how it looks from the outside, but it's a bit of a grind really, especially somewhere like this. It's hardly a hotbed of news and scandal. I get a steady flow of local stories, bread and butter stuff, that's all that's expected."

"Where do you get your stories from?"

I later discovered this is the second thing people always say to a journalist. But Kim was patient and cheerful with me.

"It's obvious when you think about it. People tell me things, you know. People want to publicise things. Then, every morning and afternoon, I ring the police and the fire brigade and the ambulance station, and then there are council agenda, and just, you know, keeping my ears open."

"But what happens if nothing happens?"

Kim smiled. "Nothing never happens. There's always something. Honestly!"

All this time, I was trying to drink in her looks without staring open-mouthed, although I know now how Kim enjoyed being admired. She was wearing a bright green jacket that made her eyes look like gems. Her lips were a perfect cupid's bow, her skin clean and smooth-looking. She made me feel clumsy and frumpy, even slightly scruffy, and yet I liked her enormously. For a start, she made me laugh. She told filthy jokes and said them so appealingly that you didn't think anything of it.

She clearly didn't think much of the local people, despite the fact that they were cold and difficult with her, and she didn't seem to care that Jim in the café gave her the kind of looks that would have reduced me to tears.

"How are you settling in?" I said. "I mean the people here can be a bit… a bit… "

"They're downright rude and unfriendly, most of them," said Kim, raising her voice a little. "But anyone who's worth talking to is alright." She paused. "I don't know what I've done to offend people, actually. Some people seem to think I'm sort of dirty, just because of my job. I think they think we all rifle through rubbish bins and hack into phones to get our stories. It's so stupid. And I suppose some people even object to women working, in a place as… " she raised her voice just a fraction again, "… backward as this."

Then she smirked at me and I smirked back, slightly thrilled. I was part of Kim's conspiracy against the backward old fogies of Dowerby. It felt like a kind of honour.

During the conversation, Kim kept smiling at Rosie too, playing little finger games with her, making little faces. She just did everything right.

Rosie was the one thing I had done right. She'd turned out so pretty and happy.

My eyes still fill up at the thought of her, how she used to laugh and stretch out her arms to me from her bed in the mornings. I don't let myself think about her too much.

Kim then said in a lowered voice, "Do you know the chief inspector? Keith Thomas? He's asked me out for dinner. What do you think?"

"Chief Inspector Thomas? I don't know him, personally, but I know who he is, everyone does. Oh god, I'm sure he's married."

"He is," said Kim. "He's nice looking though, don't you think?"

I stared at her. I wanted to say how could you even think about it, but I didn't want to stop her confiding in me, not now it had just started.

"I've never really noticed," I said, hoping I didn't sound all prim and self-righteous.

"I think he's really attractive, those blue eyes! Very distracting!"

"But he's about fifty, surely?"

"I guess. Thereabouts. That doesn't matter. He seems nice."

I took a deep breath. "Kim," I said. "When you say he's asked you out for dinner it must be, you know, because of work. To talk about stories or something." I think I knew I was lying.

"Well, that's the excuse, if anyone asks," she said with a grin. "But I guess he wouldn't be so keen to entertain me if I looked like the back of a bus, would he?"

"No," I agreed, still hoping my voice didn't give my misery away. "But you wouldn't, I mean, things wouldn't go too far, would they? I mean, in a place like this, everyone would soon know."

Kim sighed. "Don't worry, I know how to handle married men. I don't get involved. I don't expect anything from them, just a bit of fun. That way I never get hurt. No-one does."

I wanted to say apart from his wife, who would be devastated, and has he got children, for heaven's sake? But

I didn't, of course, and Kim was talking about how no-one could be hurt by things they didn't know and that she was good at being discreet.

"Discreet?" I said, in a hiss. "That word doesn't exist round here. They know what you do in your own sodding toilet!"

Kim burst out laughing and I ended up laughing too. "Honestly! They just about do!"

"Oh, Maura, you're brilliant," said Kim, watching as Jim approached, his too tall, too thin figure stopping unwanted next to our table. I looked up and found myself staring at the grease on his grey hair and beard, at his watery eyes.

"Do you want anything else... ladies?"

"No thanks, I've got to dash," said Kim, reaching for her handbag.

"I've never seen you at St Justin's," said Jim. I stared at him as he went on. "Do you go to church?"

Kim just smiled, looked at him with that very direct way she had. "No, I don't, thanks. I use Sundays to catch up with my sleep."

"There's a Saturday evening service," said Jim.

"I won't go into what I use Saturday nights for," she smirked, at me.

"Your predecessor at the *News* led the choir," Jim said. "We expect our local reporter to be part of our community."

Kim shrugged. "It's a multicultural world out there," she said, with another smile, putting money for the coffees on the table. "Each to their own, eh?"

Jim didn't bother replying to this. He glanced at me. "You take care," he said and walked away.

"Good god," said Kim, as we walked out of the café. I knew my face had flushed, but Kim looked ice-cool. "What a pain in the neck," she said, with a half-smile at me.

I touched her lightly on the arm. "Don't worry. He's very religious. If he didn't do such good coffee I wouldn't go near the place. I'll see you round."

***

Kim did of course go out for dinner with Chief Inspector Thomas. They went to a half-decent hotel with a restaurant a few miles out of town. They played it slow, as people thinking of starting an affair tend to do. They skirted around the subjects of wives and boyfriends, dropping only a tiny hint here and there that they were not happy, not altogether satisfied, would like a little extra company, if only that were possible.

Kim told the chief inspector how she was renting a flat, all alone, how it made her a little bit nervous sometimes. She asked his advice on keeping her property safe.

Whilst all the time looking up into his eyes. Corny but effective, she told me.

And he responded, of course, offering his expert advice and reassurance, suggesting that maybe he could call in from time to time, during his evening shifts, just to make sure she was alright.

And that was how it all started. He left it a couple of nights before he called round, so that he didn't seem too keen. Then he knocked at the door of her flat overlooking the market place. Kim, with some kind of extrasensory perception that came with a wide experience of men, had guessed he would call that night. She was sitting listening to Ella Fitzgerald on the CD player, an open bottle of wine on the table. Chief Inspector Thomas stayed for almost two hours, just talking. Then Kim did her favourite trick for confirming that a man was interested in her. It goes like this: you say something like, thanks so much for coming round, it's really nice of you, I've enjoyed it, and then you give him a light kiss on the cheek. But not just a peck. You let it stay there, five seconds longer than it should. And then, invariably, he'll turn his face towards you and kiss you back, right on the mouth. And you've got him. Easy. If he doesn't kiss you back, Kim said, it's okay, because you're really just giving him a formal thank you kiss. You're not left embarrassed. At least that's the theory, Kim told me. The lingering kiss trick had never actually failed to work for her. Ever.

And this is what happens next. Invariably. You'll kiss and kiss, more and more passionately, and then he'll wrench himself away with a tortured expression, and say he's got to go. And you say yes, and wipe your hair out of your face, and let him pretend that he's agonising over whether he should sleep with you or not, even though you know he will, next time.

I know all this from Kim. I was never, ever unfaithful myself, not to Nick, and had the marriage lasted I'm sure I never would have been, even though some of Kim's stories left me with a buzzing ache somewhere deep down. Nick was enough and the sex was fine for me. I was lucky.

I once said this to Kim, when she recounted how the chief inspector had given her all the usual lines, about not getting on with his wife, about being trapped in a loveless relationship.

"Good god," I said. "It's such an obvious thing to come out with, isn't it? I'm amazed men still talk like that and think you believe them. I'm really glad Nick's not like that."

Kim gave me a rueful smile and touched my hand. "Maura, love," she said. "They're all like that."

I thought she was just being cynical, that one day she'd find someone she could trust.

Later, I began to believe her.

I didn't tell Nick about most of these conversations. I couldn't make out his feelings towards Kim. Sometimes, he would say she was beautiful or funny or hard-working, and other times he would say things that didn't come out quite that way. So I didn't tell him we'd started meeting almost every day for a chat, or how I would sometimes go into her office around lunchtime when I knew she'd usually be due back from covering a story, and put the kettle on and bring her a sandwich, so that we could have a good talk. It wasn't doing any harm. But I just left it all unsaid.

One late lunchtime I went into Kim's office and she was already in, waiting for me. "Hi, come in," she said. "I'm glad you've come today. You can help me eat these." She produced a huge box of chocolates from under her desk.

"Don't tell me," I said. "Your besotted police chief."

"No, actually," she said. "Your lovely Nick brought them round, about half an hour ago."

I felt a sickly sensation in my stomach. "My Nick? Why?"

"I did a big feature on the Dowerby Fair, yawn, yawn," she said, shrugging. "He brought them to say thanks. I guess."

"Oh," I said, feeling only half relieved. "But he didn't mention it."

"The piece only went in today's paper. And they gave it a really good show because it was a slow news day. I guess he'll mention it tonight when he gets home. I think he was really pleased with the coverage. He's taking this fair thing quite seriously, isn't he?" She giggled.

I was so glad she appeared to find him ridiculous rather than showing any interest in him that I giggled too.

"Has he threatened to duck you yet?" I asked. "I'm getting sick of hearing about this wretched fair week."

"Yes, he said I have to be ducked because I'm the local reporter. No way, though, it sounds horrendous."

"Only women, too, you know. The men don't get ducked."

"Outrageous," said Kim. "Perhaps we can campaign for it to be the other way round next year."

"Some chance. It's been like this for years and not enough people want it to change. Not even most of the women."

"Masochists," she said.

We ate all of the chocolates.

When Nick got home, I waited for him to mention visiting Kim. After an hour or so, in which he'd talked about work, asked me questions about Rosie, and eaten dinner, I decided to give him a chance. "I hear there was a big spread about the fair in tonight's paper?" I said, as casually as I could manage.

"Yes, that's right," said Nick, his eyes firmly fixed on the TV.

I paused. "Did Kim write it then?"

"Yeah," he said, still not looking round.

"Were you pleased with the piece?" I asked. Nick was clearly not going to volunteer anything about taking chocolates round to Kim's office.

"Yes, it was alright I suppose." He glanced at the TV remote and notched up the volume, just a little.

I waited. "That was good of her, then?"

"Yeah, I guess."

"Perhaps you should write her a thank you note. Or take her some chocolates," I ventured. And waited.

Nick flicked a look at me. "Yeah, okay," he said, coolly, and turned back to the TV.

I cleared the dinner table and began washing the dishes as noisily as I could.

Eventually Nick followed me into the kitchen. "What's going on? Are you trying to bloody break everything?"

I turned around and glared at him. "You've already taken Kim a huge box of chocolates. Today."

"What?" A pause. "So what?"

"Couldn't you have told me?" I almost shouted.

"What? Why?"

"I've been talking to you about Kim and the piece in the paper. Why didn't you mention that you've been to see her?"

"Oh, I wasn't really listening. I was watching the telly. Sorry. What did you say?"

"Oh, forget it," I said, turning away again. Nick went back to the TV and I continued clattering, but was ignored.

When I came out of the kitchen, Nick had got in the shower, locking the bathroom door, which he almost never did. After a while, I went upstairs. He was lying in bed, with the stiff body of someone pretending to be deeply asleep.

I wasn't having it.

"Nick," I said, so loudly in his ear that he couldn't pretend to sleep through it. "Talk to me. I want to know what's going on."

"What the hell are you talking about? Nothing's going

on, as you put it," Nick grumbled, sitting up. "I want to get some sleep."

"No way," I said, the way I'd heard Kim say sometimes, on the phone, doing a story. "Why didn't you just tell me you'd taken chocolates round to Kim? It's such a stupid thing."

"Isn't it bloody obvious?" said Nick, through his clenched teeth, the way he only talked when he was really angry. "Because I knew I'd get this ridiculous overreaction. If I keep things hidden, it's only because you're so paranoid."

I turned around and marched back downstairs, furious with Nick and also with myself, because I couldn't think of a quick retort. It took me several minutes to put my thoughts in order, and then I realised that he was wrong. I wasn't angry because he'd taken Kim chocolates, I was angry because I hadn't been told.

I ran back upstairs and shouted this at Nick.

"Come off it," he replied. "Of course you're jealous of Kim, she's prettier and smarter than you are. If you're not jealous of her, you bloody well should be."

I'm afraid that at this point I started to cry, which I used to do when I was angry.

"And just for the record," said Nick, sounding satisfied. "There's nothing going on between Kim and me. And I shouldn't have to go through this scene for nothing. I'm going to sleep."

I sat downstairs trying to watch some rubbish on TV and found I couldn't concentrate. According to Nick, I was wrong for being suspicious about him, wrong for asking him about my worries, wrong for everything. Worst of all, wrong for not being as perfect as Kim. For a while, I tried to hate her, but it was difficult to see where her fault lay. My anger was really with Nick, but at the same time I didn't want to feel angry with him, I wanted us to be adult enough to talk things like this out. I'd read all the women's magazines. Talking was the only way our marriage would survive times like this. I went back upstairs into the dark bedroom and put my hand on his bare shoulder. He shook it off.

"Look," I said, trying not to sound as tearful as I felt. "I'm sorry. I just thought you were trying to hide something, that's all. I suppose Kim makes me feel inferior, or something. She's so attractive. And I feel a bit grotty these days and I just, you just... " I started to sob, against my will, sniffing hard to try and stop myself.

Nick sat up and sighed. "Come here, you silly woman," he said, his voice softening, and I leaned into his chest. He put an arm around me and squeezed my shoulders. "I'll show you who I love," he said, pushing me back on the bed and undoing my shirt buttons. The sex was fast and hard. Nick gripped and pinched at my breasts, once even biting. At this, I yelped a little and he brought his hands round behind me, grabbing my bottom and digging his nails in as he thrust faster until he came. Then he gave me a quick, dry kiss on the mouth and turned over. "I'm really tired," he said.

I lay with my arms around his back, kissing it softly, feeling cheated. When I knew he was asleep I silently got out of bed and went to the bathroom, locking the door behind me. I touched myself for a few seconds before I came, thinking about Nick making love to me, but imagining that I looked like Kim.

The next day I stayed away from Kim's office. It wasn't that I was angry with her exactly, but I was almost afraid that she would tell me something else I didn't want to hear, perhaps that Nick had been round to see her again. I thought about the night before. I still didn't think that Nick had given me an answer I could feel happy about and I worried that he'd still seemed angry during sex. But soon I missed Kim and our chats, and I thought that perhaps I could... not exactly copy her. But I could just take a few tips on how to be a little more like her, that was all. Just adapt her clothes a little, buy something in a similar colour. Mimic an action or a turn of phrase, or two. Soak up some of her, I don't know, light, or whatever it was she gave off. And then, when I thought about it, I didn't want Kim to think I was petty enough to be upset about a box of chocolates. So I knew I wouldn't stay away for long.

That morning I was listening to the radio, which I often did, as Rosie played with her toys on the rug. The local presenter was discussing one of those surveys – you know the kind, they come out every day – that claimed something like seventy-five per cent of married men admitted to having an affair. His guest was an agony aunt from one of the women's magazines. She said she wasn't a bit surprised about the statistic. I turned up the volume.

"So why do so many men have affairs?" asked the DJ, both to me and to the agony aunt. I think her name was Sandra. She talked about immaturity and boredom and she said she often wished other women wouldn't go along with it.

"What about this argument that an affair can spice up a dull marriage or relationship?" asked the presenter. I tutted to myself and was pleased to hear the agony aunt say that this was nonsense, that it was nothing but destructive to any relationship.

"At what stage are you having an affair?" said the presenter. "Is it when you first make love? When you first kiss?"

"I would say," answered Sandra, who was a good woman, by the sound of her. "I would say it's when you first ever deceive your partner. It's when you first go for lunch with someone else, without mentioning it to your wife. It's when you first have those long, intimate phone calls. You don't have to kiss at all. Your affair starts with your first little deception, your first little omission."

I looked at her – well, I stared at the radio – and I realised that's why I feel so bad about the lousy chocolates. I listened to the presenter asking why women go along with these affairs with married men, what could the women get out of it? I thought that these are very perceptive questions for a local radio jock. You're thinking of cheating on your wife too, you little bastard. I switched him off.

***

The next day when I called in to Kim's office with sandwiches and two chocolate custard doughnuts, the sort of wholesome country fare that the local baker sold, I met her just running up the steps, looking excited.

"There's been a murder," she said, panting slightly but with enthusiasm all over her face.

"Oh god, where?" I said.

"Well not here, nearby though, in Morden," Kim said. "But the girl's parents live here. Just along the road from you, actually. I got talks with them, pick-up pics, the lot. I've had a brilliant morning."

I put the office kettle on. "Speak in English," I said. Talks apparently meant interviews and a pick-up pic was a photograph the parents had of their daughter that the newspaper could copy and use. Kim told me how the girl, who was just nineteen, had been found with her skull smashed, most probably with a hammer. Unofficially, the police want to interview the boyfriend, Kim said, but he's disappeared for now. But he was too stupid to have gone very far, so they'll probably get him later today. With luck, he wouldn't be picked up not until after the paper had come out, because once someone is charged, the paper wouldn't be able to print very much.

"Did Keith tell you about it?" I asked, meaning the Chief Inspector.

Kim sighed. "No," she said. "Look, I don't sleep with people to get my stories, you know. Why do people always think reporters get stories by some underhand way? Death is a matter of public record, that's what they teach you at journalism college. In other words, if someone dies, people are entitled to know about it. That means the press, because that's who tells everyone else. You see?"

"Yes, but how can you go round and pester people who've been bereaved? Don't you think that's a bit much?"

"It's called doorstepping," said Kim. For some reason we

both sniggered. "It sounds like a sort of a dance, doesn't it?"

I grinned. "Me and my baby doorsteppin'."

Kim laughed loudly. That was the one imperfect thing about Kim, her laugh. It was noisy and she did it by breathing in hard and squeaking. I'd heard her do a controlled, artificial laugh, when she was politely responding to someone on the phone, and I remembered she'd done it a few times when she'd come round for supper. But now, I knew her real laugh and I can't begin to explain what pleasure it gave me when I made her do it. It made me blush and my whole body prickled.

"Doorstepping," continued Kim. "So called, obviously, because it's the sort of thing you can't really phone someone up about. Tactless. Better, if anything, to knock on their door on spec. And I don't actually pester people, as you put it. If they tell me to fuck off, that's what I do. I don't get paid to hang about and annoy people, not on a local rag. If something or someone's important enough, that's what the national papers do. But not us. And anyway, you'd be surprised how few people do slam the door in my face. When something like this happens, sometimes people want to sound off or just talk about it. Like today, this couple, they wanted to tell me what a lovely person their daughter was. That's what they preferred people to read, not just some sordid stuff about how she died. Sometimes it helps them."

I looked at her, raising my eyebrows.

"Alright," she said, half-smiling. "Not exactly helps. But what I'm saying is, not everyone minds as much as you'd think. Thank goodness. Otherwise there'd be no stories worth reading, would there? If real people never talked about themselves, all you'd get to read are lots of press releases from companies with too much money, telling you a lot of shit about their products."

"Oh, but, Kim what I can't understand is the way you are when something like this happens. I mean, you get all excited and it's as if you're actually pleased that someone's been murdered. I mean, that's awful."

Kim shook her head, her mouth full of bread, and waved her hands as she swallowed as quickly as she could. "No, no, no," she said, her voice still slightly muffled with food. "It's not that at all. It's like, it's like a surgeon getting a really challenging operation to do. It's not that he wants someone to be ill, but he gets a lot out of doing something that's a bit of a challenge and a bit more interesting than doling out headache tablets every day, or whatever. Do you know what I'm saying?"

I thought I did. There were things about Kim's job I did like. Telling on people, as we used to call it when I was in primary school. Or rather, exposing people who were doing something wrong. That part of it, I thought, I'd quite like to do.

"Look," said Kim, handing me a photograph of a shiny-faced, laughing young girl, who was holding a glass in her hand, Christmas tinsel around her neck. "That's the girl who was murdered. I have to take it back to her mum later on. She was pretty, wasn't she?"

I looked at the photograph and shook my head at the horrible, stupid sadness of it that didn't seem to register with Kim.

That evening, Nick persuaded me to go with him to a meeting to plan the summer fair. I didn't really want to go, but Nick said this was one of the meetings that was open to the public, and he wanted as many people there as possible. I told him I had no interest in the thing, but Nick seemed to think this wouldn't matter, all I had to do was be an extra body in the room, making it appear more full. So I reluctantly agreed.

The meeting was held in the back room of one of the pubs on Dowerby's main street. When Nick and I walked in – along with Rosie and an armful of toys and colouring books – it turned out we were the first ones there. Nick switched on the lights and I sat down on the slippery leather bench. Rosie picked up a cardboard coaster and started to play with it while I wrinkled my nose at the lingering smell of stale beer.

"Are you chairing this meeting?" I asked Nick.

"Certainly am."

"Don't let it go on forever, then," I begged. "Otherwise I'm going home."

"Thanks for your unwavering support," grumbled Nick.

Of course it did seem to go on and on. Have you ever been to a public meeting? It's really quite astonishing how long people can talk and talk about nothing and never reach a decision; how often people can interrupt and talk about something that has nothing to do with the meeting, and other people will let them do this, and not seem to notice. So there was almost an hour of this nothing-talk: apologies for absences and the minutes of the last meeting and matters arising from this, and had anyone heard from the costume suppliers because they're particularly worried that the town crier will end up looking completely wrong like last year.

Rosie and I studiously coloured in a picture of a huge mouse with long eyelashes and a bow in its hair. Occasionally, I sighed quite loudly, but Nick never seemed to notice. He even seemed to be enjoying himself.

"Item six," Nick read out. "The ducking stool. What about this water problem, apparently there were some problems last year. Are we sure it's all okay?"

"Some problems," snorted one of the local shopkeepers. "That's putting it mildly. They filled up the ducking pond and the next thing was nobody in the square had any water in their taps."

"Yes, but the water company says that was a little localised problem. Nothing to worry about this time, they said," someone else chipped in.

"It's a pain in the neck every year," said one of the other shop owners, a woman. "That stupid tank gets full of rubbish and it takes up all the space. I don't know why we keep on with it."

There was a general muttering around the room. "The ducking pond is the best bit. It's what everyone comes to see, the wenches being ducked," the first shopkeeper insisted, and most people murmured their agreement.

"It's certainly the bit I like the best, all those frilly white blouses getting soaked through," leered another man. Everyone laughed.

I decided to break my vow of silence. "Can I ask, why do you only duck women?" I said. "Why don't we duck the men too?"

There was a communal groan. The fair committee had heard this question lots of times before.

"It's history, isn't it? They didn't duck men in the old days, love. Only women. For being witches, you know."

"Yes, but they don't duck anyone anymore. Why don't we bend history a bit? Equal opportunities and all that," I said, smiling in what I hoped was an innocent sort of way, although I was aware that Nick wasn't smiling with me.

Jim, the café owner, stood up. "I've done all the research for this," he said, giving me one of his looks. "This isn't something you can bring your feminist nonsense into. It's simply a re-enactment of what used to happen, and it's got to be fairly authentic."

"Authentic, nothing," I snapped, standing up too. "If it's so authentic you wouldn't have hot dog stands and rock bands and a bouncy castle, would you? I mean, they're not exactly medieval, are they?"

"We have a hog roast too," said somebody at the back of the room.

"That's not really my point," I said.

Jim was looking quite fierce. "The point is the ducking stool is the thing that is authentic. The lynchpin of the whole fair, if you like. That's what the TV cameras come up for and that's what gets the biggest crowds." Clearly it was no joke to Jim. "Anyway," he went on, "men would be too heavy for the stool. It'd probably break after a couple of big blokes. It's designed to duck women. Simple as that."

"I don't think it's very nice, though," I said. "I mean it's not funny, really, is it, what they used to do to women, because they thought they were witches or whatever."

"Or for talking too much or just generally causing a nuisance," said Jim.

I sighed and shook my head.

"Oh, come on, pet. Have a sense of humour about it," said the man who liked watching women's blouses get wet.

I opened my mouth, but Nick cut across me in a loud voice. "Alright, let's move on, we're just doing things as usual as far as the ducking stool goes. We're not going to change the world tonight. Item seven."

I put an arm around Rosie and bent my head over her colouring book. After what I thought was a suitable interval – about ten more minutes – I got up and left, taking Rosie and her toys with me. As I went I thought I heard someone – was it Sally? – muttering something about "Kim's bloody stupid ideas." I ignored it.

As Rosie and I walked out of the pub, I saw Kim half-running towards me.

"Maura, oh, thank goodness," she said breathlessly. "Have I missed the whole meeting?"

"Oh god, don't go in there, Kim, it's so boring I've lost the will to live," I said, as Kim gave Rosie a kiss on the nose and made her giggle.

"Tell me what they've been saying," Kim pleaded.

"Oh, alright, but don't get excited. There were some complaints about the ducking stool interfering with the water supplies last year... "

"Yes, I know about what happened, I've read the cuttings."

"Anyway, the water company's promised it won't happen again."

Kim nodded. "Right. Taps won't run dry in Fair Week, promise water chiefs. That'll make a few pars. Anything else?"

"You'll like this, I said they should consider ducking men. I got shouted down, of course."

"Oh, brilliant," said Kim, getting out a pen. "Tell me everything you said. It'll make a little funny piece."

"Hmmm." I screwed up my face.

"Oh, go on," she urged.

So I went with her back to her flat and struggled to remember my exact words and those of the shopkeepers.

"I wish I'd been there now," said Kim. "But I've clearly missed the best part so I don't think it's worth going back. You don't mind, do you, if I do a little story on your stand against the old fogeys?"

"I suppose not," I said, although I wasn't sure. I had a feeling Nick would be livid. But together Kim and I wrote the story. I really enjoyed myself, even thinking of all the daft clichés that newspapers use. "Don't you hate writing like that?" I asked Kim.

"No, I don't, Miss English Literature Degree," she replied. "It's done for a reason. You have to write really, really tight, you know, you have to pack in loads of information into a tiny space, a few paragraphs. So you use the phrases everyone understands without thinking too hard. That way you get your story across without using up the whole page waffling on. It's a skill, actually," she said, batting her eyelashes at me.

Kim's story ran something like:

Battling mum Maura Wood's bid to bring a medieval fair into the 21st century has caused something of a splash. Maura, 28, tried to instil some modern-day equal opportunities into traditional Dowerby Fair by suggesting that men as well as women should be placed on the historic ducking stool. But she met with a wave of anger from tradition-lovers.

Then there were some quotes from me that we jazzed up a bit, so I was quoted as saying things like: *I said my piece but I got drowned out* and *There was a tide of anger against my ideas*. Then I told Kim what Jim had said. It sounded neat, like a real news story, the sort you actually read.

Kim picked up Rosie and nuzzled her face. "Isn't your mum just great?" she said. I found myself blushing again. I wasn't too sure Nick would think I was great, but I convinced myself he'd be pleased with any publicity the fair could get.

"I'll send this over first thing in the morning," said Kim, as she pushed her notebook onto her table, still clutching

Rosie with one arm, and the photograph of the murdered girl fell out onto the floor. "I'll have to take that back to her family first thing tomorrow, too."

I picked it up and looked at the girl's dead, flash-red eyes again and it made me shudder.

Now I suppose that girl's picture is taken out and touched up by the Photoshop artists every time there's a new reason to write about that murder. Just like Kim's picture was inked over for the story about the revival of the fair. The new version of Kim – with her dark lined lips and eyebrows, courtesy of the computers – is now clearer in my mind than the real Kim. I have to strain a bit to remember all the details of her face.

So how recognisable would I be to someone who knew me five years ago? Hard to say. But perhaps, I think, over the tinned chicken soup that Mrs Yeadon brought up to the flat, I overreacted to today's visit from the reporter. Thanks to Kim, I know a bit about how newspapers work. All I have to do is stay out of his way for a few more days and he'll get sent on another story. I've lain low for five years. How hard can a few more days be?

Chapter Three

Walking to work this evening, I feel comforted, simply by the noise and mess of southeast London all around me. I know it's a dismal place to live, really. Every day I have to go up and down cold, concrete steps to and from my flat, I walk out past a row of sour-smelling rubbish bins, tipped over by kids with nothing better to do, and past patches of grass so worn and muddy they're hardly worth keeping. But it doesn't depress me half as much as the gorgeous remoteness of the northeast countryside. If, around every corner, I can smell fried food and petrol and feel blasts of warm air conditioning, that's fine. I'm in the land of the living, as they say. I think my lungs were always too small and repressed for those great gulps of unpolluted country air. And I still feel relatively safe. Anonymous. Don't believe you can be like that in the countryside, not for one minute.

I will get by, just, without yesterday's wages. I have learned to live on virtually nothing, just so that I can stay here in London and not have to move back into some provincial goldfish bowl. I've decided that, in spite of the reporter sniffing around me, sticking to my story is my only option. The two jobs I have don't earn me a great deal, but that's the price I pay for not producing a National Insurance number and clearly lying to my bosses about my name, age, everything. It's fine. They come to expect it here, with the workers who aren't supposed to even be in the country, as well as those who're running away from their past life. There are plenty of us.

Take the wine bar, for instance. It's called Jerry's. When I applied for the job, they offered me six pounds fifty an hour and asked me to bring in my NI number. By the end of my first week, I'd told the boss I'd lost it, and I just hadn't managed to get hold of the right office to tell me what it was, and so on. On pay day, he said to me, "Alright, love, let's forget the stamp. But, you know, I reckon I may have told you the wrong wage after all. What did I say?"

"Six-fifty," I answered.

He made a regretful clicking noise in his cheek. "I meant four-fifty," he said. "That do you?"

I told him it was fine.

The café is a little better. Cash in hand, plus tips that work out at around eight pounds more a day. I like the café work better. The place is smaller and very contained (eleven tables, four outside during the summer). It means the smells of fat and cooking linger on me, but it's a wage, and better than just a wage, it's notes and coins in my hand, no questions asked.

My rent and bills eat up about eighty-five per cent of my money. I know I struck lucky with Mrs Yeadon. She felt sorry for me and she's of that generation where she feels safer renting to someone white and female, not that I'm agreeing with her. And she's getting on a bit and probably doesn't realise she could ask for a much higher rent than she does. But my life is so different to what it was, particularly during the dream-like days of working with Kim when I would buy all kinds of luxury food, sweets, make-up, magazines, flowers, expensive clothes and toys for Rosie. All that money dribbled away so easily and it didn't seem to matter. Now I'm so careful, Nick in particular wouldn't recognise me. My diet consists of jacket potatoes and tins of soup and baked beans, just like a poverty-stricken old pensioner. Porridge every morning, bread bought at the end of the baker's day just before they close the shop when it's half price. At the café, I can make a free sandwich for my lunch break and I always opt for meat, because I can't afford to buy it myself. Sometimes, too, at closing time, the manageress shares out things like large cakes, which weren't bought and are on the verge of going stale. And if there are just one or two small items going begging – scones or a Danish pastry – the other staff always say to me, "You have it. I'm on a diet," or, "My little one will only nab it and rot his teeth," or, "Those things are a bit too sickly for me."

They're being kind, I'm not stupid. But I take their charity. It's more than a stale-ish sticky cake for me, it's as much human contact as I allow myself. So I live, and it's fine. Really. And I have even managed to save a little. For four and a half years I've put a pound coin a week into the collection of jars and tins underneath my bed. When one jar gets full I push it to the back towards the wall with the others and find a new empty one, usually from the café. They say you shouldn't keep money under the bed but let's face it, what kind of a burglar will waste time and energy carrying off heavy jars full of coins? None, these days. And when you're not a real person, a savings account is pretty difficult to set up.

The plump young man leans over the bar at Jerry's and raises a fairish eyebrow at me, with an apologetic smile, which means he wants to be served. After I give him his bottle of beer and his change, he says, "Quiet in here tonight?"

"It soon gets busy," I reply and am about to turn away, but he keeps talking.

"Good bar, though. I've never been in before. I'm not really from here. You work every night?"

"Most nights," I say. Being ambiguous is a way of life for me now. Again I try to turn away, but there is no-one else to be served and again he speaks to me.

"Actually, do you do food in here at all?"

There seems to be a slight, very slight, raise in his voice. A sort of determination to keep me there.

"Sorry, only lunchtimes."

"Oh. Crisps?"

"Sure."

I find him some. I feel that he is looking at me a little too hard. I'm not used to it, that directness of stare. I haven't seen it since leaving the north. Do I recognise him at all? I don't think so, but I can't be sure. More worrying is whether or not he recognises me.

"So what's the food like at lunchtimes?" Now, he sounds as if he is trying to keep me talking and it is making me edgy.

"I'm afraid I don't know, I'm not here then," I smile. I catch sight of Cathy from the corner of my eye. She is watching. I add, with another smile, "but I'm sure it's great. Of course. Excuse me." I say the last part firmly, and walk the few steps to the other end of the bar, with my back to him so he can't keep up the conversation.

Cathy smirks at me, turns around and switches on some music to fill the bar with noise, and then says in my ear, "He's interested in you."

I frown, shake my head, and she grins, nods emphatically back at me. I am aware, as one can be sometimes, inexplicably, that he is still watching me. And I'm really grateful to see a large group of after-work office staff pile in and begin a large, complicated order for a round.

The bar gets busy and I almost forget about the fair-haired man. Then, during a lull, with the music still blasting and the place is full of voices getting louder, I glance over and notice Cathy leaning over the bar, arms folded in front of her, talking to him, smiling, and I know, as you sometimes also inexplicably know, that they are discussing me. I suddenly feel very hot and damp, and I dart through the dark wooden door into the back kitchen, where I stand trying to breathe deeply for a moment and then pour myself a glass of cold water.

After a minute or so Cathy comes in and I turn to stare at her, or that might be more like a glare.

"Hey, you alright?" she asks. She looks so genuinely concerned that I feel my eyes well up and they ache as I try to force the tears back.

"That man… "

Cathy comes over and puts her arm around me. She smells of a very sweet and strong supermarket soap, that isn't unpleasant. "He was only asking a bit about you," she says, as if to a little child. "I really think he's a bit smitten. Says he's seen you before. Asked your name and if you were local, if you had a boyfriend, like. That's all."

Now I really glare at her and shake my head, gulping the rest of the water. "Where's the harm?" she asks, part defensive, part motherly.

I like Cathy. I don't want to get on bad terms with her. "Look, he gives me the creeps. You know I live on my own. What if he's some nutcase who decides to follow me?"

She looks thoughtful. "It happens," she nods. I pause and she pats me on the shoulder. "You don't look so good, you know," she says. "Pale, like. I reckon you're still not so well and I can't say I'm surprised. I can't remember when you had any days off in all the time I've known you. We all keep wondering when you'll ever take a holiday." She glances at her watch. "Stay in here for ten minutes, then bugger off home, out the back door. I'll go out now and tell him you've gone home ill. If he follows, he'll think he's missed you." She winks a crinkly, mascaraed eye. "I won't tell the boss you've gone early and he'll never know."

I thank her, squeezing her on the arm so that, I hope, she realises how grateful I really am. She shakes her head slightly. She thinks I'm odd, I know.

After five minutes she pops her head round the door and tells me the man left in a hurry as soon as she'd told him I was gone, even leaving some beer in the bottom of his glass. "I reckon you were right, you know, so you watch yourself on that walk home, eh?"

I do, of course, frantically looking behind me every few seconds, but I can't spot anyone following me. He'd been fooled, if following me was his plan, into thinking I was long gone.

When I get home, I carry out my usual locking-up procedure. I have a chain on the door and a mini-alarm, both of which I'd fitted myself, to my great pride, shortly after arriving. This time I also put a chair against the door and I draw all the curtains before switching on any lights. Once I'm in bed I sit up, struggling to remember what was familiar about the man at the bar. I grab a piece of paper and a pen, scribbling things down as they come to mind. Hair. Eyes. Face. That had gradually appeared familiar. It takes me a few minutes, but I eventually realise that he looked like a comedian on the TV. I smile to myself. He was certainly not the comic, but he really was very similar, chubby and balding on top with his fairish hair a little too long at the back.

Something still nags away at me. I go back over the conversation, scribbling it down so that I won't forget it. The words tell me nothing. But as I recall his tone of voice, a realisation comes over me like a shower of water turning suddenly cold. He is a reporter. Of course he is a reporter. He is *the* reporter from yesterday, of course, of course, of course. I can't believe it has taken so long to click.

I'd listened to Kim interview people many times, over the phone and face to face. I myself have been interviewed, by a whole group of tabloid journalists, the whole circus. And that is why I should have known or recognised the technique. Reporters, when asking questions, have a way of sounding so casual, almost disinterested. The less interested they sound, the more important the question.

They shrug as they ask for your details. It's hardly important, you feel, although Kim told me that the lack of something like a person's age in a newspaper story would create a big hole, a major omission.

"Why?" I demanded, as do most people who don't work in newspapers, only buy them avidly and then scoff at the style. "What difference does someone's age make?"

"All the difference," Kim said. "For instance. A woman passes a degree in electronics. She's twenty-one. So what? A woman passes a degree in electronics. She's ninety-seven. That's a story, the first one isn't."

"But what if the age is irrelevant?" I continued to argue.

"It never is," Kim argued back. "Where do you go where your age isn't relevant, for god's sake? Work, a bar, a college, walking down the street. People are noting your age or how old you look all the time."

"But they shouldn't. I thought you'd be the first to say that."

"They shouldn't but they do, so it's the same in newspapers, and I write how I'm told. Anyway, it's more than that. If you work for radio or TV, you don't bother asking someone's age. Why not? Because you can see or hear the person involved.

"With newspapers you quite often have to paint a picture of someone just with words. Saying whether they're fifty-two or thirty-seven or sixteen does a bit of that. And another thing, if I leave out something like an age, I'll get a bloody phone call from a sub in the middle of the night giving me grief. It's not worth it." Kim won the day again.

As I was saying, reporters ask their questions casually, so you think they don't matter, when they do, enormously. And they can keep up that indifferent tone throughout an entire question-and-answer session. I mentioned it to Kim, once, after we'd been out on 'a job' together, so we could escape for lunch straight afterwards. "Why do all reporters mumble at you as if they're bored stiff by the whole thing?"

"I hadn't really noticed, but now you mention it, I suppose they do, especially the men," grinned Kim. "I reckon it's unconscious, but this will be why it happens, think about it. If I come up to you and ask if you left the office door open in a casual sort of way, you'll answer me quickly and without even thinking, and you'll tell the truth.

"If I ask you the same question in an urgent voice, you'll think very hard before you answer and you'll say what you think I want you to say. It's best people don't realise when they're saying a headline. They'll only get cold feet."

So you see I know quite a bit about the art of newspaper interviews. I should have recognised the tone in that man's voice as that of a reporter, desperately trying not to sound too interested. I run my fingers through my hair. Stupid, stupid, stupid. I had outwitted the blasted reporter only by sheer luck and no doubt tomorrow he will be back, either in the bar or outside it at closing time. How did he know where I worked? Has he been following me? He must have been. Christ. For how long? Kim told me that if a reporter wants to know something, really wants to know something, they will find it, if they're even halfway up to the job.

Have you ever thought that you were the only one to know a secret, only to discover it's something everyone else knows too? It feels as though your life has been turned inside out.

It was when I went into Jim's the morning after the committee meeting. It was one of the first warm days of that late spring, when Rose was wearing a little yellow dress and I felt vaguely happy. It was Sally who shattered my peace. She came and sat at the table with me, tickling Rosie under the chin, babbling at her in the kind of pointless baby-talk that Nick and I always avoided. "How's your little friend?" she said to me, in a poor attempt at sounding casual.

"What little friend?" I said, though I guessed she meant Kim. I didn't have so many friends I had to think hard.

"Your little glamour-girl," said Sally, now unable to disguise the sneer in her voice. "I see you spend a lot of time with her."

"Not really," I said, and then thought maybe that was a little disloyal. So I added, "I like her though. She's a good laugh."

Sally gave a little snort. "I don't suppose Elizabeth Thomas thinks she's a good laugh, do you?"

I stared at Sally. She was talking about the chief inspector's wife. I found myself going hot and red. "What do you mean?"

I knew I was even worse than Sally at sounding casual. We were having a farce of a conversation. Say what you damn well mean, Kim would have said.

Sally leaned forward and spoke in a low voice. "Oh, come on, Maura. The little bitch is having an affair with Keith Thomas. Don't say you don't know, because you're well in with her. I don't know how you can look at her without spitting in her face."

"I don't know what you're talking about," I said. "But I think if you're going to accuse Kim of having an affair, you should say it to her. I don't know why you're talking to me about it."

"You're her friend, I was just saying to Nick how you're always popping into her office, with your little picnic lunches."

I flinched. I hadn't exactly told Nick I spent so much time with Kim. I didn't think too hard about why I didn't tell him. It was just easier not to.

Sally continued. "Don't you think you should have a word with her? Tell her to find her own bloke and keep her mucky fingers off other people's?"

"I don't think it's anything to do with... "

"Do you know how long they have been married? Twenty-four years. They should be having their silver wedding anniversary next year. The function room at the White Horse is already booked. And that little slag comes along and ruins it all."

"Shut up," I said. "I don't want Rosie repeating words like that, if you don't mind, Sally."

"But you don't mind Rosie being with a woman like that," she snapped. "Look, none of us know the little, the little cow, except you. You tell her. Tell her to get her hands off our married men. Before she does some real bloody damage."

"I'll do no such thing. Kim's private life is just that. I'm not going to tell her how to live. It's nothing to do with me."

Sally shook her head in a self-righteous way that infuriated me even more.

"What if it was your husband, eh?" she said. "What if it was Nick she had her little claws into? Wouldn't you want someone to say something to her then?"

"Well, it's not Nick, and if it was... well... I'd still think it was no-one else's business," I stammered.

Sally just smirked.

At that moment I hated Sally, hated every detail about her, like her faint smell of cigarette smoke, her thick black eyeliner, her shiny plump face. I knew it was irrational.

"Anyway, you've got no evidence that Kim's having an affair," I said.

Sally grunted an artificial laugh.

"You know what I think?" I went on. "I think Kim's funny. I think she's bright. I think she's the best company I can find in this backwater. And I think you're jealous because she's so lovely and you're so... fat!"

I knew it was a childish thing to say, but I couldn't stop myself.

Sally laughed loudly, but she looked furious. I picked up Rosie, who was looking at me in that startled way that young children have, when the usually sensible adults around them raise their voices, and I left the café. I walked home, my head and insides burning, and when I closed the front door behind me I burst into furious tears.

It was about an hour later, when I'd cleaned up my face, had two cups of tea and used some deep-breathing exercises that Kim had taught me, that I thought I'd better go and tell her what had happened. If people were talking about me, whether it was true or not (in fact particularly if it was true) I think I'd want to be told. So Rosie and I walked round to Kim's office. The ground-floor door was locked but I'd had a key for ages, ever since the last time Kim had locked herself out and decided someone else should have a spare.

"Come on, Rosie," I said. "We'll go in and wait for Kimmy and make her a drink." We went up the stairs to Kim's office and I twisted the key to open the next door.

Then I stood there open-mouthed. In front of me on the chair I could see a man's bare outstretched legs, and moving over them, slowly up and down, was Kim's smooth naked body. I must have only been there for a second or so, gaping stupidly, when the man – it was the chief inspector, of course – made a loud choking noise and half-flung Kim over to one side.

Kim turned and leapt off him, laughing. "Oh god, Maura, what a fright!" she squealed. I started to laugh because I simply didn't know what else to do, and instinctively covered Rosie's eyes with my hand. The chief inspector jumped up and grabbed the first piece of clothing he could from the floor and used it to cover up his shrinking penis, which I noticed even though I tried hard to look somewhere, anywhere else. Purple in the face, he grabbed up the rest of his clothes and dived into Kim's toilet, which adjoined the office. He slammed the door behind him.

Kim looked at me and we both burst out laughing again. "Oh god, Kim… I'm going. I'm really sorry."

"It wasn't your fault," said Kim, picking up a pair of lacy knickers and wriggling into them. "Was it something important?"

"Well, yes, but it'll have to wait," I said, rolling my eyes towards the toilet door. It opened. The chief inspector came out, now wearing his trousers, a crumpled shirt and socks. "Look, er… er… " he started.

"This is Maura," Kim said, still only wearing her tiny knickers but wriggling into a bra, still clearly desperate to laugh. "Maura, Keith, Keith, Maura."

She made us shake hands. Keith couldn't look me in the eye. "Maura," he said. "Listen. Please don't… I mean, I'm sure you wouldn't… this is very… "

I shook my head vigorously and Kim interrupted. "Maura's a close friend, she wouldn't say a word. Honestly. There's really, really nothing to worry about."

She placed a hand on his chest. I noticed the way he looked at her. It was kind of sad and hopeless. He placed his big, policeman's hand on her head and sort of patted her. Then he put on his tie, his shoes and jacket and left as quickly as he could. Rosie waved him goodbye and so, his face going red all over again, he had to wave back to her on his way out of the door.

Kim, now wearing an open shirt over her bra and knickers, hugged me as we continued giggling. I could smell sex and her perfume intermingling.

"Shall I stay or do you want me to disappear?" I said.

"Stay," said Kim firmly. "I don't know about you but immediately after a shag I always feel like having chocolate biscuits or something, preferably with a real mate. It doesn't always work out so well."

I made the tea while Kim got dressed.

"So what was it you wanted to talk about?" she asked.

"Well, the thing was... I was going to tell you... oh, you're not going to believe this. I was coming to warn you to be more discreet about Keith." We both shrieked with laughter again. When we'd calmed down, I told her about my conversation with Sally.

Kim shook her head in amazement. "So she's watched Keith and me at nights and she's watched you coming here at lunchtimes. She must have no life whatsoever."

"Most likely," I said. "But that's not really the point. The point is I got the impression that she, or someone else, is going to start causing trouble for you. They might even tell Keith's wife and then all hell would break loose, wouldn't it?"

"They wouldn't tell his wife? Surely not?" she asked, her eyes wide. "I mean, who'd be hurt the most? She would."

"I know that," I said. "But in a way, Kim, I can sort of see the way Sally and her cronies are thinking. That Elizabeth has a right to know that her husband's mucking her around. They're thinking if that was happening to me I'd want someone to tell me too."

"Would you? Really?" She gave me a strange look.

"Yes, I think so," I said after a pause. "And they're thinking that, okay, telling the wife would cause ructions but it'd put a stop to your affair once and for all. And that's what they're after in the end."

"But why? Why do they care?" asked Kim. "I mean, why would they want to be involved in someone else's relationship? I can't understand why anyone thinks they have the right to tell me or anyone else what to do with my private life."

I thought about this. "It's because affairs are so close to home. On a basic level, they think, she could nick my man next. And in a place like this you can't be discreet, everyone knows your business. And they want to think that people who live here just don't do that sort of thing."

"What bollocks," snorted Kim. "You're probably right about the way they think, but the way they think is bollocks. As if I'd be interested in bonking Sally's disgusting boyfriend or any of the other local apes."

"So what are you going to do?"

Kim stuck out her lower lip and exhaled hard, so that her breath lifted her dark fringe and let it flop back down over her forehead. "What I feel like doing is dancing naked down the front street shouting, I am screwing a married man... " She started to sing loudly and wave her arms in the air. "I am screwing... a married man... la la la... and he has a wonderfully big chunky dick... tra la... and he is a police inspector... and we have used his... HANDCUFFS... in bed... what are you all going to do about it... LA LA... !"

I smiled. "It didn't look that big to me!"

Kim squeaked with laughter again. "What do you expect? He'd just been caught in the act by a strange woman clutching a young child. It was enough to make anyone shrivel!"

"Assuming the naked dance isn't an option," I said. "What are you going to do? I don't want to be accosted by the holier-than-thou brigade every time I go outside the door."

Kim stopped giggling and took hold of my hand. "Oh,

Maura, I'm really sorry about that. I had no idea something like that would happen. Look, don't worry. The thing about all affairs is they have a set time limit. They can't last very long, because one of three things happens. Either I start whingeing at Keith to leave his wife, so he bottles out, which, incidentally, I'm not going to do. Or, she gets suspicious and it gets harder for him to continue the affair, which I gather is happening anyway. Or else, the scarlet woman, a.k.a. me, finds someone else because she's bored with spending time on her own when he's taking the Missus to Marks and Spencers. Which is a distinct possibility too."

"So you're going to finish it?" I asked, giving a deep outward breath.

"Yes, that was always the intention, in fact I was going to do it very shortly. But I don't want Sally and Co to think I care what they say, so I'll hang on just a bit longer. Just to irritate them."

"You don't actually care about Keith then? Not at all? It's just I don't see the point of the whole thing, Kim. You know you could have anyone you wanted. You're beautiful. Why go to all the trouble of having an affair with someone who's married, when you're not even all that interested in him?"

"I could explain, but you won't believe me," Kim said, shrugging.

I gave her a mock glare. "Try me."

"No, really, Maura, you won't believe me. No-one would believe me if I explained what I think. Let's just say I don't believe in all that falling in love stuff. It's not real. There's just sex and laughs and presents if you're lucky."

"Commitment?" I said. "Children?"

"Commitment doesn't exist. You can get children out of your relationship if you want them. I don't. But commitment, it's only temporary."

I started shaking my head and Kim shrugged again. "I said you wouldn't believe me. But I am right."

"You think like that because you haven't found the right

person," I said. I elbowed her gently. "And you're naturally cynical, you hardened old hack. But honestly, Kim, you're wrong. Some men are genuine."

"Show me one."

"Well, I think Nick is, at least, I'm pretty sure he wouldn't actually have an affair," I said.

Kim looked down at the floor and shrugged.

"What I mean is, we have rows, quite a few recently actually, but in general I think he's right for me. We have a sort of bond, we're very close. I can't imagine being like that with anyone else. And he feels the same. I know he does."

Kim just shrugged again and gave me a sad kind of smile. "You see," she said. "I feel like the child in that fairy story. Remember the Emperor's New Clothes? The little kid knows he can see the truth, but not one other person will be honest and back him up. I think I'm the only person who's worked out that love's a complete swindle."

"Are you saying I'm stupid? I don't suppose it's occurred to you that it just might be you that's wrong. You know, that some people actually have good relationships and that they last?"

"No," said Kim. "At least, I've seen no evidence of it. But people will always, always believe what they want to believe. Believing in something called true love and even imagining that you've found it, it's a comforting thing that we take on instead of fairies and angels and Santa Claus. But it is just a story. A kind of good advertising ploy."

"For what?"

"You name it. Chocolates, sexy knickers, make-up, diets, holidays. The continuation of the species. It sells men to women and women to men. But it's a lie, Maura. Oh, I wish I could make you see it."

I shook my head. Much as I liked Kim, what she said felt like an insult. "Sorry, Kim, but I can't accept that. I think you've probably had a bad time with one relationship and you're bitter. But I don't know what gives you the right to go round writing off everyone else's relationships and feelings as false. Really, Kim. It's a bit arrogant, when you think about it."

Kim gave a self-mocking smile. "Yes, I know how it sounds. I wouldn't even try to tell anyone but you. And I suppose you're not going to believe me until the day you find that you're bored stiff with Nick and in love with a new Mr Right, or else you find Nick in bed with someone else."

"Don't."

"Sorry, just ignore me. You're right. Bitter and twisted. That's me."

She picked up a bar of chocolate from her desk and held it by the edge of its wrapper, swinging it from side to side in front of my face like a hypnotist's watch. "You are feeling... very... sleepy... you will forget... that I have just been very rude... and you will partake of my fattening chocolate... "

Then she snapped her fingers and Rosie jumped and chuckled. We shared the chocolate and dropped the subject.

I was feeling a little better when I started walking home. On the way, I had to pass the newsagent and I spotted Nick standing outside, holding that day's paper and chatting to a man and a woman from the fair committee. I recognised them from last night's meeting: one was the wet-blouse man. I pursed my lips and walked over to meet them. Nick's face was hard to read. He gave me a smile, but when you've been living with someone for years you know when it's not a real one.

He held up the paper, open at an inside page. The headline said: *Play fair at the ducking pond, demands judge's wife*. It was Kim's silly story from the night before. I'd forgotten all about it. Funny how it seemed such a laugh when we put it together, yet it looked so much worse in black and white.

"I was just saying," said the man, with a chuckle, "that Nick's wife was all over Page Three." Then he gave a great bellowing laugh at his own joke.

Nick's fake smile widened. I gave him an apologetic wince. "Oh, god. I'm so sorry. I chatted to Kim about it and I didn't realise she was really going to write it all up like that."

"You do know she's a reporter, don't you?"

I cringed at Nick's sarcasm. "I didn't think."

"Well, never mind," the woman chipped in. "Look at this." She ran her finger down the page and read out the last few lines, which were all information about the fair, when it was on and what the attractions were. "You never know, it might get people interested, people who've never been before. We shouldn't worry about it."

I gave her a grateful smile, but I could feel that my face was hot and red. I wasn't, at that stage, a very practiced liar.

As soon as we'd got nearer home, and were out of earshot of anyone else, Nick's face changed. "You are so bloody stupid," he said, through gritted teeth.

We kept walking, Nick taking long strides and me hurrying alongside, trying to keep up. "Maybe that woman's right, though. It's like an advert, in a way?"

Nick put his key in the door. "Is that what Kim told you?"

I followed him inside and he slammed the door behind me.

"She didn't say anything, I didn't expect the piece to go in," I insisted. "I mean, it's obvious I didn't really say all those daft things, isn't it? No-one talks like that."

"So where did she get it all from? She wasn't there."

"One of her police contacts?" I ventured. My heartbeat had quickened a little. I hated rowing with Nick. I wanted more than anything to smooth this over.

"You made me look like an idiot. It was embarrassing enough when you were sounding off at the meeting and now it's all over the paper. People will be laughing at me." He threw his jacket at me.

I fumbled with it and hung it up. "They're not, Nick, they're not. You're being… " I thought better of suggesting he was overreacting. "You're doing a great job, everyone says so all the time."

"It's a good thing everyone else is taking it so well. Otherwise," Nick stepped towards me and jabbed me in the chest with his finger. "Otherwise it would be much… " he pushed me again, so that this time I stumbled backwards a little. "…much worse for you. Remember that." He turned and walked upstairs.

I blinked at him, my arms wrapped around my chest. "I'm sorry. It won't happen again. I promise."

The next day I didn't go round to Kim's office, not because I was angry with her – it really was difficult to stay angry with her, she was one of those frustrating people who can talk you out of a bad mood in no time – but because I sometimes felt that she might prefer me not to call round every day without fail. Maybe, I thought, she'd rather do something else in her lunch hours. Kim, however, called round to see me, something she'd hardly ever done. I let her in and again felt slightly embarrassed about the old-fashioned decor I'd chosen for my living room.

Kim dropped into a chair. "Look, Maura, I have something to ask you. It's so brilliant. How do you fancy a job? With me?"

"What are you talking about?"

"It's like this. My boss has been promising me for ages that I can have help. A sort of office junior. Someone to answer the phone and deal with some of the post and the small ads for the paper, that sort of stuff. Put some of the stories I've written onto the website. Make sure the paper still has a presence in the district when I'm not there. They advertised on the jobs pages a few weeks ago, but they didn't make it clear it was to work in the Dowerby office. All the applicants were expecting to work in the city centre and it turned out none were keen to work thirty or so miles out of it. Understandably.

"Anyway, now they're stuck and my boss asked if I knew anyone who fancies working in the office with me, for a few hours a day? I said I knew the ideal woman. They'd have to interview you, but it'd be pretty much a formality. The money isn't brilliant but, well, you spend half your day with me anyway and I don't fancy some dumb bunny from

Dowerby job centre being sent my way. Oh, go on, Maura. Say you'll go for it!"

"Hang on, hang on," I said, taking all this in. "I hadn't really thought about going back to work yet. Rosie's pretty young and I'd have to find her some grotty childminder."

"Ah, but, you could bring her in, couldn't you? You know she's ever so good, she sits and plays. We can bring her toys in. We'd keep that little arrangement between ourselves, of course. The hours would be flexible and to suit you."

"Nick and I always agreed that I'd stay at home until Rose started school," I said, doubtfully. I had a feeling Nick wouldn't be happy about the idea of me working with Kim.

"But why? To save him the childcare costs, I'll bet. And so you're there to make his dinner every night. Oh, Maura, I know the work's way beneath you, but it'd be easy and I really want you rather than anyone else. We get on, you understand what my job involves and you could do the admin with your eyes closed. Think about it, at least."

I was thinking about it. I did like the idea and Kim was, of course, right in everything she'd said. I liked the promise of earning some of my own money, too, even if it wasn't very much. I said I'd think about it some more.

The following day, Kim called round again. "You have to fill in an application form online. Come round and use my computer to fill it in. You are going to do it, Maura, aren't you?"

"The thing is, I haven't had a chance to talk to Nick yet," I confessed. "He was at a fair committee meeting till really late last night... "

"No, it was over by quarter past eight," Kim interrupted in the sharp way she sometimes interviewed people over the phone. Then she smiled. "Sorry, I happen to know because Keith was there to discuss policing the fair and he was round at my flat by quarter past. He said it was all over, I mean, he didn't leave early or anything."

I shook my head. "Not much gets past you, does it? All

right, I sort of didn't get round to mentioning it. It's a sticky subject, me going back to work. When I was pregnant, I got the impression he couldn't wait for me to give up work and I really don't think he'll be all that happy about me going back."

Kim looked at me with an open mouth. I knew what she was thinking, how could I defer to Nick's wishes so much. Even as I was saying it, it suddenly annoyed me that I had to consider his views at all when really, the decision was my own.

And there was another thing that I didn't admit to Kim. Nick hadn't come home till around ten-thirty last night. He'd given me a whole speech about how the meeting had dragged on and how tired he was. He went straight in the shower and I don't remember him getting into bed because I was already asleep.

I just couldn't tell Kim that. I knew she'd jump to conclusions. Anyway, maybe Nick and a few others had things to discuss, once the main meeting had finished. It wasn't worth having an argument, I told myself. And if I hinted to him that he wasn't being honest with me, there would be a row.

"Don't you want the job? I mean you, not Nick."

I blinked. "Yes. I'd love it, it sounds ideal," I replied.

"Well, look," said Kim, shuffling up the sofa to be right next to me. "Let's just get the ball rolling. Talk to Nick about it tonight, though it'll take head office a few days to get sorted out anyway. You don't have to take the job in the end, if it's really going to cause a problem. But just fill in the form."

So I filled in the application form, with Kim's help, and pressed the Send button with a shaking finger.

That night, I bottled out of talking to Nick again, imagining that I had a few days' grace. As it happened, Kim phoned me at nine the next morning.

"They're about to call you any minute to ask for an interview this afternoon. I know it's short notice, but I'm going into the city anyway to drop off some photographs, so

I'll give you a lift there and back. You'll be back by half-past three. I'll take Rosie round the toy shops while you're in with my boss. Get your smart suit out!"

"Oh, help, Kim," I said. "I haven't worked for ages. Years. I haven't had a job interview for... I don't know how long!"

"Oh, well. Interviews are always horrendous, however often you have them," said Kim, not very consolingly. "But in this case, they're desperate to offer you the job. The interview is just to check that you haven't got three heads. Put it this way, you're the only applicant!"

"But imagine if they decide I'm still not suitable? I'd be mortified."

"God, Maura. Only you could think you're not going to get the job when you're the only person in for it. Just sort out some smart-ish clothes and I'll pick you up at one."

Sure enough, moments after Kim's call ended, the phone rang again and it was the personnel office from the newspaper, asking me if I could come for interview that afternoon at two and apologising for the short notice.

I'd never actually been in Kim's car before and I was surprised to find it was quite messy with CDs, newspapers, sweet wrappers and post lying strewn over the floor and the seats. It smelled of her perfume. We listened to the one o'clock news bulletin on the local BBC radio station just to make sure there weren't any stories Kim didn't already know about. After the bulletin finished, Kim plugged in her iPod and we both sang loudly to some cheesy Eighties hits, with Rosie humming tunelessly along in the back seat.

Kim had everything worked out. She parked her car in the small underground car park at the back of the newspaper office. I stayed in the car with Rosie while she dashed inside with a set of photographs to be copied. She came out a few minutes later and opened the passenger door for me.

"Now," she said, addressing Rosie. "We are going to look at the toys in the shops while your Mum sweet-talks my boss." She picked Rosie out of the car, locked up and handed me her keys.

"We'll be back in one hour," she said. "You can let yourself in if you escape a little early. Go for it, Maura!"
It was the first time I'd been anywhere near the newspaper's head office. Kim showed me the revolving front door that led me into a beige-coloured reception area, a Sixties building, last decorated years ago before the visit of some minor Royal. I felt jittery, but the receptionist was friendly and so was the secretary who came to take me to the editor's office.

"I'm Carol," she said, in the practised, soft tone of someone used to putting people at their ease. "You'll see Mr Bray in just a few minutes. Would you like a coffee?"

I told her no, thank you, knowing I'd probably spill it down my shirt. After a short wait I was taken into the editor's office, which was decorated in Seventies-style brownish Anaglypta, with walls that were covered in framed front pages and awards for newspaper design and journalism. I noticed that the awards, too, dated back some years.

Bray was a huge, glossy-faced man with slicked-back hair, just my idea of a caricature newspaper editor. But he had a broad grin and a painful grip of a handshake. "So," he began, still grinning. "You've got to know our Kim. What do you make of her?"

I paused. "Oh, I think she's… "

He didn't wait for my reply. "Quite a character, eh? Shaking things up out there in the sticks, is she?" And he gave a bass chuckle.

Then he glanced down at my application form, asked a few polite questions about how I'd enjoyed my degree course and if I got on with people in general.

Kim would have probably answered saying she was actually a borderline psychopath and she'd still have got the job. But I gave the expected answers.

Then Bray stood up, leaned over his desk and held out his hand again.

"You've got Kim's approval, she's the one that has to work with you and you can clearly do the job. Can you start next week? We're keen to get going on this one. Doesn't look good for the paper when there's never anyone in to answer the phone, or the reporter forgets to put their charity event in the listings page. We can rely on you, I know. Welcome to the *News*!"

It sounds silly but I was almost tearful with happiness.

I spent the rest of my time in the newspaper office being taken into the personnel office, filling out more forms, and being given a whistle-stop tour of the building. The bit I liked best was watching the paper coming off the computerised presses. Kim had said that was quite a sight, although not quite as exciting as watching the old-fashioned printers. But I was thrilled.

As I found my way back to the car park, I met Kim walking along with Rosie who was clutching a carrier bag.

"Well?"

"Kim, I got it!" I squealed, and I kissed her and then Rosie. Rosie thrust the bag at me and I looked inside to find a small bunch of freesia, a box of chocolates and a toy kitten.

"Congratulations!" grinned Kim. "Incidentally, the kitten isn't for you. That's for Rosie."

"Oh, Kim, you shouldn't have. And thanks for all this. I'm really excited! I'm starting Monday. I'm going to earn almost as much working part-time as I did full-time for the charity. I'll be rich!"

"Well, hardly," laughed Kim. "But it is brilliant, isn't it? We can now legitimately gossip half the day and both get paid for it."

It was only on the way back in the car that I made myself think about what Nick would say. I couldn't possibly tell him I'd applied for a job, attended an interview and then accepted the post, all without saying a word to him.

Kim kept up her small talk all the way back to Dowerby and it was only as she dropped me off outside my house that she patted my knee and said, "Nick'll be fine. Don't worry. Tell him about the money!"

"How did you know I was worrying about that?"

"Just a guess," Kim smiled. "But I'd tell him now, if I were you."

I put Rosie to bed as quickly as possible after our meal that night. Fortunately, Nick was in a chatty mood, preparations for the fair week were going smoothly and his day at work had been good. I sat down and told him about the job at Kim's office. I skirted over the actual series of events. I didn't tell him about the application form and the interview, only that Kim had offered me the job herself, informally. And I was quick to mention the money. Nick raised his eyebrows.

"Not a bad wage, just for answering the phone," he said. "But what about Rosie? What would happen to her?"

"Kim says she can come to the office with me. It'd just be like looking after her at home, really, I'll just be going through emails and things like that."

I paused and Nick shrugged.

"What do you think?" I asked.

"Why not?" said Nick, casting an eye down the TV listings. "We could do with the money. And if it doesn't work out you can always pack it in. Sounds fine to me."

I went over and kissed him hard on the cheek. "Thanks," I said. My relief must have been so obvious. "I thought you might give me a hard time. You know, we said I wouldn't, but it seems like such a good chance."

"You must think I'm a real sexist pig," Nick grumbled. "I'm not against you working, you should know that by now. Honestly, Maura. You always think the worst of me."

"Sorry." I hugged him again. I just didn't always know what mood he would be in. I suppose I'd hit lucky.

So the following week, Rosie and I went to work in the newspaper office. The job, as Kim had said, was extraordinarily simple. It involved filing away paper cuttings of Kim's stories, opening the post and going through emails. I answered the phone and fielded some of Kim's calls. It was astonishing what silly things people called about and I could see how Kim, who had to produce a certain number of news stories a day, would be too impatient to deal with them. People would call to complain about something that would have nothing to do with Kim, a misspelled small ad in the previous week's paper, or an error in a story done by another reporter entirely.

I used the soft secretarial tones of the women in the newspaper's head office and became expert at telling people I was sorry they were upset, that their complaint would be looked into.

People also called up to ask for information that had nothing to do with the newspaper, for trivial general knowledge facts, shortwave radio frequencies, late-duty chemists, bus timetables, addresses of organisations. I had the time and the patience to find out these things while Kim got on with her job. I started typing the details of jumble sales, school concerts, Women's Institute meetings, all directly into the computer. Kim said it saved her hours. I started translating wedding photographs into extended picture captions: turning the basic details of names, churches, honeymoons and dress materials into readable paragraphs, by looking for a newsy angle. I actually enjoyed it. And all the while Rosie played with her toys on the soft new rug Kim had bought for the office. I had time to read to her and play with her too.

As the weather warmed and became more spring-like, Kim, Rosie and I took walks in the local woods and along the beach during our lunchtimes, if Kim wasn't out on a job. I loved hearing about the news stories she'd done each day. In fact, I knew as much about the people she'd interviewed as Kim did herself. I knew her daily routine well. Sometimes, first thing in the morning, I even did the calls to the police, fire brigade, ambulance and courts myself, scribbling down the details of all their overnight incidents, leaving them for

Kim to rewrite into news stories. We seemed to laugh a lot. It was just as Kim had said, some days, it felt like we were being paid just for having a good time.

Neither of my two jobs are like that now, the café or the bar. Of course there's still the odd laugh, but I'm careful not to get close to anyone I work with. When I started work at both places, I answered their questions about my family and life outside of work so tersely that the small talk stopped. Twice, Cathy, who works at the bar, asked me over to her house, once for a birthday party and once just for a drink, probably because she'd taken pity on me. Both times I said I couldn't. I didn't want to risk being pressed too closely on my past, where I'd come from before London, where my family were now, all of that. So the invitations stopped too.

I don't mind. Life's very, very simple, almost empty. I'm still sorry to have missed a day's work yesterday thanks to the reporter's visit. Work's my only, slight contact with other people and of course I couldn't really afford to lose the pay. And now the reporter knows where I work, in the evenings at least. He's persistent, I'll give him that.

I peep out of the side of my curtain onto the street below. Is that someone hanging around, close to the bins? I shrink back, holding the edge of the curtain, glad it's one of Mrs Yeadon's heavy, lined things that can't be seen through, even when my light is on. The figure puts something in a bin and moves away. I breathe out and drop the curtain back into place. This is no way to live. I already know what it feels like to be constantly watching my back. I really don't want to feel like that again.

As far as I can see it, I have three options. One. I could do another runner. But I have no idea where to, and if someone found me once, perhaps they'd just find me again. Two. I could try to brazen things out and claim I'm definitely not the person he thinks I am. Somehow, I don't think that's going to wash. I'm pretty sure he's rumbled me.

Or three. I could come clean and find out what he really wants. Don't like the thought of that one at all, but I may well be forced into it. After all this time. The months, weeks, years of leaving my past behind me. Everything, and everyone, I've given up. Could it all really unravel, just for the sake of a reporter's next byline? For what Kim always called 'tomorrow's fish-and-chip wrappers'? I put out the light and try to sleep, but I can't. I stare into the dark until my eyes are sore, headlines flashing around my mind.

Chapter Four

Today is Friday and I think that if I can get through today then I will have most of the weekend off – and so, probably, will the reporter – which will give me some breathing space. I haven't slept much at all. Ever since that reporter first rang the doorbell, I've had a queasy feeling in my stomach and I lie awake playing out stupid scenes in my head. But I get up on time as usual, have a quick shower to convince myself I am feeling better and walk to work, without, as far as I can see, being stalked. On the way, I call into a hardware shop and buy a cheap, hand-held personal alarm. Kim would've laughed to see that they come in pretty patterns these days. Who thought that if you're being attacked, you'd rather have a pink alarm than a plain one? I toy with the thought of pressing the alarm if I spot the reporter following me again. Chances are, though, no-one would take any notice. And if they did, then they'd probably call the police. And I really don't want that. I didn't think that onc through. Just wasted £4.95, I tell myself. Idiot.

The café is busy. It's a pleasant day and we set up the outside tables, which always makes me feel vaguely cheerful, as if summer is on its way and that's something to be glad about. We get more tips in the warmer weather, too. Perhaps the customers are conscious of being able to sit and enjoy the sunshine whilst the waitresses are working and they feel a pang of guilt. Who knows.

One of the other women, Julie, she's younger than me

and hasn't been here long, is entertaining us with tales of a drunken night out she had last night and how bad her hangover is today. I listen to everything, anything to take my mind off the fact that at some point today or this evening the reporter will turn up again. And presumably this time, he'll be certain not to lose me, until he gets what he wants, whatever that is. All I know is that the constricting armour of guilt I've worn ever since leaving Dowerby prevents me from simply asking him and putting my mind at rest.

It's about midday and there is one spare table outside and yes, there he is, moving into the seat smoothly, as if he has been skulking somewhere, waiting for it to become free. I turn to Julie and ask her, in a whisper, if she wouldn't mind serving that table, but she shakes her head looking pale, and says she's sorry, but she'll have to take a break right now because she isn't feeling too well. There's only me. I curse the conspiracy of events that have left me so vulnerable. I walk up to him, notepad in hand and he looks up, smiles, gives a sort of wink and says, "Well. Hello again."

I give him what I hope is a blank look. "Sorry?"

"You obviously have a poor memory for faces," he says, still smiling. "I was in the wine bar last night and you were serving. I was on my own."

I shrug. "I can't remember everyone who comes in there. What can I get you?" I reply, hoping he didn't catch the tremor in my voice.

"I would remember everyone if I worked there," he continues. "I have a really good memory for faces. I could remember someone straight away, even if I'd only met them once, years and years ago."

"Good for you," I answer. I know what he's saying now. He's saying he's in no doubt about my identity. His voice isn't hostile but then, it wouldn't be, I know all their tricks. "I'm sorry," I say. "But if you're not eating you'll have to free up the table."

"Right. I'd like black coffee and… a tuna salad sandwich. And a chat."

"Brown or white?"

"Eh?"

"Your sandwich."

"Oh, brown. But if you could just hold on a minute... "

I am already walking away towards the kitchen, and then Julie appears, slightly grey in the face, and gives me a weak smile. "Think I'm a bit better," she says. "Shall I see to that bloke for you?"

I thank her and disappear into the back room where we have our lunch breaks, and I sit there for my allotted half-hour. When I come out, he's gone, but Julie hands me a note he's left, written on lined paper, from a reporter's notebook, I'm sure. I look down at the scratchy handwriting.

Hello. Please read this. I don't want to frighten you but I would like to have a drink with you. There's really nothing to worry about. Please give me a call. Paul Hollings.

There was a mobile number.

"I'm sure that's for you, although he hasn't put a name on it," Julie says, raising her eyebrows at me.

"I'm not interested. Actually, he was in the wine bar last night too and he's becoming a bit of a pest," I tell her.

She frowns. "Really? I'd thought he was okay," she says, shaking her head. "If he comes in again I'll see to him. He'll soon get fed up."

I feel I have beaten him once more and I'm almost smug for the rest of the afternoon. I start to rationalise things in my head. Reporters may be persistent but they're paid to produce stories. He has to give up eventually or his bosses, his news desk, will get fed up and send him on some other job that'll get results. I just have to be smart for the next few days and then surely, surely, he'll be told to go and pester someone else. I haven't survived the last five years just so some grubby, podgy hack can blow my cover for the sake of a byline and a few good expense claims. I am coming out of shock. I am getting my strength back.

May, five years ago. A fantastic month, even in cold, windy

Dowerby. On the way into the town is the war memorial and surrounding it are cherry trees, small, parasol-shaped, which explode like pink popcorn in the very late spring. All around Dowerby, the fields are virtually floodlit with rapeseed crops, luminous yellow, with an acid smell that catches your throat as you pass, even in a car. Finally, the trees start to leaf and the grass needs to be cut, with that clean, sweet smell that you have forgotten is so good, which Kim said she would spray on, bathe in and wash her clothes in, if only it could be bottled. Were those few weeks as good as I remember them? I struggle now to recall the dull or the difficult times and there were some, of course, but not many.

I worked in Kim's office between ten and two. At least, those were my official hours, for which I was generously paid, although in fact I was often there much longer than that. We found Rosie a place in the nursery class attached to the local school.

'We' was really just Kim. She did a small feature on a little garden created for the nursery class, and on a quiet news day – was it the first May Bank Holiday? – it got a huge showing, with colour pictures. The teachers were thrilled. They called to thank Kim but the head teacher spoke to me instead. "Oh, it's Mrs Wood, isn't it? We were just wondering whether you would be bringing your little one to us sometime soon? There are one or two places in the nursery and it does the little ones so much good, you know."

I didn't need asking twice. I took Rosie along one morning to meet her teacher and left her for an hour, to see how she'd settle. When I came back, she was absorbed in a painting and reluctant to leave. The teacher beamed at me. "She's been no trouble at all. Settled in straight away." Of course she did. That was Rosie: the people pleaser. I probably taught her to be that way.

And so she started school, effectively, and loved it, and was endearingly serious about it. Nick hadn't put up any arguments against Rosie joining the nursery. Maybe he thought the teachers were a better influence than Kim. Or maybe, more likely, he had other things on his mind. We were all proud of her, though, Nick, myself and Kim, who didn't mind covering the office walls in Rosie's splodged works of art.

Now that I no longer have Rosie in my life, it pains me to remember how much I then enjoyed being without her. It seemed such a freedom, to let the nursery school worry about amusing her, while I chatted and drank coffee, or worked, or went for drives and walks with Kim. I cringe when I think of how much I liked leaving her. Rather like the one and only memory I have of smacking her hand when she was much younger. I have never stopped hating myself for that smack, even though I grabbed her and hugged her and apologised straight away. I didn't appreciate her and now I've lost her for good. It's easy to say this now, of course, but it's as if I didn't see anything clearly back then, not really.

I didn't know how much I needed Kim, the wise, funny sister-friend I'd never managed to have when I was younger. I didn't realise how much I loved Rosie and how I should have put her first. I also had no idea how much my relationship with Nick had started to slide. It seemed that I was having less and less to do with my own husband as many of his evenings were now taken up with the organisation of the fair. Late meetings, a couple of times a week, and even occasionally at the weekend. He rarely discussed this with me and I thought this was because he knew I found it all ridiculous. When I think about it now, it wasn't like Nick to just let this happen. Someone else must've been listening to him and telling him how wonderful he was.

Also, I was tired at nights, with my new job. It seemed all I could do to make a meal, bath Rosie, switch on the washing machine and stagger into bed. Nick and I would turn away from each other and go to sleep. And for some reason, it didn't occur to me that this wasn't right, especially for a man like Nick.

But I looked forward to my working days very much.

Kim was never, ever in a grumpy or unreasonable mood, in the way that almost everyone else I knew, myself and Nick included, could be. She was what some might call relentlessly cheerful, but I loved it, because Nick could be moody, and I'm the type to soak up other people's moods straight away. I can be brought down as quickly as I can be cheered up. Every morning, Kim had a huge smile, some funny story to laugh about, little things like punnets of strawberries to have with our first coffee, new kinds of biscuits, some article she'd pulled out of a magazine because she knew I'd be interested. Very little things, I suppose, but I thought she was the funniest, kindest woman I had ever met. I remember one morning, she said, "In the winter, Maura, we'll get an office toaster. Crumpets and toast and teacakes. Loads of butter." I looked forward to it. But of course, the winter never came, not there, not for Kim and not for me.

I say she was the sister-friend I'd always wanted and it's true. I did have – do have, I suppose – an older sister. She's seven years my senior, and always, when I was growing up, seemed as much of an adult as did my own mother. Certainly she didn't help me through the pains of being a shy, skinny, not particularly popular little girl, and a shy, skinny, not particularly popular teenager. She seemed more like a sort of extra disciplinarian. My overriding memories of Veronica are of turning round to find her watching me doing something I shouldn't. Usually something as heinous as trying on some make-up or writing a pathetic love letter to some current crush. 'I'll tell,' was her usual response. And the times when I would run inside crying because no-one would play with me or someone had teased me – or any of those things that seem so tragic to a five-year-old – her response was always, 'You must have asked for it.' I certainly couldn't have asked her advice about anything. She decided when I was born that I was stupid and never changed that opinion.

As for friends, I had the misfortune of being acceptable but not particularly popular. I think, in a way, this is worse than being totally alone and rejected. You can see what you are let in on and what you're excluded from, what you're invited to and what was only for a more select group. You can be part of only some conversations, but listen to others without understanding them fully. You're the one left out when numbers are tight and you have no idea why. So at school I had friends, of a sort, but none that I really trusted or who trusted me, although I longed to be important enough to be taken into someone's confidence. And when most girls my age were dreaming about boys or pop stars – and I did too, some of the time – I was fantasising about having a best friend, who I could go around Boots' make-up counter with and giggle, whose nails I could paint, who would have a terrible boyfriend she could tell me about, who would always, always take my side. She never materialised, this imaginary friend. Not until the very real and technicolour Kim came along. It seemed that every day she did or said something kind, which I took home with me and thought over, and knew I was lucky.

I thought I'd stopped being jealous of her looks, even though in the summer months she seemed to get even prettier and sexier, while I just felt clumsier and more exposed. One Monday morning, she walked into the office wearing a bright, white shirt. Her bare legs were smooth, shiny and brown, her arms golden. She looked fantastic. "Where did you get that tan over the weekend?" I asked.

"In the bathroom," Kim grinned.

"It's fake? You're kidding."

"Well, I haven't been abroad for the weekend and it hasn't been that hot here, has it?" The thing about Kim was that she didn't mind me asking her everything, where did you get that, how do you do that, whatever.

"What kind is it? How much is it?" I demanded.

She told me the brand, then told me all the tips she could for putting it on. "You put it all over, I mean, all over. Get Nick to do your back, although I warn you, it always makes blokes horny to do it and they end up pleading to do your tits as well.

"Then you really scrub your hands, otherwise your palms go dark brown too. And then you sort of smear the backs of your hands over your bum or somewhere and it picks up enough to tan them. Just wear an old tshirt for an hour or too because it can stain your clothes."

"How come the hairs on your arms are blonde and your hair's really dark?"

"Bleach them. Before you put on the fake tan!"

"Oh god, Kim, it sounds really complicated. I know I'll end up looking like some sort of orange ripple ice cream."

So at lunchtime, Kim took me out to buy one of the tubes of tan and then locked the office door behind us when we came back in. "Alright, girl. You are one of the very few people in this world who is going to go home from work looking fitter than when she arrived."

"I can't put that stuff on in here!"

"Clothes off," Kim ordered. I took some persuading but eventually, of course, I did what she told me and there I was standing, goose pimpled, blushing and completely naked in the middle of the office floor. Kim helped me get the technique right, although we were falling about laughing most of the time. Only when I was covered in the stuff did Kim tell me I shouldn't put my clothes back on for another half an hour and we got just about hysterical when the doorbell rang and Kim had to go downstairs and keep someone talking, without letting them set foot inside the office.

Another lunchtime, she booked me in to get my legs waxed. This was much less fun, but afterwards I always preferred waxing to shaving, and felt generally sexier because of it. I think during that time I looked and felt better than I ever had, not that Nick seemed to notice. One time he told me some lipstick looked a bit tarty, another time when I was getting ready for bed he told me my thighs were getting dimpled and it didn't look very nice. I felt sick about that comment for days. But then I realised he just shouldn't say that sort of thing. He's in the wrong.

But Kim and I were getting closer and closer, or so I felt. If asked, I would have described her as my best friend and I tried not to think too hard as to whether or not she would have said the same about me. In my mind I clung to all the things she confided in me and assumed she hadn't told them to another soul. The only time I got frustrated with Kim was when the subject of her affair with Keith Thomas came up, and that was because I simply couldn't understand why she was doing it. Why would someone I loved so much do something I hated?

The subject came up again one glorious afternoon when Kim, with typical efficiency, had written a handful of stories to file later in the day, and so had made time for the two of us to drive out to the beach and have a picnic. This became quite a regular occurrence during the warm weeks of May. At some point in the morning, I would nip into the supermarket and pick up things like baguettes, soft cheese, fruit and sometimes a half-bottle of wine and off we'd go for a couple of hours. Once or twice we had to sit in the car because there turned out to be a stiff breeze, but on this day the air was still and the sea glittered. The dunes were deserted and as warm as your bed in the morning. We nestled down on Kim's car rug and started tucking into the lunch. Then, as I said, the subject of Kim's wayward love life came up, I can't remember how.

"But don't you think," I said, conscious of sounding like a head teacher, like the class creep, like someone's mother, whining, "Don't you think you should take some responsibility for getting involved with someone else's marriage. I mean effectively breaking it up?"

"I'm not breaking it up. She doesn't know a thing about me," said Kim, deliberately missing the point.

"She could though, very easily. Someone could tell her any day now, you know they could. And then you'd have broken up a twenty-five year marriage. I mean, Kim... "

"Me? I'd have broken it up? Not her philandering husband, then?"

"Well, yes, of course, him. He's to blame too. But shouldn't you be... I don't know... "

"You mean if I was behaving responsibly, Keith wouldn't be unfaithful? Well, bollocks, actually, because he's done it before – although he says it was never like it is with me, ha ha – and I'm damn sure he'll do it again. And he'll say the same thing again. They all do, Maura. Every one of them."

"Even if they all would, which I'm not sure I believe, they couldn't if women didn't give them the chance. I can't understand why a woman would want to have anything to do with a married man. You hurt another woman and you get bugger all out of it."

Kim smirked. "Not true. At least, not necessarily. You get their best behaviour and their best presents and their best moods and their best sex. And you don't get any of their crap. Most wives don't get to know and so it doesn't hurt them, not directly. And I'd only get hurt if I expected him to leave her for me. Which I don't. And anyway, why should women have to be responsible for men's behaviour?"

I shook my head. "They must know, the wives. Surely. She must know. How can your husband be seeing someone else and you don't know? I'm sure I'd notice if Nick was."

Kim looked at me for a long moment. "How?" she asked. "Let's say he was seeing someone at work. Or on the damn fair committee. How would you possibly know?"

"I'm just sure I could tell," I said. I knew I sounded limp, even though I believed it. "Anyway, I wish you wouldn't go on as if all marriages were some kind of sham and that no-one has any commitment to anyone else. I know you're wrong. I don't see what gives you the special insight to say the things you do."

"Experience," said Kim, looking at the sand. "I do have some, you know."

I could hardly challenge her, knowing nothing of her past relationships before she came to Dowerby and also being so hopelessly inexperienced myself. Falling in love with someone you knew at college, marrying them and never even thinking about anyone else didn't really count as experience.

"Go on," I said.

"Alright," said Kim, sighing, as if she was being forced to tell me something she'd rather keep to herself. "Although you won't be convinced, I know it. Once – " she grinned, self-deprecatingly " – once upon a time, in what feels like another life altogether, I fell in love with someone and I believed it was the absolute, the total, the perfect relationship. And it went wrong and it taught me that all relationships are pretty cheap and interchangeable. There."

"Kim," I groaned. "You're right, that's not very convincing, for god's sake. Tell me more. Go on, all the gory details. Make me believe you."

Kim looked down and wriggled her toes deep into the sand. "What a great feeling that is," she said. "It exfoliates your feet, you know."

"Don't change the subject."

"Alright, alright. Don't laugh, then. A couple of years ago, no, four years ago, I met a bloke at work. You know how they say you have a sort of blueprint in your mind about how your future partner should look? He was it, just the way I'd always wanted. Not obviously handsome but lovely to me. Not too tall, dark hair, green eyes. Glasses. I've always had a weakness for glasses. Fantastic smile, really wide. Crinkly. I mean, when he smiled his whole face sort of wrinkled up into these deep creases in his cheeks, and then when he didn't smile these lines were still there and made him look all ravaged. I thought it was sexy.

"Anyway. We both liked each other and we used to have these so-called platonic lunches. We became closer and closer friends, you know the way it happens. Then one day – I'll never forget how it made me feel – one day, he just blurted out that he was in love with me." She paused and laughed. "We were both sharing flats with other people from work and we didn't want everyone to know about us, not straight away. The newspaper office is so gossipy. Naturally.

"So we kept it all a secret for a while, although not for long, then we sort of went public and we were thinking about moving in together."

She rolled over and lay on her stomach. "The thing about it was, well, it sounds so corny. We were so close. Thought we were, I mean. We knew what each other was thinking and we could spot each other's moods from a single look or by saying one word on the phone. The sex was just incredible, lovely, I mean, sometimes we would just stop making love and hold each other and cry."

Kim paused and I said nothing. She was stirring her index finger round and round in the sand, making a dry whirlpool. She exhaled hard. "I shouldn't do this."

"Why not?" I asked, dreading that she might stop, that I'd never hear the end of the story.

"It ruins your nail varnish. Sand, I mean."

I reached across and cuffed her lightly across the top of her hair. "Get on with it."

Kim grinned and looked at me from the corner of her eye, as if to ask if I believed her, or if I thought she was taking the piss. Then she sighed again. "So we were planning to move in together. We went round looking at houses to buy and we were agreed on every little detail of how it was going to be. How the house should look. Which countries we'd travel to. How we'd not get married and have no kids, but live together forever. All that stuff."

"How long had you been going out with him then?"

"Two years by the time we decided to buy a place together. The only hold-up had been that he had to sell a flat in London, where he'd lived a while before, and he'd paid too much for it and it wouldn't sell. Otherwise we'd have been living together from the beginning. But then one day it did sell and we were all set to go."

Kim poked her finger hard down into the little sand-hole she'd made, bringing it out with damper sand under her fingernail. She inspected it for a moment. "So then we had this stupid row. Over something really little, I mean, I can't even remember what it was about. We didn't speak to each other for two weeks. I was so unhappy I was ill, I mean, I couldn't eat or sleep and all that business. Then he rang me up and cried on the telephone and said he was desperate to see me again and we got back together. I thought everything was going to be fine.

"We booked a week's holiday to celebrate, it was January and we got this cheap deal to Tenerife. We had five fantastic days in the heat, I don't think we stopped touching each other for more than a minute or two, we just walked around draped all over each other. We lay on the beach melting together like two big blobs of sun cream, we showered and slept wrapped around the other.

"When he was hot – just a stupid thing, I don't know why I remember this – his skin smelled just like toffee. His back was as smooth as a statue. Tiny arse, you know, all that, and it was just bliss, bliss, bliss.

"And then… " here Kim gave a deep, resigned sigh. "And then, on the sixth night, we were making love, and he said… " she stopped and blinked. "… He said no-one had ever turned him on like I had. He said, when we'd fallen out he'd fantasised about someone else and it hadn't turned him on anything like as much.

"I was supposed to think, great, he's more attracted to me than anyone else. But of course I didn't, I thought… "

Here, she looked up right into my eyes and smiled, that smile you give to a best friend who understands you, and it seriously made me love her all the more. "Well, you know what I thought."

I nodded. "You thought, why was he even thinking about anyone else, how could he have thought about anyone else, and who the hell was it he was thinking about?"

Kim gave a small laugh and shrugged.

"I would have thought that too," I said.

"So of course I froze and said, who were you fantasising about? And he said, oh, you don't want to know, it's not important. He said it was just one of those fleeting thoughts you have about other people, that you'd never act upon, you know the sort of thing, and I said no, I didn't know the sort of thing, actually, and that ever since I'd known him I'd never even glanced at anyone else, not for a single second. Which was true.

"And he said, oh, come on, everyone thinks about other people, not that you'd ever do anything about it. And I said I didn't think about anyone else. And at first he said that was just not true, not possible. Kind of weird, even.

"Then he said if that was true, then he wasn't good enough for me, because all men think about other women, and anyone who says they don't is a liar."

She started to push sand back into the little hole, carefully, looking down at it fixedly.

"Well, we had the sort of row you might expect. I wanted to know who it was he'd been thinking about, and he eventually named some silly, shiny blonde from the office, who he'd always claimed to despise. And he tried to blame me, you know. He said he'd thought we'd split up and what was he supposed to do?

"And then I felt like a real sap for being so pathetically devoted. I realised, that the big L.O.V.E., the big Heathcliff'n'Cathy thing, it was all just in my head. All the things he'd said about being so close to me couldn't have been true because he was able to think about someone else. He could just switch me in his head for the last woman he'd seen across the office. It was all spoiled."

Kim looked up at me, shrugged and gave a resigned sort

of smile. "And there you have it. Just an everyday tale of love and romance."

I shook my head. "Oh, but, Kim, that was just one shitty relationship, you can't write them all off because... "

"Ah, but, you don't get it," Kim interrupted. "It wasn't just one shitty relationship, not at all. It was The Relationship, the Big One. I've had all the little shitty ones that don't really count. I had them before and I've had them since.

"But I know, I just know, that if that relationship could go wrong, when we were so good with each other, then they're all pretty cheap and interchangeable. And since then everything I've seen of other people's relationships has just convinced me even more. I've seen people being shat on by their so-called lovers time and time again, and it doesn't matter how brilliant you are, how beautiful you are, how long you've been married, how many kids you have, no-one is really devoted to anyone any more. The depressing thing was, Maura, he was being honest with me. People go round with half an eye on someone else, all the time, no matter how much they think they love their partner. And if only men and women would just get that into their heads and stop expecting the earth then we'd probably all be a lot happier."

"So from now on you won't get truly involved with anyone? No matter how great they are?" I asked, frowning at her.

"Nope. I'm really good at not getting involved." Kim rolled onto her back again and stretched out her arms wide, inhaling deeply, closing her eyes to the sunshine, smiling.

"Don't you feel, I don't know, like you're sort of, disconnected?" I asked, struggling to say what I meant.

"Not at all," said Kim. "Who says you have to be permanently linked to a man to be a whole person? I get male company, I get female company, I get sex, I love my friends, I love my job, I help people out, I mean, I'm not inhuman. I've just made a choice about not being anyone's permanent partner."

"What happened to the bloke? You know, Heathcliff?" I asked.

"Oh. Him. Well, he begged and pleaded with me for months.

He just couldn't get it, you know, couldn't see what he'd done that was so wrong. He seemed to think it should only matter if he'd actually, physically, screwed someone else. Didn't see anything wrong with just thinking about it, in other words, just wanting to. Even thought he should get merit points for being so honest.

"But that was it for me. I was totally disillusioned and nothing would make it better. So I just stopped answering his calls, and eventually he left me alone."

"And did he find someone else? What about the shiny blonde?"

"No idea," said Kim. "I left that office pretty soon after. But don't worry about me, Maura, I'm actually happy. I like my life."

I reached across again and gave her hair a little stroke, a daring move for me, who had rarely been patted or cuddled as a child and who never touched anyone other than Rosie and Nick. Kim gave me a smile, for a moment more subdued than usual, and then she seemed deliberately to broaden it out and grinned, as if to say everything was okay. Then she wiped her eyes. "Sun's making me squint," she said.

Now I think about that day, trying to imagine myself back on a warm beach, trying to imagine Kim still alive, but, as usual, it's impossible. I cannot have truly pleasant memories of Kim anymore because of my part in her death. The word 'haunted' comes to mind and I realise it's the right word. I am dogged by guilt and if that was not enough, some news reporter is now effectively shadowing me, appropriately enough one of Kim's own kind. It's what I deserve, I suppose.

Saturday morning. After a late night working in the bar, I sleep until after ten. I don't feel any better though, I must've been exhausted, that's all. There was no sign of Hollings last night, or at least, I didn't really spot him anywhere. That didn't stop me imagining I saw him in every other punter, my heart beating faster every time a stocky man came towards the bar. Cathy noticed my jitters. "If he comes in here, darlin', I'll tell him he's barred. I don't have to give a reason. He'll back off in the end."

But not yet, I think. He's not giving up. He's just giving me a chance to get in touch with him. I won't, of course, and then he'll be back, spooking me. But I can't miss any more shifts at work. Keep it up, I tell myself, he'll have to quit eventually. I'm trying to ignore the sick feeling I've carried around for the last few days.

I get washed and dressed. I try to go out for a walk on a Saturday morning, rather than sitting in the flat watching rubbish TV. Should I go out? Will he be skulking outside ready to pounce on me? Outside, there is a spring sky, light blue and soft. I could go out, not very far. Chances are the reporter has the weekend off. He'll be sitting at home with his kids or heading off to a football match. He won't be working, not on a Saturday, surely. I'm close to a park. It's not a particularly nice one and one of its worst features is a collection of huge grey and brown model dinosaurs created in some sort of reinforced plastic material and meant for children to play on. The ex-mother in me suspects that most kids would probably find them terrifying, but anyway I ignore them, and the children too, because I still twinge inside when a child, for some silly reason, reminds me of Rosie. I walk around the patches of muddy green and the carefully-placed daffodils and tulips, red and yellow. They remind me of a time when Kim and I went to a similar park back in Dowerby. Kim said you could tell the flower-planting had been done by a man because the blooms were all in such straight rows. We'd turned the corner and there, on his knees by a plot of soil, was the park gardener with a trowel and a tape measure, carefully checking that the distances between his bulbs were equal. We'd found this terribly funny at the time. It is a stray, happy memory of Kim, which takes me by surprise and makes me smile as I wander back to the flat.

I'm met on the stairs by Mrs Yeadon. She has a silly grin on her face. "I've got a visitor for you," she says, almost giggling. My stomach flips unpleasantly. "Your brother," she continues. "He's come all the way from Leeds and you were out, so I let him wait with me. It's been so long since you've seen each other I just couldn't let him go."

I stare at her. I'm about to say that I don't have a brother, when out of her door steps Paul Hollings. He gives me a wide, slightly apologetic, smile.

"Hi, sis," he says. "You're hard to track down. Long time no see, eh?"

I try to glare at him without making it too obvious to Mrs Yeadon. Then I force myself to look pleased. Or I show him my teeth, more like. "You'd better come up," I say and he thanks Mrs Yeadon charmingly, before following me upstairs into my flat. I close the door and round on him.

"How dare you?" I say, my voice shaking. "I am sick of you following and harassing me. I made it quite clear that I want nothing to do with you. Now, you con your way into my landlady's house and effectively force your way into mine. What the hell do you think you're playing at?" I find I am actually wringing my hands. I don't know how to stand or where to look. I can't believe this man has got inside my home. And I let him in.

"Maura," Paul Hollings says, as if I've somehow hurt him. It's a few seconds later, and too late, when I realise I haven't corrected my name. "Calm down. I just want to talk to you." He pauses. "You could always have told Mrs Yeadon that I'm not your brother. She'd have chased me down the street! I can tell she likes to take care of you. Why didn't you tell her, Maura?"

I breathe out hard. "Because... because... you know why, because I don't want her to think I've got newspaper reporters chasing me. What name did you ask for?"

"The name you're using now, of course. I don't want to get you in trouble. Look, can we just have a civilised chat? Please? I'm on your side. And I've got something you might want."

I swallow hard and wave him towards the kitchen, where he sits down near the small formica table. I can see him looking round, taking everything in. Not that there's much to see.

"Come on then," I say. "What's the story?"

He smiles and opens his hands. "Relax. You're not in trouble. You don't remember me, obviously. But I remember you. You gave me my first big story when I started reporting. Dowerby Fair? Kim Carter's death?"

I say nothing.

"I was a junior reporter when that fair thing happened. That was my first real story. I was one of the reporters you spoke to just after it happened and you gave me that photograph of Kim.

"I know it was bloody awful for you, Maura, but for me it was a big break. You were really helpful. And I never forget a face, especially not someone I've interviewed."

"No," I say, and when I breathe out, I can feel myself still shaking. "You said that."

Hollings continues. "A couple of weeks ago, I ended up doing the story about the revival of Dowerby Fair. I always believed what you said back then, and I never thought the whole thing was properly resolved.

"Now, someone else who was at the fair that day has approached the newspaper and let's just say I think we've got a big story on our hands. I started trying to track you down straight away, but I was drawing a blank. You did a pretty good job of disappearing, didn't you?

"Then, as luck would have it, I saw you just over a week ago. Just saw you there on the street. I had to do a double take. I couldn't believe it. Then I followed you here. The more I watched you, the more I knew for definite who you were. Look, Maura, I can guess why you ran away and why you want to put the past behind you. But I think you should listen and think about talking to me. Seriously."

I stare at him directly as he speaks, his voice becoming intense, urgent, not like the usual, casual-reporter act. Then I shrug. "No," I say, and I can't seem to stop shaking my head.

He looks at me. "What do you mean?"

"No. I'm sorry. I'm sorry you've had a wasted few days following me everywhere and lying your way into my friends' confidences, but I have no reason to talk to you. The more you follow me, the more I'll say it. I'm not talking to you, not a word. Now, please, just leave."

His mouth drops open slightly. He's not used to being turned down.

I indicate towards the door.

He gets up. "Maura… "

"No. I said no. I mean it. Don't push it. I know you have to keep asking and people do change their minds, but I won't. Just go." I walk to the door and hold it open for him.

"Please," he says. "Just listen to me. Just hear what I have to say. Please. I don't want to blow your cover and I don't want to get you into trouble. But… "

I push him, lightly but firmly, out of the doorway. He turns and sticks his foot in the door, just like they say reporters do, although I'd never seen Kim have to do it.

"Alright," he says, reaching inside his jacket pocket. He pulls out a thick brown envelope. "Let me just tell you what's in here."

"I don't want money," I say.

He gives a little laugh. "It's not money."

I try to push the door shut, but he's a big, solid man and his foot stays where it is. "Photos," he says, as I keep pushing at the door.

I pull the door back and then bang it hard against his foot and in a moment of shock he jumps. I slam the door closed and almost laugh.

Then he lifts the letter box and speaks through it. His voice is very gentle. "Photos of your daughter. Photos of Rosie. I thought you'd like to see them."

Chapter Five

"Pictures. Recent ones. I thought you'd like to see how your little girl is doing. Don't you miss her, Maura?"

I am briefly dumbstruck. I'm furious that my heart is beating so hard and loud, it sounds like a fist inside my own head. "I don't believe you," I eventually say.

Hollings sighs and drops the letterbox flap. I hear a rustle of paper and then the opening lifts again, with a little creak. Slowly and deliberately, he slides through part of a colour photograph. I can see a girl's feet wearing shiny black buckled sandals, and legs wearing knee-length white socks. It's pushed in a little further to show a white pleated skirt and the edge of a peach-coloured jumper. Then it stays still.

I make a grab for the edge of the photo, but Hollings has anticipated this and holds tight. I can't pull it away from his fingers.

Then, it is as if we both realise at the same time that the photo is about to tear, and we both seem to relax our grip a little. At the same time, we both give a small, reluctant laugh.

"For god's sake, Maura," he says.

"Alright," I say and, taking a deep breath, I open the door. Hollings sits down on the sofa.

"Give me the photo. It could be any little girl," I say.

"But it's not, it's your little girl. I'll give you the picture when we've had a chat."

"I can't tell you anything new. And I'm not saying a word until I know this isn't a trick."

"Alright, look. Here's the pic and there are some more. You can have them when you've heard me out, but you have to promise to listen to me, properly. Deal?"

I nod and he hands me the slightly bent photo. The little girl in the picture has a wide, gap-toothed smile and very long hair, in two bunches, tied with coral-coloured ribbons. I have not seen Rosie for almost five years but it is unmistakably my daughter, with her lovely brown-gold hair and that huge, eager-to-please smile. She's holding a little tabby kitten up to her face. She looks happy. I hold my breath but I can't stop hot tears from trailing down my face.

Hollings gets up and goes into the kitchen, where I hear him filling the kettle and clinking a teaspoon into two cups. I try to compose myself, although it's not easy.

"Help yourself," I call sarcastically, although I know this to be unfair, that he's making tea to help me calm down.

He ignores me as the water boils then he comes in with two cups of tea. "I haven't put sugar in because I couldn't see any. Okay?"

He sets the cups on the small table next to the sofa and sits down. "You are one awkward woman," he says, with what sounds almost like affection.

I give a small laugh and blow my nose. Then I snatch up the photo again, in case he takes it from me. "Can we just get this over with?"

"Maura. Please stop being so hostile. I am not about to do or say anything that will hurt you, okay? Now. Five years ago you gave me an interview, your version of what happened at Dowerby Fair. You stuck your neck out and I know that's why you ran away from home. Right? Now, a couple of weeks ago my paper printed a story about the revival of the fair, five years after that girl, your friend, died.

"Someone read the story and called me up. Someone who was at the fair that day and saw some stuff which backs up your story."

I sniff. "So what? No-one took any notice of me then. Why are they going to listen to this person now?"

Hollings drinks some of his tea with a noisy slurp.

"Because," he says, grinning at me, "this person – he's called Brian Guy, but it doesn't really matter, you don't know him – this person has the whole thing on film."

"How do you mean, the whole thing?"

"I mean, the whole thing. What happened to Kim. He and his wife happened to be visiting Dowerby that day, just as a tourist, he's not from round there. He videoed the whole thing from start to finish. I've seen the tape and boy, is it conclusive. You were right, Maura. It all happened."

"You don't have to tell me I'm right. But this, this Brian, why the hell is he coming forward now? Why not then?"

Hollings' grin widens. "You'll love this. He did come forward at the time. He gave his tape to the police. The local plods told him that, in the opinion of the police and the coroner's officer, it didn't really add anything to the evidence. And then, get this, they told him they'd lost the tape. What a shame, eh? Fortunately, my man had made a copy, because he'd hoped to flog it to the local TV station if there was a trial. There wasn't, so he didn't.

"But something told him to hang onto it. And when he read my story, he came and offered the tape to me."

I think about this for a few minutes. I really, really don't like the sound of it, for all sorts of reasons. "Alright. I can see that this could become a good story for you. But where do you go from here? I mean, where do I come in?"

"Right. My first thought was to contact you. I went back to Dowerby for a weekend and I found that you're no longer there. That no-one knows where you are. I found your ex-husband in the same house. I gave him a bit of a hard time because, to be honest, my first thought was that he'd done away with you. I know, I know. It wouldn't be most people's first thought. But he wouldn't be the first angry husband to bump off his wife. It seemed very fishy that you'd just disappeared and left your little girl behind."

"I didn't exactly leave her."

"No, I know, you took her to your sister's before you disappeared off the face of the earth. But Nick came and claimed her back. You knew that?"

"Not exactly. But I thought that would probably happen."

"Anyway, I'd given up on you. And I had other stories to chase. And then a couple of weeks ago, you walked past me in the street. I nearly had heart failure. In fact I thought I was imagining you. But after I'd watched you for a while, I was sure I was right. I'm sorry, I had to follow you. Do you understand that now?"

"How long were you following me?" I thought about how completely I'd let my guard down, thinking so much time had passed that no-one was interested in me anymore.

"Not long, okay? Just long enough to convince myself it was really you."

"Alright, I'll forgive you, just about. But listen, did you tell Nick about this video tape?"

"Not exactly. Well, no, not at all. I just asked him loads of questions about what happened at the end of the fair, until he got a bit hostile. And then I politely left. But what we're thinking of doing, Maura, is passing the tape on to the Director of Public Prosecutions and asking for the case to be reopened. What do you think?"

I pause for a long time. "Would I have to get involved?"

"I think we need you. You're a key witness and there's only one other, the camera chap. We could argue for you to get a certain amount of protection, like not giving your address to the defence solicitors, that kind of thing."

"Oh, god. I don't know." My insides feel like water. I hesitate. "Look, you have to tell me about Rosie. Was she okay?"

"She seemed pretty okay to me." Hollings gives me what's meant to be a consoling smile. "I mean, she seemed clean and healthy and cheerful and the house was full of toys and Nick's new partner seemed genuinely fond of her. Honest."

"New partner?"

"Ah. I guess you wouldn't know about that, would you? Sorry, that was a bit tactless of me. She's called Sally. She was a plump sort of a girl, long blonde-ish hair, definitely dyed. *Local lass*," he added in the Dowerby accent. He shrugs, "Nothing like as good-looking as you."

"I think I know who you mean, actually. It's not that much of a surprise. Look... Rosie... she... "

"What else can I tell you? I got the impression she's a smart kid. Told me she likes school. She likes drawing and writing stories and music. She was out in the garden most of the time I was there, though." He pauses and looks at me, with what seems to be genuine concern. "She didn't say very much to me. But my guess is she'd love to see her real mum again. Don't you think?"

I shake my head. "Don't. That's just not fair and you know it. If Nick finds out where I am, well, he'll just go mad."

"Yeah. Maybe, although he's got a new life now. But, what if something happens – you know what I'm saying here – and he's not around to look after Rosie any more? I don't think that Sally would be keen to take on someone else's kid on her own. Shouldn't you be stepping in there now, to make sure you're around if Nick isn't?"

I shake my head again, staring at the floor. It is too much to take in.

"Listen," says Hollings. "How about this. How about we go out, say, for dinner, top restaurant, the *Jet* will pick up the bill, and you just give me your side of the story again? Start to finish. I'll take notes on an off-the-record basis. And you have a think about what I've told you. About what might happen. About what you want to happen.

"And then when you feel a bit clearer we'll decide what to do with your interview and whether you want to go any further. How about that?"

I find myself nodding, without really wanting to.

He gives me a huge grin again. It's quite a nice grin, boyish. "Right. What are you doing Sunday night?"

I can't think of a reason to put him off. "Nothing."

"Okay. I'll come here and pick you up. We'll go somewhere really nice. And don't worry about it. I won't print anything without your go-ahead."

He gets up to go, then turns back. "Oh, almost forgot. Here you go."

He hands me the envelope, thick with photos of Rosie. I grasp it without saying anything. Just before he goes out of the door, I suddenly ask, "Paul. How did you get these photos?"

He gives another grin, rather sheepish. "Oh, well there was a pack of photos on the table at Nick's. You know, I think I picked them up by mistake along with my notebook. Stupid me, eh?"

We both smile at each other now, conspiratorially.

"Stupid you," I say. And it's the first time I've felt like laughing for years.

During that late spring and early summer, five years ago, I was having too much fun at work to think very hard about anything else. Kim was so good at picking up stories, chatting to people and writing at breakneck speed that we had endless time during the day for walks, picnics, long lunches. At least that's how I remember it. We also developed a habit of picking Rosie up from nursery at three o'clock and driving into the city for an hour's shopping. I knew I was spending money recklessly and I was often quite late home. Nick had to make do with heat-up meals from the more expensive supermarkets, but he didn't really seem to notice that. He only noticed when I was home later than he was, and then he would complain.

What were his grounds? It's hard for me to remember. I simply can't understand how I put up with being a good little wife. I know I couldn't do it now. But I used to feel nervous about going home when I was late, because I knew there'd be a row. I also got into the habit of hiding things that I'd bought on my shopping sprees with Kim. A pair of shoes lay hidden, unworn, under the bed for so long I forgot all about them and for all I know they could still be there. I bought clothes for Rosie and if Nick noticed that they were new, I almost always lied about the price and made out they were much cheaper than they really were. I wonder if he got a terrible shock the first time he ever had to buy children's clothes himself.

None of this seemed to matter at the time, though. What mattered was keeping up my friendship with Kim, which I still believed was getting closer and closer.

One day, a wet Thursday, I seem to remember, as we sat in the office and Kim tapped in a bored manner at her keyboard, the telephone rang. I answered as usual and put Keith, the Chief Inspector, through to Kim, who made a bored face, curling her lip as she picked up the receiver. I walked out, as I always did when he telephoned. I liked to think this made me appear very discreet but deep down it was because I couldn't stand to listen.

First I went to the toilet and lurked in front of the mirror for a few minutes. Then I came back in to signal to Kim that I was popping out to buy the early edition of the newspaper. Kim was talking in a low voice into the telephone, with her head bent down over the desk and her other hand raking through her hair. I went out quickly and when I came back with the newspaper, she was sitting at her desk, the conversation over.

"Something up?" I asked.

Kim used both hands to smooth her hair back off her face and sighed. "You could say that."

"What is it?"

"You won't believe this. The stupid old fool wants to leave his wife."

I stared at her. "But you don't want him to, do you?"

"No, of course I don't. Oh, bloody hell."

I sat down. "What did you say to him?"

Kim sighed again. "Well, this has been on the cards for a little while and I sort of guessed it was coming. I kept meaning to break up with him to avoid things coming to a head. I just kept putting it off because I was having a good time.

"We went away last weekend and I thought, maybe, I could finish it shortly after then, maybe the end of this week. But he's just rung up and told me he wants to tell his wife tonight and then leave home. He seemed to think he could move into my flat."

"What did you say?"

"I told him not to be so stupid. I said I wanted the relationship to finish anyway. But he can't seem to get it. He seems hung up on the idea that if he wasn't married any more I'd be happier. I can't make him see that I just want it to be over, whatever. And I really don't want to break up his marriage."

"So what did he say when you told him that?"

"Didn't take it in. I don't think he got the message at all." She paused. "Listen, Maura, I think I'd better disappear for a couple of days. I'm going to head off now and go and stay with a mate. I won't tell you where I'm going and then Keith can't put pressure on you to tell him. I'll ring in sick for the next couple of days."

"What do you want me to do?"

"Just act as if nothing has happened, but if anyone asks say I'm not well and I've gone off to stay with friends. Say you don't know who they are and you don't know when I'll be back. Just come in and answer the phones as usual."

As she spoke, Kim was switching off the computer and getting her things together.

"When will you be back, then?" I asked.

"Er... a couple of days. When I feel up to dealing with the silly old fool."

She almost ran out of the door.

I switched the computer back on and finished off writing Kim's story. It only needed two more paragraphs. I hit the button to file it to the newspaper. I was tidying up before getting ready to go home when I heard heavy footsteps on the stairs. The door burst open and Keith came in. "Where is she?"

"Not well," I replied. "I think she said she was going to stay with friends."

Keith swore and I raised my eyebrows at him.

He apologised. "Just tell me where she's gone."

"I can't, I'm afraid. Honestly. She didn't tell me."

He looked directly at me and I met his eyes and shrugged. "Tell the truth, Maura," he said. "She would tell you where she was going, I know it."

"Sorry," I said. "She said she wasn't telling me so you couldn't ask me. That's the truth."

He sat down heavily in the office easy chair. "You know she's given me the boot, don't you?"

I nodded. "Never mind. You still have a nice wife at home. Go back and forget about Kim. That's the best thing."

Keith shook his head. "That marriage has been over for years. I should've left a long time ago. Kim just... "

"Not that old line, please," I snapped at him. "Listen. I'll tell you what Kim said to me. She said she doesn't want you to leave your wife. She said she was going to end the relationship anyway. So just go home, take your wife some flowers and be nice to her. You had your cake and ate it, no harm done. You've been bloody lucky."

"You despise me, don't you?"

I shrugged.

"You think I'm a typical married man using your friend and messing her and my wife about. But you're wrong. I love Kim. Honestly. I've never loved anyone like this. I've decided to be honest to my wife and everyone else, by leaving Elizabeth and standing by Kim."

I shook my head. "You're not listening. She doesn't want that."

"You're wrong," Keith insisted. "She's just saying those things to protect herself. If I wasn't married, there wouldn't be a problem. She'd feel so much better about me if I left my wife, I know it."

"No, she wouldn't," I almost shouted. I felt like slapping

his face. "She never wanted a serious relationship. If you leave your wife you're making a huge mistake. Why would I say this if it wasn't true?"

"Because you believe it," Keith said, shaking his head. "But I know Kim. If I leave Elizabeth, she'll come round. It'll be hard at first and people will be hurt, but then things will settle down and I can be with Kim. And that's all I want." He paused and then stood up. "If you see Kim, tell her."

As I watched him go down the stairs to leave, I wondered which of us was right. Perhaps what Kim had said was indeed all bravado and she did want to settle down. I hoped, however, that I was right. And I also hoped that Keith would act true to form and lack the courage to leave his wife in the end. Just so the whole thing would be over.

As a result, I was late for picking Rosie up and then I took her into the supermarket to buy something for dinner. When I got home Nick was waiting, having come home early for some reason. He was holding a letter and he waved it in my face.

"Know what this is? It's your bank statement," he told me. "So?" I asked.

"You're overdrawn," he said.

My stomach turned. I hadn't particularly realised I was overdrawn but neither had I kept much of a check on my spending that month. "Oh," I said, casually. "Well, I get paid in a few days' time."

Nick looked pale with anger. "Do you know how much you're overdrawn? Six hundred and twenty pounds, just about. What the hell have you been playing at?"

"I don't think that's right," I lied, even though I guessed it was probably quite correct.

"Oh yes, it is. I rang the bank manager."

I glared at him. "How? It's my account, not yours."

"Because I know him, he's on the fair committee. I thought it must be a mistake so I rang him to sort it out, to save you having to do it. Only it's quite right, because he went through all the spending you've been doing on your card, to clothes shops and kiddies' shops and god knows what else."

I marched Rosie through into the kitchen and slammed the shopping down on the kitchen table. "He had no business to do that without my consent."

"Why?" Nick almost snarled. "What have you got to hide?"

"Don't be ridiculous. Nothing at all. He still shouldn't do it."

"That's not the point, anyway. The point is you're six hundred and twenty quid overdrawn. How are we going to manage next month?"

"I am going to manage by putting my wages in and being a bit more careful next month," I shrugged.

Nick waved the letter in my face. "What I want to know is, what the hell have you been buying?"

"I don't know," I shouted back. "Bits and pieces. Stuff for Rosie. It's my money."

"No, it's our money! Why should I have to sub you if you can't manage your own wages properly?"

"I'm not asking for a sub," I shouted.

Rosie started to wail because we were yelling, and Nick snapped at her and sent her upstairs.

"Don't take it out on her," I screamed at him.

"I'll do what I bloody well want. And I do sub you. I give you money for food and you're spending all your wages on clothes and make-up and crap. I don't know why you bother. If you're trying to look like Kim you're wasting your time, because you never will."

"It's not that," I said, blinking back tears. I was so angry I really felt like walking out, but of course I had nowhere to go and no money.

"Make my bloody tea and see to Rosie," Nick ordered.

"Who do you think you're talking to?" I asked.

"A stupid extravagant bitch," he spat and smacked me across the face. I went to slap him back but he struck me across the head so hard I reeled backwards. He came towards me as if he was going to hit me again and I shrank back against the kitchen sink. He just turned and walked into the living room, switched on the TV and sat silently, glaring at the screen.

I was crying by now and took a few moments to recover, dousing my face in cold tap water. I shoved a pre-cooked lasagne into the oven and went upstairs to Rosie's room, where she was sitting on the bed, whimpering. I gave her a cuddle and staved off her questions about why I was crying and why daddy was shouting.

I bathed her, finding her satin skin and beautiful smell calming me. Then all three of us ate the lasagne, more or less in silence.

Once Rosie had gone to bed, Nick looked at me and sighed. "You have to see it from my point of view. You're in a right mess." I realised for the first time since I'd started working for Kim that I was back in a position of feeling dependent on Nick. I was surprised by how much I hated it.

"I've negotiated with Charlie, your bank manager, that you can pay off half the overdraft this month and the rest by next month's pay day. But you'll have to be really careful and I mean it. You can't spend anything on clothes or make-up or anything for a few months."

"Thanks," I said, my insides boiling.

I may have known then that our marriage was probably no longer going to work, but it was barely a conscious thought. My overall feelings were sheer embarrassment and anger, nothing more coherent than that.

I can't explain what a relief it was to get out of the house to go to Kim's office the next morning, although I badly wished she was there. She telephoned at one point and I told her about Keith's visit. We had a long chat about her situation but I found myself unable to tell her about Nick or the overdraft. Money problems were just too private, much more shameful than sexual or emotional problems, for some inexplicable reason.

Outside it was pouring with rain and the noise of it was powerful on the old roof of the office building. Wet weather made the office smell even mustier than it usually did. I was sitting having a lunch break, reading the paper and eating a sandwich, when the door was pushed open. I looked up, more or less expecting to see Keith again. Instead it was a tall woman with long, grey hair in a loose bun, wearing a long green mackintosh. She had no umbrella and was dripping rainwater from every part of her body which gave her a slightly mad appearance. She didn't say anything, just stared at me, her mouth slightly open.

"Hello," I said, brightly, standing up. "Can I help you?"

She frowned and narrowed her eyes at me as if she hadn't quite caught what I'd said.

"I'm afraid Kim, the reporter, is away," I continued. "But I might be able to help you anyway."

"Away," the woman repeated, with a slight shake of her head. More drops of water fell onto the carpet. Then she blinked hard. "So you're not her. I should have realised that."

I suddenly knew that this woman was the chief inspector's wife. I'd say she was approaching fifty and still beautiful, although she seemed older than her husband. Elegant was the word that came into my head, in spite of the fact that she was dripping wet.

"I really don't know when she'll actually be back," I went on. "So... "

Elizabeth Thomas' long body practically folded in two and she sat down heavily into the office chair, as if the anger that had brought her here to confront Kim was all that had kept her on her feet. I stared at her helplessly for a minute and then reached over and clicked the kettle on. Recently boiled, it switched itself straight off again and I offered her a cup of tea. She didn't reply but sat looking at her soaked, probably ruined, shoes. I made tea anyway, strong and sweet, as they say you should do for people in shock.

"I know it's frustrating," I said. In so many ways I was

on this woman's side. "But she really has gone away for a couple of days and she wouldn't leave me an address."

I picked up the telephone receiver and held it out to her. "If you like, you can call her head office and they'll tell you the same thing."

She shook her head and waved the phone away. "I will have that tea though," she said and her voice was deep, pleasant, just a little shaky. "You are... ?"

"I'm Maura. I'm just her assistant."

"Do you know who I am?"

I nodded. "Yes. I'm really sorry," I added, uselessly.

Elizabeth wiped a strand of wet hair out of her face and looked at me directly. "What's she like?"

I was mortified. "In what way?"

"Beautiful? Intelligent?" She half-smiled. "Dumb?"

I shook my head. "Not dumb. Quite, quite pretty. Quite intelligent, well, sort of sharp."

Elizabeth nodded slowly. I wonder if she realised I was playing down Kim's attributes to make her feel better. "What does she want?"

I shrugged. "Not this," I said, honestly. "She didn't mean things to go this far." I paused. "That's, that's why she's run away for a while, I think. She's horrified."

"Oh." Elizabeth looked stricken. "So, it's not her, then. It is what he wants, after all."

I said nothing, just made what I hoped was a sympathetic face.

She took a sip of tea and looked at me again. "And what do you think about it all?"

"Well, it's not really any of my business."

"But I'm asking you. For an opinion."

"I hate it," I said. "I wish it had all never started. I think she was mad and... " I looked at Elizabeth. "... I think he's mad too."

She took a deep breath. "He's quite adamant, though." She put down her mug, carefully, and gave me another sad smile. "Thank you very, very much for the tea and sympathy, anyway. I'm sure you'll tell the young lady I was here, but, there isn't a message."

She stood up and walked out, with a stoop to her shoulders that hadn't been there on her way in.

I hated being alone in the office and suddenly I didn't know how I felt about my new best friend. The thought of going home, where I was somehow expected to show Nick some signs that I was saving money, didn't appeal at all. For the first time in ages I felt deeply depressed.

My first instinct was to go out to the nearest shop and buy something to cheer myself up, but that, of course, was off limits too. I knew I needed hair shampoo but had to think hard about whether I could bring home my preferred expensive brand from the local hair salon, or whether Nick would spot it and complain. I decided I would have to buy a cheaper one from the chemist just to ensure that Nick didn't get annoyed. The ridiculous, burning resentment I felt towards him, over this small issue, came as something of a shock.

I was suddenly snapped out of my thoughts by a thudding noise on the door downstairs. I knew that it wasn't locked, but it didn't sound like anyone wanting to come in, more like someone kicking or punching the door itself.

Tentatively, I went down the stairs, with their familiar, damp, old-carpet smell making me feel slightly sick. The noise stopped. I opened the door and put my head outside, but no-one was there. I glanced at the door. It was covered in something, white, powdery, sticky. Flour and eggs. And someone had chalked the words 'Fucking slag' along the top of the door. I ran outside to the soaking market place and stared around. All I could see were a few people, buried under their umbrellas and hooded coats. No-one was looking my way. There were no obvious culprits, but I knew that somewhere, they'd be still around, watching for a reaction. I went back inside, slammed the door, ran upstairs to get my things and then left for home.

I needed to talk to someone and the only person I had

was Nick. As soon as Rosie was in bed that night, I told him what had happened. He gave a sigh. "I could see that coming," he said.

I rolled my eyes. "So why didn't you warn me? I'd have stayed at home today," I growled.

"I don't exactly mean the door thing," he said patiently, patronisingly. "I mean there was bound to be a reaction to what Kim was doing. You know what people round here are like."

"Oh, yes, I do. What do you mean, what Kim was doing? She wasn't doing it by herself, you know. I bet no-one's thrown flour at Keith Thomas' door."

"But she was breaking up a twenty-five-year marriage."

"She wasn't the one who was married," I said. "How does she get all the blame?"

Nick shook his head. "You are totally on her side, aren't you?"

"Yes. Totally. She's my friend."

"*She's my friend.*" Nick's mimicking drove me mad with rage. I couldn't speak so I walked out to the kitchen and Nick followed. "Maura. I didn't like to say anything but everyone thinks Kim is a really bad influence on you. She's turning you into something you're not. You're not a glamour girl with money to fling around, but you're acting like you are. And the two of you are so close, you're like a bloody witches' coven. It's okay for Kim but you're married with a kid and you're acting like a silly schoolgirl." There was such venom in his voice as he spat each word out. It almost felt like he'd been waiting for this moment, all that spite building up inside.

I glared at him dumbly. I was close to tears and I wanted to scream and punch him, all at the same time.

"I think you should pack that job in. It's not doing us any good and that Kim is just going to get you into trouble."

I slammed a plate down on the bench. "Who do you think you are? My dad or something? I'll choose my own friends and... "

The next thing I knew, I was stumbling backwards and half-falling against the oven. Nick had struck me hard across the side of the head and now he was standing over me, grasping my ear and a clump of my hair, so close that I was breathing in his breath and feeling tiny flecks of spittle on my skin.

"I'll tell you who I think I am. I'm your fucking husband and I earn the money that you live on. I'm the one who's subbing your stupid spending habits and I'm the one who's sat back while you've made me look like a prat, behaving like a twelve year old with the town whore.

"It stops now. Do you hear me? It stops. Tomorrow you will ring that fucking editor and pack that job in. And you will start acting like a proper wife and a proper mother. And you will stop seeing that slag you call a friend." He shook my head, by the grasp he had on my hair. "Well? What are you going to do?"

"Pack in the job," I answered, dully, trying not to move my head.

"And?" He shook me again.

"Stop seeing Kim."

"Right." He let go, turned his back on me and walked into the next room.

I stayed in the kitchen, shaking, trying to stop, fighting back the tears that I thought would annoy Nick even more. I rubbed my throbbing left ear and the side of my head where my hair had been wrenched. I was sore but that didn't matter. What mattered were two things. First, Nick was taking away the things that made me happy. And secondly, I was deeply humiliated. I knew at that point that I would never forgive him. But I also knew that I was afraid of him. I was afraid of the person I lived with.

We spent a dreadful weekend together, not because there were more rows, as I was careful to avoid them, but because I had to pick and choose every word I said. I felt I couldn't mention anything that had to do with work, with Kim, or with anything that involved spending money, even on reasonable things. It felt as if the slightest thing might spark off Nick's anger. On the surface, he seemed to have cooled down considerably and spent most of his time playing with Rosie, and keeping up a relatively pleasant front. He was good at that when he wanted to be. But my own shame and fear were still there, following me around.

I persuaded Nick that the editor could not be contacted over the weekend, and made up my mind that as time went on, I would try to gently talk Nick out of making me resign. I wasn't sure how realistic this was.

I walked slowly to the office on Monday morning. It was the first time I had ever felt really reluctant to go there. I made sure to go early and, armed with a damp cloth, I rubbed away the chalk words. They had been added to over the weekend, to include more obscenities about Kim.

Then I realised the door was already unlocked and went slowly, very cautiously up the stairs. With relief, I saw that it was Kim who'd beaten me to the office.

"I was cleaning the door," I said, foolishly, waving the raggy cloth at her.

She gave me a small smile. "Thanks. Kettle's on."

"How was your weekend?"

"Good. It was really great to get away. I know it looked like running away from the mess, but honestly, I did a lot of thinking and I talked to some good mates and I really feel like I can sort myself out." She looked at me. "God, Maura. Are you okay? You look awful."

"Thanks!"

"No, I mean, you look like something awful has happened. What's up?"

I told her everything, from Keith's visit, to his wife's visit, to the row with Nick, although I left out the violence.

Kim listened, made tea and put her arm around my shoulders. "He wants me to quit this job and stop seeing you. He means it, Kim. I don't want to but I don't see what else I can do."

"Tell him to sod off."

"I can't he's my husband and, I'm skint and he's having to bail me out. It's such a mess."

Kim sighed loudly. "Right. Let's think. Tell him you've spoken to the editor and you have to give three months notice."

"Will he believe that?"

"It happens. Tell him there's a financial penalty in your contract and you have to stick to the notice period or pay back some money. That gives you a bit of grace. In the meantime, I will be on my best behaviour. I've officially given Keith the elbow so that's all in the past. I could even go and see Nick and sweet-talk him for you. When things are a bit calmer."

"Best not." I longed to blurt out to Kim that Nick had hit me. But something inside me stopped the words from coming out.

The day went quickly, probably because being in Kim's office was so much easier than being at home. It was shortly after two, when I was about to leave, that the telephone rang and Kim picked it up.

"*What?*" she said, in such a tone that it made me freeze. I looked at her face and saw that she had gone very pale. I listened.

"Oh, god. Oh, no. I'm so sorry. What do you want me to do?" Then, after a long pause, "Yes, yes, you're right. Oh, bloody hell. Look, thanks for ringing. You take care." She placed the receiver down and put her head in her hands. From underneath her heavy hair, she said, in a tiny voice, "Elizabeth Thomas has killed herself."

I dropped my bag and ran over to her and held her tightly. For the first time ever, I felt Kim start to cry. I felt useless.

"Was that Keith?" I asked.

"He found her this morning. She'd taken pills or something. He's in a terrible state. He was telling me because he thinks there'll be more trouble, you know, more people vandalising the office, or worse. He's advised me to get away again."

"Oh god, Kim."

I'm ashamed to say one of my first thoughts was whether or not Nick would hit me for this. It sounds terrible now, but at the time my instant reaction was to think of myself and Rosie. Would there be another scene? With Nick being the way he was, I couldn't risk any harm coming to my daughter, nor did I want her listening to her mum and dad fighting again.

But I held Kim and stroked her hair and listened to her as she talked. She told me she would call her editor and ask if she could work in the head office for a couple of weeks. She'd be straight with him about what had happened. He'd find out anyway.

"Maura, will you keep an eye on my flat? You've got the keys. I just think some of the local nutcases might take it on themselves to smash it up or something."

I promised her I would. We hugged and kissed and she left, quickly.

I went home feeling completely alone.

Saturday afternoon.

I delve under my bed and take out one of the heavy, dusty coffee jars full of pound coins. I have to shake off a thick cobweb from my fingers. I tip the jar and count out fifty pounds, one by one. Almost a year's savings for me, these days. Then I tip out another of the jars. I wrap the coins in some old cloths to stop them from jangling too much and put them in my bag, then go out to the shops.

The bag is ridiculously heavy and the shop assistants sigh as I count out all the payments in single coins. I apologise and make a joke about it, saying I've been saving up my pocket money. Sometimes they smile, sometimes not. I haven't spent anything on myself in this way since leaving Dowerby and it feels almost like a criminal act, hugely extravagant. Soap and aqueous cream for my face, because my skin feels dry, are the only luxuries I usually buy.

I look at windows and items that I would normally pass

without a glance. First, I buy a glossy magazine, a new one. It costs £3.90. Once, I would have bought several of these every month. These days, I only see the ones that get left behind in the café or that the other girls bring in and let me read in my lunch break. I flick through it in the way Kim and I both used to do, to see the sorts of clothes that people are wearing these days. Purple-type colours seem to be very 'in'. Clarets and mauves, that sort of thing.

Next, I go into a cheap clothes shop, the kind you often find on small high streets. Badly-made, throwaway clothes, I know. But this is the limit of my budget. I try to ignore the fact that most of the customers in this shop are teenagers, effectively buying fast-fashion clothes they'll only wear once or twice. As I'd hoped, I find a bargain. It's an aubergine-coloured dress with a belt, a cheap version of the designer dresses in the magazine. I try it on, and it looks better than I'd even hoped. It only costs £24.99.

Then, into Boots, every woman's second home, as Kim used to call it. I buy a wine-coloured lipstick (£6), a black mascara (£9), a hair-dye kit called 'Golden Honey' (£8.75), a blusher (£5) and a tube of foundation (£12). For 75p, I buy a trial size bottle of a new oil to put in the bath, and for £1.05p, a sachet of face mask. At the perfume counter, I persuade the assistant to let me take away some tiny samples of two types of scent and matching body lotions. My next stop is at what I always call the local bucket shop, one of those odd-smelling bargain discount shops that sell everything. I buy a small, plastic photo album for £1.25.

It's only on the way home that I ask myself the question I've been pushing to the far corners of my mind. Why had I suddenly felt the need to buy all those things? I'm going out tomorrow night, I argue back at myself. I haven't had any new clothes for more than five years, I only have the handful of outfits I took away with me, which are faded and worn. I'm going to a nice restaurant somewhere and I want to look halfway decent. What's wrong with that?

So, I've spent more than a year's savings on almost nothing. The money's just sitting there. What else is it for? I know the answer to this, of course. It's for an emergency getaway. An urgent cab or train fare. But there's still some left. Enough. Probably.

As a last stop on the way home, I call into the bakers and buy a fresh cream cake to have with my tea when I get home. I realise I have really enjoyed myself. For the first time in years.

I get back to the flat and put on the hair dye, then run a hot bath. When I come out, I sit around in my tshirt and have my tea and cake. I arrange the photos of Rosie in the album. There are fourteen photos: several of Rosie at a farm, petting and feeding various animals, and more of Rosie playing with the little tabby kitten, in the old house back at Dowerby. She'd always wanted a kitten. I'd promised to get her one when she was old enough to help look after it. There's a picture of her sitting at the top of a slide in the local park and one of her in a Brownie uniform. I marvel at how long and thick her hair is now. She gets that from Nick, not me. There's one of her in her blue school jumper, proudly holding a little certificate. I squint and peer but, frustratingly, I can't see what it is she's won. I feel this like a little stab. I can't even guess what it is that my own daughter is so good at. It could be reading or it could be drawing, she was always good at those things. Or she could have discovered she is better at science, like her father. It could be for good behaviour. I rather hope it's not.

That evening, I have to go to work in the wine bar. I've experimented with the new make-up. "Wow, you look great," says Cathy. "I've never seen you with make-up on. What's the occasion?"

"Nothing."

"Don't believe you," grins Cathy, nudging me gently. "It's a fella. It is, isn't it?"

I find, irritatingly, that I am blushing, and for no reason. "It's not. It's really not. I just, I'm going out tomorrow with, er, with my brother and I haven't seen him for a long time and I thought I'd treat myself."

She weighs me up, a knowing expression on her face. "Your hair looks good too. I like the colour. Your *brother* will be really impressed," she says, with a wink.

"Don't," I plead.

Cathy drops the subject for an hour or two. Later, when we take a short break, she for her cigarette, me for a long glass of iced water, she tackles me again.

"You know, you're such a dark horse. One of the girls was saying the other night that you never come out with us. We like you very much, you know. But sometimes it's as if you don't trust the rest of us. Not enough to tell us anything. We don't really get it."

Standoffish, cold, she means, just like Nick used to say. I look away from her.

"There was a girl here a while back. She'd run away from a bloke who used to beat her up. I think she was nervous of saying anything, at first. But eventually she spilled the beans, and you know, it meant we could sort of look after her. We could make sure no-one answered any questions about her, check that she always got home alright, that kind of thing. We stick together, here." She pauses and looks at me. "No-one here would think any the worse of you. No matter what the story was."

I take a deep breath out. "Cathy, the thing is, you're right, I'm running away too. I really don't want my husband, or anyone who knows him, to find me. So it's hard for me to get friendly with people. That's all, really."

Cathy pats me on the shoulder. "Okay, love, don't worry." Then she grins. "But who's the new fella? Tell me that much. Give us a bit of good gossip."

I sigh. "I don't know him very well. I don't think I want to get involved but, hey, I'm getting a night out and that's unusual for me. So I'm making the most of it."

"Good for you," says Cathy.

She is one of those people who can't resist helping out. Before the shift is over, she has arranged to drop off some of her younger sister's clothes that she no longer wants at my flat the next morning. And she also arranges for me to give her three rings on the telephone every night, from the call box in my entrance hall, just to let her know I'm okay. We'll start this tonight.

This is nice. This is a bit like having a friend. I'm never very sure how it's supposed to be, real friendship, only how I imagine it should be, how it is in little girls' stories, before the boys come along.

Cathy is as good as her word. At around 11 o'clock the following morning she buzzes the intercom and I let her into the flat. She is only the third person to come inside since I moved here five years ago. I can see her looking around with interest as I make her a cup of coffee. "You are far too bloody tidy," she comments, and I smile. "You can't half tell you've never had kids."

She's brought a bin bag full of dresses, skirts, trousers, tops. "My bleeding sister. She spends a fortune on clothes and she hardly wears them. I'm sure she's about your size. We'd just throw these out otherwise, or put them in the charity bags, so you might as well take your pick. Just dump what you don't want."

I'm grateful. Yesterday's shopping spree has taught me how rarely I can buy new clothes, should I want to. I listen as Cathy fills me in on her family's likes, dislikes, habits. Then she waits for me to reciprocate.

Carefully, I tell her that yes, my husband was violent, and yes, I am effectively in hiding. I say he lives in the northeast. I tell her I have no other family.

"Apart from your brother," she grins, and I'm embarrassed.

"So it's all that time since you've had a fella. Or a decent night out," she says. "Bloody hell. Well, look. Don't let him come up here after your night out because you don't know him well enough. Tell him you've got a mate staying over at the moment, so he doesn't think you're on your own. And make sure you give me a bell, no matter how late it is, so I know you're okay."

I nod.

When she's gone, I look through the bag, and find I like most of the clothes. There are also two bottles of perfume which seem to have been opened, sniffed and discarded unused, several pairs of shoes and sandals, size 5, hardly worn, and even some cheap jewellery, chains, bangles and hair slides. I feel as if it's my birthday.

Then something deep in the pit of my stomach nudges me back into reality. I think about the conversations I've had with Cathy. I have almost convinced myself I am going out with some new boyfriend. When in fact I am going to meet a journalist, to pick over the horrible details of the worst time of my life and the worst thing I ever did. What on earth made me imagine I was going to enjoy myself? Momentarily I panic and tell myself I can't possibly go. But something makes me take a bath, put on the new make-up and the new dress, coupled with Cathy's sister's sandals and one of her bracelets. My insides, though, feel as if I am at sea.

Paul Hollings arrives at 7.30, prompt. Journalists are always on time, Kim used to say, unlike photographers, who're always late.

He gives a little start when I open the door and then a huge grin. "You look stunning," he says. I mumble something contradictory and we go downstairs where he has a cab waiting. These days, I keep imagining there is someone hanging around outside my flat, and again, for a moment, I think someone is standing beside the row of plastic bins, smoking, just watching. But I can't see them properly and we drive off straight away. Paul takes me to a restaurant somewhere around Covent Garden, where a pianist is playing quietly and the lighting is very subdued. I spot someone from a TV soap and try not to be too impressed.

Paul excuses himself and goes to the toilet where, he later tells me, he called his news desk to check that the actor in question is with his legitimate partner, which, it seems, he is. "So what if he isn't?" I ask. "What would you do?"

"We'd get a photographer out to snatch a pic," says Paul. He looks at me. "Do you think that's wrong?"

"Not as wrong as two-timing your wife," I shrug.

Paul spots an in. "Nick wasn't exactly faithful, I gather," he says, by way of a question.

I twirl my fork around my plate. "Well, no. But I didn't know that for ages. Kim used to say that any man would be unfaithful given the chance, and I used to argue with her, but now I think she was right."

"Tell me all about Kim, then."

I don't have much appetite when it comes down to it. So I start to tell him everything, from the beginning. I'm about to tell someone about the worst thing I've ever done.

Chapter Six

It is hard at first, trying to tell Paul Hollings my story. I stumble over the right words, make several false starts, leap too far ahead. I wish I had rehearsed this better in my head. All this, along with trying to pick at the first three-course meal I have had in five years, and fight back the nauseous feeling inside.

But Paul is patient. There is something about his babyish face and his wide smile that makes it easy to talk, although I keep trying to remind myself that I am not confiding simply in him, but, potentially, in several million readers of a national tabloid newspaper. My story is to become Paul's story, which becomes the newspaper's story. Is it then still my story? Or, if I sell it, as Paul is suggesting, can I no longer claim to own it?

At intervals such as when I am particularly hesitant, Paul interrupts with some kind of unrelated small talk, about the food, the pianist, the weather, his work. It is a technique which gives me some relief and lets me sort out my thoughts before going back to the subject. He is a kind interviewer, gentle, non-adversarial, so that you are inclined to keep talking. He's also very good company, or so I am finding as the evening progresses. He has a fund of funny stories about his job, his friends, his family. He makes me keep laughing out loud, even though I am so out of practice.

The weather at the beginning of that June, five years ago, was disappointing, as people called it. What they meant was it was raining almost every day and there was usually a stiff, cool breeze to accompany it. It was depressing to look out of the window every day and see the colourless sky, and even the trees and shrubs seemed weighed down with too much moisture, their darkening greenery looking heavier every day. Even the lipstick-coloured roses that filled most people's gardens in Dowerby couldn't cheer up the scenery; their heads drooping and nodding like old alcoholics, rain-drunk. The annual coach loads of trippers who visit Dowerby every summer traipsed around the town centre in hooded waterproofs looking cheated and glum, and they filled up the tearooms for hours, with their smells of wet anorak. Nick was concerned that the fair was going to be a washout so he started becoming slightly obsessed with long-term weather forecasts. He also started being much nicer to me. For a while, there were no more rows. He became markedly more affectionate. He told me I was a nicer person when Kim was not around. I think he meant I did what I was told.

I spent a miserable two weeks alone in the office. Without Kim, the place felt dingy and cold. I noticed damp patches and curling strips of wallpaper I hadn't spotted before. Even the stories I tapped into the computer felt dull and pointless. On the day of Elizabeth Thomas' funeral, I went in to find two of the windows had been smashed. Taped to one of the half-bricks thrown through the glass was a newspaper photograph of Mrs Thomas, taken some time ago at a charity function. Taped to the other was one of those corny notes made up of newsprint words. It said: Dead because of you Whore.

I called the local police and they said it was unlikely someone would get out to see me today as many of the officers were at a funeral. They finally sent a young female police officer the following afternoon, by which time I'd had to clear up the mess myself and arrange for the windows to be replaced. She said I probably shouldn't have cleared it up if I'd wanted the vandals caught. She asked me if I had any idea who had done the damage. I said I hadn't. We both knew that nothing would be done about it.

I went round to Kim's flat to find what looked and smelled like dog dirt smeared around her front door. It was Nick, to give him credit, who came round to help me clean it up and splash disinfectant around. I was relieved to find that whoever had done it hadn't got inside the flat.

Kim didn't turn up again until a few days after the funeral. I was sitting at the computer typing up what Kim called 'overnights', little, relatively unimportant local stories which could be safely held over to the next night's paper. Kim sometimes called them the 'teddy bears' picnic' stories because they often involved things like school projects and fundraising events. I heard her voice coming up the stairs and was overjoyed, until the door opened and I saw she had someone with her, another young woman, a colleague from the paper's head office. "My god, I see what you mean, darling," the woman said, looking around the office and then at me, wrinkling her nose. "It's a bit Third World."

"Hi, Maura," Kim said, coming to give me a hug. "This is Nicky, she works with me in head office. Maura, I'm not stopping long, I've just come to pick something up. I'm going to work at base for a few more days. How are you getting on?"

I decided not to mention the vandalism and she didn't notice the new windowpanes, although they were markedly cleaner than the old ones. I also didn't want to tell her about what had happened at her flat, not until things had settled down. I gave her a bland update about the calls we'd had and I handed her some scribbled messages that I hadn't got round to forwarding her by email.

Kim kept giggling with Nicky about some private joke. All she told me by way of explanation was that it related to a party Nicky had held the night before, from which they were still rather hung over. It got annoying very quickly, the way stories do when they're about something you missed.

Then Kim took a white box out of a large canvas bag and opened it. It contained glossy photographs, professional studio portraits of her face. She handed one to me and one to Nicky. "Go on then, what do you think? Be honest."

She was talking to Nicky.

"They are really good. Gorgeous. You look great, darling. They'll never turn you down."

Kim glanced at me. "I've applied for some TV jobs," she explained. "Just regional ones, you know. But I had to have the photos done to go with the applications. So, what do you think?"

"You look fantastic, of course," I said. "Like a model. They're gorgeous."

Kim grinned. She took out some of the photos, put them in an envelope and put the rest in her desk drawer.

What I was thinking, of course, was that Kim could have told me earlier she was applying for other jobs. It was obviously no surprise to Nicky, her new best mate. My mind raced ahead to the idea of working with another reporter, perhaps a man, perhaps a woman that I didn't get on with, perhaps someone like Nicky who would wrinkle her nose at me. I didn't like the thought of it.

Kim was already making her way out of the door, with Nicky in tow. "I really don't want to hang around. I don't want to get spotted by anyone with, you know, evil intent," she said, only half-joking.

"Bye," I said, unhappily.

After she left, I felt as if there was a heavy stone in my stomach, and I tried to rationalise it. It was partly that Kim was likely to leave and that meant my own job would change dramatically. But more than that, it was the feeling that I'd been kidding myself about our friendship. Kim wasn't really concerned about me. If she left the newspaper she would barely keep in touch, I knew it.

She'd turned out just like the half-friends I'd had at school.

I was a good fall-back for her, but there was always someone cooler, funnier, more interesting to spend time with. Just like those girls years ago, Kim had a whole other social life going on, and I was not good enough to be invited.

That evening at home, Nick made me laugh by parading around in the judge's costume he'd have to wear at the fair. "You look daft," I giggled, although carefully.

"You can't say that, I'm the judge," Nick said, pretending to sound stern. "I could sentence you to a ducking." Then he made a grab for me and chased me, laughing, into the bathroom, where we had a mock scrum, and he ended up taking off my clothes and pushing me into the shower. "Duck, you wench," he grinned, pulling off his own clothes and jumping in beside me.

Afterwards, he was kind. He dressed and brought me a glass of wine and wrapped his robe around my body. "We are good together, you know," he said, which was something he used to say a lot. "We are totally compatible. We fit together."

I knew that what he really meant was that he wasn't too tall and he liked me for being much smaller. Nick was the sort who couldn't cope with a woman being above him in any way. But I took it in the spirit of the moment and held him closer. I ended up confiding in him about what had happened that day. "Kim made me feel really, you know, left out," I said. "I'm so pissed off with her."

"She was never a real friend," said Nick. "I could have told you that ages ago. I could tell you some more things about her that would prove it, but you don't want to hear them."

"What do you mean?"

"You don't want to know. Just don't ask."

I had to press him for some time, but eventually he sighed. "Okay. But you really won't like this. She made a pass at me."

I swallowed my wine too quickly and coughed. My stomach lurched. "She didn't. I don't believe you."

"I knew you'd say that. That's why I never said anything before. But she did, Maura. Some mate, eh?"

"When was this?"

"A few weeks ago now. Remember that row about the box of chocolates? That's why I didn't want to talk about it. How do you think I felt?"

"How do you mean, she made a pass at you? What happened?"

"She obviously thought that I'd brought her chocolates because I fancied her. She just came up and said thanks, and put her arms around me and gave me this, this really obvious hug. I didn't know where to look."

"Are you sure she meant... "

"Oh, yes. She was angling for a real snog, I could see it. It was really hard to get away."

"You should've told me," I said, with a hideous, burning feeling deep inside.

"Look, don't say anything to her. I'm sure she's embarrassed about it now. And she's probably leaving soon. Let's just forget about her, eh? Maura, she's not worth it."

I think it was the next day that Sally poked her unwanted face around the office door. "Is the slag still away?"

"Stop it, Sally," I said, more out of dislike for her than loyalty to Kim.

"Yes, alright, although why you keep sticking up for her I'll never know," Sally grunted, and sat down, uninvited. "I just wanted to see how you were doing. All on your lonesome in this grotty hole."

"Dowerby, you mean?" I said, sulkily.

"No, I mean this crappy office," she said. Thick-skinned as ever. "Look, Maura, I know we don't always see eye to eye. But I think your Nick is a nice bloke, really hard-working and he's putting all his energies into the Fair week, which is a big thing for us. Everyone in the town is grateful."

"Why are you telling me?"

"Because it's obvious you just don't appreciate him.

You've been swanning around with that sl... with that Kim, like bloody Thelma and Louise and you're making him look like a prat. He doesn't deserve it.

"And I know you think you've got no friends round here. But people really like you, or at least they did before that Kim arrived. They just don't feel they know you very well, but they want to, you know. Why don't you give people a chance?"

It occurred to me, later, that I used this moment as an excuse to get all my anger out, on someone for whom I had no real feelings. "A chance?" I said, deliberately raising my voice and screwing up my face for some high drama. "A chance for what? A chance to turn me into one of you morons, I suppose?"

Sally started to say something but I just kept going. "A chance to help me to become really stupid and really prejudiced. A chance to spend all my time in church and then come out slagging off all the other women in sight, in case they turn out to be competition. A chance to turn into a total housewife, because it's just not done to have a job and a bit of independence, even though my daughter spends most of the day at school. A chance never to enjoy myself or have a bit of a laugh. A chance to become a typical country vegetable."

I knew I was ranting and not particularly making sense, but I didn't care. Sally stood up and glared. "Fine," she said. "I only came here to help Nick. I think there's something wrong with you, Maura." She pointed to her head and waved her finger around. "I think you need to see the doctor."

"Fuck off," I yelled after her as she made her way down the stairs. When she'd gone, I started to laugh at myself. Then I slumped back down at the desk.

Of course, I knew she'd run straight to Nick and tell him about my performance. I was worried that he'd be angry and I prepared a different version of the story, in which Sally had been insulting first. When Nick came home, he asked me what had happened and seemed to buy my version entirely.

"I'm sorry," he even said. "It's my fault. I said I was worried about you and that you were a bit lonely. She insisted on going round, although I know you're not keen on her. What could I say? I thought she meant well. I suppose she can be a bit of a cow."

I was so grateful that he was on my side that I ended up hugging him. I could almost feel Kim judging me.

Paul listens to all of this, carefully. Every now and then he makes a scribbled note in the jotter by his plate, but I can't read it as it's in shorthand. Kim did that kind of shorthand. I'd always meant to learn.

I realise I've been talking for some time and he has finished his dessert while mine is in front of me, untouched.

"Hey," he says. "You'd better eat that thing up, or I'll do it for you. Give your tonsils a rest, eh?"

I'm grateful for the break and start to eat the chocolate torte. There is so much chocolate in it that I physically shudder when I take the first mouthful.

"That Kim. She was quite a girl, wasn't she? I wish I'd known her. She sounds like a laugh."

"She was. I mean, she was trouble as well. But she didn't deserve what she got."

Paul gives me a sympathetic look. I find I am starting to like him, quite a lot. I think he's clearly good at his job. I always admire people who are good at what they've chosen to do. Kim was a great reporter, even though everyone assumed she got stories out of people because of how she looked. Paul, on the other hand, is what Kim would have described as no oil painting, plump and slightly balding on top, with short, chubby fingers. And yet, I think, there's something about him, a gentle way of talking, that slightly bashful smile. Confiding in Paul turns out to be no trouble at all. But then I think about what Kim would have said. It would be something along the lines of never trusting a journalist and that I could do better than that.

We end up among the last customers in the restaurant.

"Listen," says Paul. "I'll get us a cab. I think I should see you safely home and then I'll push off. But we'll need to arrange to meet up again. We need to get through the rest of the story. Is that alright?"

"Um, yes, I suppose so. Am I waffling?"

"Not at all. Retelling all this must be painful for you. I want you to feel okay about it."

I want to say that, in a strange way, I have enjoyed it, but I think this may sound weird, so I just turn away and look for my coat.

When the cab arrives outside my block, Paul asks the driver to wait a few moments, then he walks up the stairs with me and lingers as I put my key in the door. I turn towards him. "Thanks for the meal and everything," I say. I feel vaguely dirty, as if I've been doing something much worse than talking. "Er... when do you want to... you know... "

Paul gives me a card. "Ring me on Monday. That's my own mobile number, you can call it any time, day or night. We'll get together again very soon. Hey," he says, "and take care." He smiles and gives my shoulder a soft nudge with his fist.

I go inside and wait a few moments. Something makes me feel uneasy. There is a smell. I can smell cigarette smoke. At first I try to tell myself it's lingering from the cab, but it's just too strong for that. The thing is, I hate the smell of cigarettes. I always have. And I can't think why it should be so strong here, inside my own flat. I slowly walk into the living room, the bathroom, the bedroom, flicking on the lights and opening cupboard doors. There is no sign of anyone here. When I'm sure of this and certain that Paul has left, I head back for the door. I haven't forgotten to call Cathy to let her know I'm okay, and there's an old-style payphone on the landing below mine. I give her three rings and hang up, the coin dropping back down with a clunk. There's a thought that won't stop gnawing at me. Paul found me by a stroke of luck, he says.

His good luck, my bad luck, maybe. But if he can find me, then so could anyone. I go back inside and close the door, instinctively still using the deadlock, chain and the little alarm. The smell, though, lingers.

Chapter Seven

I don't know what to make of the whole evening. I don't even know how I feel about it. Sitting at that restaurant, one I'd never be able to afford, made me feel so special. Nick would never have taken me anywhere like that. I really liked Paul's company too, but I know I should keep my guard up. Journalists are very good at being nice to you when they want your story. If you bother them afterwards, they get fed up with you and behind your back they'll call you a 'journo-groupie'. Maybe that's what I am. It's the whole pull of knowing the gossip before everyone else, being part of a really cool clique. I think Kim would understand what I'm doing. Maybe she'd even give it the okay. But I have to think about what I'm saying. Tell the story so that I come out of it in one piece. It won't make me look very good. But after all this time, I just need to tell the truth.

Monday night. I'm working at the bar and Paul strolls in. I'm relieved that Cathy isn't working tonight, because she has him down as a stalker, but I'm baffled to see him. He greets me and doesn't call me Maura, which is also a relief. Over a pint, he asks me if we can talk again, soon. He's keen to finish the story and I am taking too long over it, I guess. But I've been lying in bed, rehearsing my words, so that I know how I am going to tell it. I say I don't work Wednesday evenings, and straight away he confirms our next session for then.

It's one of those situations where afterwards I think I should have said no. But I didn't. If I'm honest, the thought of having company on my night off gave me something to look forward to, almost. The smell of the cigarette smoke has gone, thanks to a few squirts of some eye-wateringly strong air freshener, but it's left behind an atmosphere. The thought that someone may have been inside my flat is too frightening even to entertain. And there is always the consolation that I might have just imagined it. There were no other signs of anything different after all.

Wednesday night comes around and there is Paul, pouring me a glass of cold white wine and sitting with his legs squashed under my tiny table, his notebook placed casually next to his hand. I don't usually drink these days. Paul has a black coffee. I breathe in the citrusy smell of the wine. It smells of giggly evenings at Kim's flat. And so I start my story again, where I left off.

Dowerby's miserable June days dragged on, chilly and grey. Everyone, but particularly the visitors, grumbled constantly about the weather. Shop assistants could be heard trying to cheer up the tourists: "We're used to it here, there's lots of things to do anyway. Have you been in the castle yet?"

Or else snapping at them, "Surely you didn't come up here for the weather!"

Or if all else failed, blatantly lying, "And yet last summer was beautiful... "

None were as downhearted as the members of the fair committee.

"All this work," moaned Jim from the café. "I'm telling you. You can bust your guts and it doesn't matter. If we get a wet week, no-one will make a penny. No-one wants to step outdoors when the weather's bad these days."

Someone suggested buying in a bulk-order of plastic hooded macs, printed with the Dowerby Fair logo, to sell to drenched tourists.

"Now there's a sure-fire way to make the sun shine after all," grumbled Jim.

"Great idea. And you can keep them for next year," Nick said.

"I'm not storing them," warned Jim.

"They can go in my loft, then," said Nick, anxious to maintain morale, such as it was.

"Anyway," Jim added. "There's no way you could get them now, at such short notice."

Everyone sighed.

Working in the newspaper office on my own, I lost count of the number of trumped-up little stories about the fair I typed and sent over in a desperate attempt to win it some regional publicity. The shortage of buckets for the ridiculous beer drinking competition. The need for beds for a brass band, visiting from overseas. The naming of the fair queen. The town crier losing his voice (to regain it, miraculously, just before the fair started). The local bookmakers taking bets on the weather with the odds-on favourite being seven wet days out of seven.

Kim, meanwhile, had continued to hide away, as Nick described it, in the newspaper's head office. It was a complete surprise when one afternoon she popped her head round the door. "Hey," she said, beaming. She was about the only person I'd seen smile in weeks. "Hold the front page. Have I got news for you. And other clichés."

"What," I muttered. "Let me guess. You've got a new job."

"No, not me. Not yet, anyway," Kim said, unfazed. She had a good way of letting sarcasm slide off her, although I'm sure she noticed it. "Put that kettle on, Maura, I am about to change your life."

"*My* life?"

Kim flung herself into the battered old chair and giggled. "Wait till you hear this, Maura. I've been chatting with the editor and we both think it's probably best if I don't come back to this office, for one reason and another. You know.

128

"But obviously we need someone out here. And to be honest, this can be a tough role to fill, because it's kind of isolating, and not many people want to live out here, that sort of thing."

"So who am I going to end up working with?"

"Aha. We're thinking of staffing this office with a new trainee."

I pulled a sulky face.

"You," said Kim, with an ear-to-ear smile. "The editor's thinking of training you up as a journalist. He thinks you've got the knack." She looked hugely pleased with herself. "So? What do you think?"

I couldn't find any words.

"I know. You're going to miss me dreadfully. I understand that," grinned Kim. "But just think, Maura. It's a proper job, if you can call journalism such a thing. More dosh. You'll go on our in-house training course and get a qualification. You'll get the car and you'll manage the office yourself. Aren't you pleased?"

"It'll be full-time. I can't drive," I finally said.

"So what? Rosie's starting school shortly. You can take driving lessons. You might even get the paper to pay for them if you haggle. Remember they're desperate to fill the office and no-one wants the job. God, Maura, I can't believe you're throwing obstacles in the way. I thought you'd be pleased. It was my idea, actually."

"Well, thanks," I said, not terribly gratefully. "I'll have a think about it."

Kim sat for a few moments, staring at me with raised eyebrows. "Alright, Maura. What's up?"

"Nothing," I said. My voice came out flat and unconvincing.

"Yeah, I believe that. Come on. Out with it." I paused. "I'll just go on and on at you until you tell me. Have I done something to upset you?"

I snorted. "You could say that."

"Well?"

"You have got some nerve, Kim. Nick told me."

"Told you what?"

"What happened between you and him."

Kim visibly flinched. So it was true. She even flushed slightly. "He told you? God, I didn't expect that. What on earth made him come out with it?"

"I thought you were my friend, Kim. I stuck up for you when people slagged you off. What the hell did you think you were playing at?"

Kim sat forward, her mouth slightly open. Then she gave a short laugh. "Maura. What did Nick tell you?"

"Exactly what happened. That you made advances on him. A couple of months ago."

"And you believed him." She sat back in the chair again, shaking her head. "Is there any point in telling you my version, or will you believe whatever your darling husband tells you?"

"What do you mean?"

"Maura, it happened the other way around. Nick told me a load of bollocks about how you weren't really getting on. Then he made a grab for me. I was in a horrible position and I'm telling you, if he'd been anyone else I'd have smacked his face. But as he was your husband I had to push him away as politely as I could." She sighed. "But I don't suppose you want to hear that. I suppose it's easier on you if I was the bad guy. Even though everyone knows... " She stopped and shrugged.

"What? Everyone knows what?"

"Oh, Maura. I shouldn't stoop to this, but, what the hell. Nick's had affairs at work. Two at least. All his workmates know. I found out from some of them I met out on a story a while ago. I wasn't going to be the one to tell you, but, well if Nick's saying that about me. He's a philandering little shit and you deserve better. That's the truth, Maura. You think what you like."

I struggled to take this in. My stomach felt like someone

had their hands inside me, pulling and tugging. "Who? Who has Nick had affairs with?"

"There was someone called Rhoda, a lab assistant. Very young."

"She babysat for us for a while. Then she stopped," I said.

"Yes, and some canteen woman. Elaine. Little fat thing."

"I've met her, too. Are you sure? Who told you?"

"A bunch of people from the factory. I met them out in a pub near head office. I was covering some charity event they were doing. We got chatting and it seems your Nick has a reputation. You might not want to believe me, Maura, that's up to you. But if I were you I wouldn't trust him. That's all."

I put my head in my hands and wiped them backwards through my hair, a gesture I'd picked up from Kim. "I suppose I should thank you for telling me."

Kim sighed and looked down at her feet. "No. I feel bloody terrible. What are you going to do?"

"I have no idea," I said. I felt as if I could easily throw up.

After Kim left, it occurred to me that perhaps I owed her an apology. Her version of events seemed much more likely to be true. But I didn't want it to be. Somehow I couldn't find it in me to call her or send an email. I was just left with the heavy feeling that I couldn't trust anyone any more.

I went to fetch Rosie from nursery. I did it the way people say they do things, on autopilot, and afterwards they can hardly remember how they got there. My head felt so heavy and confused it was like a bad hangover. Rosie, though, was excited because she had made a Father's Day card for Nick and I was charged with hiding it for her until the weekend. It must've been this that snapped my head back to normality, if it was ever going to feel like normality again. I thought that perhaps the adult thing to do would be to say nothing to Nick about Kim's accusations, and just to let it go. For Rosie's sake. She shouldn't have to watch another row and if Nick and I split up, which is where a confrontation like this could end, who's to say what effect it would have on her.

Funny. I never thought of myself as someone who would put up with being treated badly for the sake of someone else. But here I was and that was exactly what I was talking myself into doing. If you'd asked me a few years ago whether women should stay with bad partners for the sake of their kids, I'd have had no grey areas to consider. No-one should put up with unfaithfulness. No-one should put up with violence.

I decided to test myself. If I could get through tonight without blurting anything out to Nick, then that would be the hardest part over. I would probably feel slightly better tomorrow, and the next day, and the next. That queasy feeling inside that you carry around even when you're thinking about something else, it had to fade away eventually. Surely, sticking it out for Rosie's sake would be the sensible, unselfish thing to do, the best for everyone. What a good mother would do, I was sure.

In order to get through the evening, I mentioned the idea of my training as a journalist. I didn't say Kim had visited the office, I made out I'd spoken to the editor on the phone. Nick was surprisingly supportive. Maybe without Kim there, the whole job seemed less of a threat. "How much more money?" he asked, quite quickly.

"Er, he didn't go into details yet," I shrugged. "But obviously the prospects would be really good. What do you think?"

"Give it a shot. If you don't like it, you can always quit."

I knew I'd like it. I concentrated my mind on the idea of training for a new career and tried not to think too hard about whether or not my husband was a serial adulterer. By the end of the evening, I was mentally planning a diet and some new clothes, a haircut. Maybe I would eventually become so dazzling, so interesting, with my job and my new look that Nick would never stray again. It was worth a try. For Rosie if nothing else.

The next morning when I arrived at the office, Kim was already there.

"Hi. Your girlfriend's back and there's gonna be trouble," she sang. Then she gave me a sheepish look. "Are we? Friends again?"

I shrugged, rather gracelessly. "I suppose so. I can hardly blame you because my husband's a git."

"It is what's called shooting the messenger," grinned Kim, looking relieved.

She picked up a large brown envelope and waved it at me. "This is for you. It's blurb about the newspaper training scheme. You need to fill in a form and send it back to the editor's secretary. Bet you haven't mentioned it to hubby, though."

"I have, as a matter of fact. And believe it or not, he was okay about it," I replied.

"So you're going for it? Fantastic! You'll be great, Maura, I know you will."

Over a coffee, we filled out the course form and read through a shiny brochure about the training scheme.

"Normally," explained Kim, "They only guarantee you a job somewhere in the newspaper group, which could be anywhere in the country. But in your case, the editor specifically wants you here in this office, so you at least know where you're going to work and you know the area. It's a fun course to do, I did it and you can have all my books. Except for the law one, which is probably a couple of years out of date now, so you should buy a new one. You'll love it, Maura, honestly."

I already knew I would. It was strange for me to take on something new and big and yet not feel apprehensive. Perhaps, deep down, I thought it would never really happen.

"I'm staying on here until the end of June, sort of handing over to you, and then you'll take on most of the work yourself until September. The editor reckons you can handle it, pretty much, although if there was some really big story – ha, ha, not very likely here – they might send up a senior. Then it's over to the big city for your course. You'll come back as a fully-fledged reporter. And I'd guess this job is yours for as long as you want it!"

I found I was smiling rather stupidly. "God, Kim, who'd have thought it? It hasn't really sunk in yet."

"Only thing is, Maura, do you think Nick might hold you back a bit? I mean, if you end up working late and things, will he kick up a fuss?"

I sighed. "I'm not sure. I can only wait and see, I suppose. But so far he's been fine about the general idea. I was surprised, actually."

"Me too. I think he's so preoccupied with this bloody fair that he hasn't really grasped it yet. He might prove awkward once things start. How will he feel about the money issue?"

"What money issue?"

"You'll be earning more than him, once you qualify. Bet he hasn't realised that."

"Really? I didn't work that out. Are you sure?"

"Yep. I know what those factory guys are on and I know what you'll be on once you've passed the course. You'll beat him by a couple of grand a year. Think he'll feel emasculated?"

I laughed. "No idea. Hopefully he'll just enjoy the extra cash. And stop complaining every time I spend money."

It all sounded too good to be true, as if so many of my troubles were about to be solved. I should have known.

The day started going downhill when we decided to go out for a celebratory lunch. Kim's treat, she insisted. First we tried Jim's as Kim said she thought the cream cakes were worth going for, in spite of the atmosphere. But when we walked through the door, Jim turned around and walked towards us, abandoning the couple whose order he'd been taking. "The café is full. No seats," he said, firmly.

"What about that one?" I pointed to a table behind him, which, I naively imagined, he'd overlooked.

"Reserved," he snapped. "So are all the others." He stared at Kim, very pointedly. "You'll have to leave."

"What... " I started, but Kim touched my sleeve and lightly tugged me towards the door.

"Come on, Maura, it's not worth a scene," she said, under her breath, and we left.

I stood outside on the pavement, breathing hard, red in the face. A couple of people in the café were staring at us out of the window. "I can't believe he did that."

"I can. In fact, let's hop in the car and go somewhere a bit further away. I don't fancy being turned away like a leper more than once."

So we drove to a tiny, pretty village on the coast, some four or five miles out of Dowerby, and went into a pub for a seafood lunch. But the whole incident had left a sour taste in our mouths.

"I'll tell you what, Maura, I won't be sorry to see the back of this place," Kim admitted, licking salt off her fingers. "I'm sick to the back teeth of the parish-pump mentality and the bleeding moral majority. And I'll tell you something else. My goodbye present to Dowerby is going to be a nice, juicy story about all the corruption on the council. I've been working on it from head office."

"Wow," I said. "Tell me the details."

Kim told me she'd managed to persuade an ex-employee of the council who'd moved to another authority, a long way out of the area, to give her an anonymous interview. It was coupled with documentary evidence about planning applications that had been given the nod without proper consultation and against council guidelines. There were also allegations that leading councillors were taking bribes from certain local builders.

"It gets better," she told me, speaking quietly, but enthusiastically. "There've been some really dodgy coincidences. Like, one week, this guy I've interviewed was told to rubber-stamp the planning consent for a huge extension to a local magistrate's house, right out in the countryside and completely against the sort of guidelines they have for that area. He was told it wasn't important enough to go to the council committee for discussion. My chap argued that it should go to a committee and the chief planner told him, effectively, that he had to do what he was told, or else think about his future.

"So he does what he's told. Now get this. Two days later, on a Saturday morning, the magistrates' court is opened, even though there've been no overnight arrests to deal with. There are two cases heard, with no court list and of course, no press or public there. Both cases are drunk-driving. One is the chief planning officer and the other is the councillor in charge of the planning committee, both copped on their way back from the same bash a couple of weeks earlier, well over the limit. Neither of them lose their driving licence as they both plead that it's vital for their jobs. They both get £500 fines, which is hardly a punishment for either of them. Who hears the case? Only the magistrate who's just been allowed to build a bloody great monstrosity out in the green fields."

"Bloody hell, Kim. Can you prove all this?"

"Yes, every word. It's taken some digging around but I reckon the story's cast-iron now. They can sue if they dare. There are other things too. When he was still working for Dowerby council, my little mole was taken out and wined and dined by a local building firm who wanted to put up six whopping great luxury houses, again on greenfield land, just up the road from here. The planner and the councillor were there too. The way the conversation went it was pretty clear that both of them were getting backhanders from the builder. My man was offered free trips abroad and some cash, but he made his excuses and left, as the saying goes.

"A couple of weeks later, the housing scheme got the green light, even though there were objections from local people and the nature lobby. Again, it didn't fit in with the council's own guidelines on greenfield development. It all happened under the last reporter's watch. She never bothered covering any of it. Too busy in the church choir, I suppose."

I breathed out. "God, Kim. This is not going to make you any more popular round here, is it?"

Kim just laughed. "Oh, well. If I can really annoy some of Dowerby's biggest stuffed shirts then my time here hasn't been wasted. And in a place like this, the best time to do a major story is when you're about to leave. Because no-one here would ever speak to me again."

"Damn right they won't. Do you think they'll speak to me? Or will I be tarred with your brush?"

Kim swallowed a mouthful of her drink and waved the suggestion away with her hand. "No, of course you won't. Don't worry about it. They like you, it's me that's seen as the bad apple. Just disassociate yourself from me when I've gone. It'll be fine."

I watched her as she took out her tiny silver compact from her bag and checked her reflection in the mirror. As I looked at her, I found my eyes narrowing slightly. I had the uneasy feeling that my dream job might actually become nothing of the kind. It might be what a newspaper would call a poisoned chalice.

That evening, Nick came in with a large carrier bag. "I've got a present for you," he announced.

"Really? What is it?" I had some doubts. Nick had an irritating habit of saying he had something for me, when what he meant was he wanted sex. That had made Kim fall about with laughter when I'd confessed it once over a few drinks.

"Great present, a man's dick," she'd snorted. "Give me bubble bath any day."

Nick waved the bag. "A new dress, go and try it on."

"Thanks," I said, surprised. I took the bag in the bedroom and opened it. I pulled out a hideous, long, frilled, blue and white gingham dress. I turned to see him sniggering in the bedroom doorway. "What the, what is this?"

"Your costume for the fair. I knew you'd never get round

to getting one, so I hired one for you. I'm not having my own wife refusing to dress up."

"It's horrible!"

"Hey, you should've seen the others. I got first pick. You'd better tell Kim to sort her costume out quickly because there's going to be very little left."

"I don't think she's planning to wear one."

"She has to. She's the local reporter. Everyone's expecting her to dress up."

"I really don't think she will, Nick."

"Fine. Not wearing a costume is a ducking offence. I reckon if we decide to duck Kim, I could sell tickets."

I guessed he was right.

Paul Hollings takes more shorthand notes this time and makes me go back over some of the details several times. He's very interested in the council corruption angle. "I remember the story, you know, but I don't think she got a byline," he said. "No-one followed it up because there were threats of legal action flying everywhere. But she was quite a good reporter, your Kim, wasn't she?" His voice has a tone of slight surprise.

"More than quite good," I say. "She would've been on national news or something by now. If she hadn't... " I can't finish the sentence. A hot ache at the back of my eyes and nose tells me I'm going to cry. I have to dash to the bathroom and when I come back Paul has rinsed out his cup and is making to leave.

I see him to the door and wait to hear him close the external door to the flats. But I can overhear him talking. Another man's voice. My insides flip. I creep a little further down the stairs and peer down the stairwell. I can hear Paul's saying no to someone. "No, mate, sorry. I can't just let you in, this isn't where I live." The other man says something, too low for me to catch. "Sorry, pal, you'll have to wait for your friend to come back then, won't you?" I hear the outside door slam. I scuttle back up the steps and into the flat. I race to the window. My heart's beating hard and fast. I see Paul getting into a cab. He must've called for it while I was drying my eyes in the bathroom. There's a figure of a man, watching him, giving him the finger gesture as the cab drives away. Does he then look up at my window? I'm sure he does. But just for a split second. Then he turns and walks away.

I check that all my locks are in place. I pour myself another glass of wine and sit at the window, the curtains only half-open, looking at the black sky and the lights of south London. Usually I'm able to tune out the traffic but tonight I try to listen to its distant grumbles and hooting, if only to make myself feel a little less alone. I think about what it would be like if Kim was here, now. She'd put something I'd never heard before on the clunky old CD player and bring another bottle of wine from the fridge. We'd talk about our day. And we'd laugh. I don't usually let myself think this way. Perhaps it's the wine. I end up doubled over, clutching the emptiness in my stomach, sobbing like a baby.

Chapter Eight

I still haven't told Paul everything that happened. I'm dragging it out like a storyline in a soap. I don't even know why, although part of me recognises that, for the first time in a long time, someone is paying me some attention and it feels good. He has this nice way, when it gets hard for me to keep talking, of telling me funny stories. He's got enough for a book, I've told him. And it's been a long, long time since someone's made me laugh. So much so that I hardly recognise myself doing it.

I really wish I could talk to Kim about it all. Once, she warned me that journalists are never really your friend, even if you think they are. They don't really have friends, they have 'contacts'. They would use you for a story without a second thought, and if they have any qualms about it then they're probably in the wrong job, Kim said. I mustn't get used to Paul being around. But talking, having someone listen, getting the inside story on the latest news, it all feels so good. I think to myself that maybe Kim would not begrudge me that. If only I could ask her.

Another night where I've hardly slept. The creeping insomnia is making my brain feel as if it's only half-working. There are moments, and they only feel like moments, when I drift into blackness but then the slightest sound makes me jump awake. So when I stop trying and get up, my eyes feel sore and my face is white and puffy. Kim would've had me lying down with some sort of eye mask on, trying to sort me out. But I don't deserve to pamper myself like that any more.

It's only seven in the morning when the buzzer sounds. In all my five years living here, the buzzer's only sounded a handful of times, and most of those times the caller wanted to leave a parcel for someone else. And of course, there was Paul. This time, I wonder whether to answer it at all. It buzzes four times before I find the will to push the answer button. "Yes?"

And after all that, there's no answer. Just the sound of the street, traffic and someone's footsteps, striding past. I swear under my breath. The sounds have just clicked off and I'm heading for the kitchen when it buzzes again. This time I'm quicker. "Who is it?" No-one says anything. But I think I can hear breathing. Someone is standing quite close to the intercom, and listening. "What do you want?" I say, and I'm trying hard to sound strong. No reply. I stop answering and after another four or five buzzes, it stops.

The first day of Dowerby Fair was a Sunday and it finally arrived. As everyone predicted, it rained. Heavily. So heavily in fact, that some of the drains burst in our street and a sickly brown-coloured rivulet poured past the parked cars. Nick swore when he looked out the bedroom window. "It's going to be a total washout."

"You won't need to use the ducking stool," I said. "Everyone's going to be drenched anyway."

Nick didn't laugh. "Is your photographer coming?"

"Yes, the picture desk promised."

"Make sure they do," Nick grunted.

Rosie and I had a good giggle at Nick when he put on his ridiculous red judge's robes and old-fashioned white wig.

"Right, folks. Let's just try to make the best of it. Put your costume on, Maura."

"It'll get ruined, in this weather."

"Don't worry about that. Just get into the spirit of it, because if we don't, no-one will."

Reluctantly, I put on the hideous blue and white checked frock, over my jeans, tshirt and trainers. Rosie had another giggle and for some reason, this cheered me up.

We walked into the market square. The rain kept coming, hammering loudly on the stall tarpaulins as the sellers set out honey, fudge, candles and crafts. An overpowering sweet smell came from the van selling fresh doughnuts and there was a constant electric humming noise from the generators. A huge children's bouncy castle was waiting to be inflated and there were other rides like a little merry-go-round and some swings, still covered in plastic sheeting. Rosie begged to get on the rides straight away and took some persuading that she'd have to wait until they were all properly set up.

Some people from the fair committee came up to Nick. One of them was Sally, wearing some sort of black and pink lace concoction with a plunging neckline and a huge feathered hat. "God, Maura, what're you? Some sort of dairymaid gone mad?" she smirked.

"Blame Nick," I glowered at him. "He chose the thing." I couldn't help wondering if he mightn't have found me something a bit better.

At 11 o'clock, the tinny town hall bell rang out, and everyone was lined up for a procession around the town's main streets. Rosie loved to see all the people dressed up and clapped as the procession went by, laughing when they splashed in the puddles and trailed their silly skirts and cloaks along the wet cobbles. Nick was trying hard to make everyone as cheerful as possible, constantly cracking jokes and gee-ing people up when they complained about the rain. But the crowds were thin and the faces of the stallholders were as glum as the weather.

By lunchtime, there was no sign of the paper's photographer. Nick asked me to check up on him. I nipped into the office, struggling up the stairs with the stupid, now sopping wet dress getting in the way. I called Jack, the picture editor, and asked if a snapper was on their way.

"What's the weather like up there?" Jack asked.

"Not great. Bit wet."

"Hmm, thought so," he said. "Look, Maura, think we'll leave the pictures till tomorrow. The forecast's better. The pics will look really crap if we do them today."

"Oh, but with today being the first day I think they could do with the publicity."

"Sure, but we're a bit short-staffed and the paper's pretty full looking for tomorrow anyway, so we'll just leave it. We can get the pics any time this week, can't we?"

"Well yes, but the fair needs to… "

"Sorry, kid."

I started down the office stairs. I wasn't looking forward to telling Nick this news. Halfway down, I tripped on the hem of my long dress and struggled to stop myself falling, grabbing the stair rail and ripping the bottom of the dress. "Bugger it," I hissed, examining the long tear in the material. Then I realised this meant I couldn't wear it any more. "Every cloud," I grinned to myself, hoisting up the long skirt into a bunch so no-one would notice the tear.

I pulled Nick away from the group of committee men and told him that the photographer wouldn't be coming until tomorrow. He looked furious.

"What's the point of you working for that bloody paper if you can't swing us a bit of publicity when we need it?"

"Do you mind? I've written stories about this sodding fair until blue in the face. And I'm not the editor, I can't tell them how to organise their staff."

I stomped off home and got out of the mothball-smelling dress as quickly as I could. Rosie asked if she could try it on. I let her tramp around the house in it most of the afternoon, making sure the tear got even worse. I'd read a note that came with the dress, which said that any damage was covered by insurance, but that wearers were asked not to attempt their own amateur repairs to any of the costumes. "Good, that's me costume-free for the rest of the week."

Nick came home at around six. By that time, I'd started to feel a bit sorry for him so I'd cooked a full roast dinner, which I knew he'd enjoy. I wanted to avoid any confrontation in the slightest. If Nick took his bad feelings about the fair out on me, he might start laying down the law about my job. I didn't want anything putting that at risk. I know this was cowardly. It was bound to catch up with me, sooner or later.

"Sorry I went down your throat earlier on," he said. "It's just such a pisser, after all the work that's gone into the fair, to get rained on like this."

"The forecast's better for tomorrow," I said. "But surely there've been wet fair weeks before. Why aren't you more prepared for wet weather?"

Nick shrugged. "I don't know, really. I tried to make the committee think of more indoor events, but they keep putting obstacles in the way, and I can only do so much. I'm relatively new, you know."

"I'll keep badgering the news desk to get more stories in," I promised.

The next morning, the skies were grey but it wasn't actually raining. Nick's mood didn't lift, though. I took Rosie to nursery as usual and went straight into the office to phone the picture desk.

"He's on his way," Jack told me. "So you can stop panicking."

I rang Nick to tell him. He sounded relieved.

Mid-morning, I heard footsteps coming up the office stairs and the door slowly opened. Ned, a cheerful young photographer who Kim always called 'Deadhead Ned' for no apparent reason, gave me a mock salute.

"Here we are again," he said. "Every year the same, Dowerby Fair. Got a passenger with me."

Kim followed him into the office. "Hey," she said.

"What're you doing here?"

144

"Hell, Maura. You'll need to learn to be more diplomatic when you're a fully fledged reporter."

"If, you mean."

"No, when." Kim pushed an envelope at me. "I told Bray I'd deliver this myself."

I opened the white envelope. It was from Mr Bray, the editor.

Dear Maura,

This is to confirm that from July 15th your role for The Northern News *will change from Office Assistant to Trainee Reporter.*

As you know, the role will entail you becoming our full-time district reporter based in the Dowerby office. Although you will take up the role immediately, we will also send you on our in-house day-release training scheme, which will start in September.

A new contract with terms, pay and conditions will be sent out later this week.

Well done and thanks for all your hard work!

It was signed by the editor.

I rushed up out of my seat and gave Kim a hug. "This is down to you," I told her.

"Rubbish. If you couldn't do it, there's no way Bray would take you on. We'll drive out to that pub again for a celebration lunch if you like. But first, I need your help with a little job."

"Okay, it's pretty quiet." As soon as I'd said this, a brass band started playing outside in the street. The noise was dreadful. Kim, Ned and I all burst out laughing.

Ned said he was going to go out and get some shots of the fair. "I'll be about half an hour," he said. "You can explain to Maura what we're going to do next."

I looked at Kim as Ned thumped noisily down the stairs. "Well?"

"Maura, remember my exposé of the councillor and his chief planning guy?"

"Yes, of course I do. When's it going in?"

"It's just about done. What I need to do now is the worst bit, I have to front them up."

"What does that mean?"

"It means I have to go and doorstep them, you know..." Kim and I did a few steps of our made-up 'doorsteppin' dance and giggled. "I have to go and see them in person and put the allegations across. It's always a horrible job but you have to give them a chance to reply before you print anything like that. They'll probably tell me to fuck right off, or words to that effect. Anyway, Ned's going to try and get a snatch pic after I talk to them. And we just thought it would be a good idea if you were there too, taking notes, because then we'd have a backup version of whatever it is they say. If they say anything printable, that is."

"Sounds quite exciting."

"Well, I guess it's exciting for a local paper. I have to say, Bray's really twitchy about this story, even though we've had it legalled so many times I've lost count."

"So I just stand there with my notebook and write down anything they say. Or do."

"Yeah, that's about it. You don't really have to, because Ned'll be there to back me up too. But I thought it might be a good bit of experience for you and it's always helpful to have an extra witness, just in case they start getting funny afterwards."

"Sure. When do you want to go?"

"We'll go when Ned gets back. There's a council policy meeting going on this morning, which I reckon should finish in about an hour. We'll just lurk around the council chamber and when they come out we'll ask if we can have a word with Councillor Black and Mr Christopher in a private office." She rubbed her hands together. "And then we'll put it to them that they're a pair of crooks."

I grinned. "But more diplomatically than that, I expect."

"Yes, of course," said Kim, giving me her most demure face.

Ned came back up to the office, shivering and blowing on his hands. "Those people must be mad," he grumbled. "I don't see the point of it, myself."

Kim laughed. "Maura can tell you, her husband's the mad judge."

"Oh, sorry," said Ned.

I shook my head. "It's alright. I think it's a bit mad myself. But Nick's very into the idea of promoting the town and getting visitors in."

"I suppose it does that, though not in this bleeding weather. Any chance of a cup of coffee before we go and ruin these councillors' lives, Kim? I'm cold to the bone."

We re-boiled the kettle.

"The thing with Dowerby Fair is that it's the same every year, isn't it?" complained Ned. "You know, the same stalls, the same daft ceremonies, the ducking stool. That's weird, I reckon."

"Well, it's history, isn't it?" grinned Kim. "You can't change it even if you want to. Bit like Dowerby itself, eh, Maura?"

I rolled my eyes.

We made our way to the council chamber, a grey stone Victorian building that had been gutted inside to make way for safety doors, offices and meeting rooms full of new wood and smelling of carpet. Ned waited on the steps outside the building. Kim and I stood for around ten minutes in the deadened quiet of the corridor outside the council chamber. Eventually, the door swung open and people started filing out of the meeting room. Kim stopped one of the clerks. "Hi, we're from the *News*. Is it possible to have a word with Councillor Black and Stuart Christopher?"

The clerk said she'd fetch them for us.

They came out one after another. "What's this about?" asked the councillor, a tall, craggy-faced man with thick brown hair that looked like a wig. "Something your editor's put you up to?" I'd seen him before at meetings about Dowerby Fair. Like anyone who was anyone, he was on the committee. Kim gave him an apologetic shrug and a smile. "Could we have a chat in an office somewhere?"

"We can go to my office," said Stuart Christopher. "I've got ten minutes, then I've got to go to another meeting."

We followed them along the corridor and through a door that needed a security pass to open, with the councillor chatting all the way about the fair and the poor weather.

Once inside the office, Stuart Christopher waved us towards a couple of seats. "My name is Kim Carter. You know Maura."

"Yes, of course," said Black, smiling. "Your other half's a stalwart of the fair committee. Great bloke."

Kim went on. "Maura's training as a reporter for the *News*, starting shortly, so she's shadowing me today."

They both nodded kindly at me. I shifted in my seat and looked away.

I heard Kim taking quite a deep breath. "Councillor Black, Mr Christopher, the *News* is investigating some serious claims about the conduct of certain members of the planning committee and also some officers."

The expressions on their faces changed. They stared hard at her as she continued.

"The newspaper has documents which suggest that a number of planning consents have been made which are against council policy, particularly in greenfield areas. The evidence suggests that one of these was to the magistrate John Partington's house and that it was granted around the same time as both of you were given a very lenient sentence by him for a drink-driving charge."

The councillor's face went white and he started to bluster. "How dare you suggest… "

Stuart Christopher coughed and held up a hand. "Just a minute, just a minute. Can we be absolutely clear about what you're saying, Miss Carter?"

"It appears," said Kim, flicking through her notebook, although I was sure she wasn't reading anything from it. "It appears that on Saturday January 12th, the magistrates' court in Dowerby heard two cases of drinking and driving, the drivers being yourself and Councillor Black, who'd been arrested on the same night after a council function, for driving while over the limit.

"The court was effectively held in private and unusually, neither of you were banned from driving, although you both pleaded guilty to the charges. You were in fact given small fines."

"We told the court that... " began the councillor, but Christopher put a hand on his arm and shook his head.

"It can sometimes be legitimately argued, Miss Carter, that to take away someone's driving licence may cause them unnecessary hardship, and the courts do have discretion to waive this penalty in exceptional circumstances."

"Yes, I realise that," said Kim. "But it appears that only the week before the court case, you recommended that planning permission should be granted to a large extension on Mr Partington's house, in spite of this being in an area where the council policy is to restrict development. Councillor Black as chairman of the planning committee agreed to this. Do you feel that this may, to some people, appear to be more than a coincidence?"

"To some, very cynical, persons, perhaps," said Christopher, before the councillor could speak again. Black's mouth opened and closed. "But in fact, in the report, you will be able to read our reasons for granting this permission. I'm afraid, Miss Carter, there is no story to be found here."

Kim paused and turned another page of her notebook.

Inwardly I smiled because Kim had once told me that a sure-fire way to wind up a reporter was to tell them they didn't have a story. They would always make sure they did get a story after that.

"The thing is, Mr Christopher, we also have extensive interviews with a former employee of the planning department.

He has gone on record as saying he believes that corrupt practices went on there. He can detail expensive holidays, meals and gifts which were received by yourself, Councillor Black and other members of the planning team, from builders who were later given permission to develop in and around Dowerby, again often against council policy."

Christopher stood up. "Miss Carter, you seem to be making very serious and, I should warn you, false allegations against myself and Councillor Black. We will, of course, need to see any documents you say you have which may relate to these allegations.

"We will be consulting our solicitors immediately with a view to suing you personally for making these slanderous statements in the presence of a third party." He nodded in my direction. "We will also be contacting your editor to warn him that if any of your... " he coughed then raised his voice, "... lies are printed, then the newspaper will also find itself in court. I think this meeting's over." He got up and held open the door.

Kim finished scribbling in her notebook. "Thank you, Councillor, Mr Christopher." She walked out, jerking her head to me. I followed, hot and red in the face.

"Did you get all that?" Kim asked.

"Think so. Kim, he said he was going to sue you. And the paper."

Kim shrugged. "Of course he did. I expected him to. He might even try it. But honestly, you should see all the stuff we've got on him and Black. I promise you they won't get very far. Bang to rights, yer honour. In fact, perhaps we could just get Nick to put them in the stocks right now!"

Ned was still waiting on the council steps. We told him what had happened.

"They haven't come out yet," Kim said. "Give them ten more minutes and then drop it. We can always use stock pics of them if we have to."

She raised her eyebrows and smiled at me. I was still

feeling a bit shaky. "Lunch?" she said, punching me lightly on the shoulder. "You can celebrate your new job and I can celebrate putting the wind up those two old gits."

She phoned her news editor and told them what had happened. She said she'd be back later that afternoon to write the finishing paragraphs to her story, which she was expecting to be the next day's front page lead. And then we drove out to the pub on the coast where we'd had long, happy lunches before.

Kim was on a high. She persuaded the barman to give us two glasses of champagne, which he didn't want to do and he blatantly charged us far too much for them, but Kim was past caring. She chatted for a long time about her big story. It was, she said, the best one she'd ever done.

She hoped it might even help her get away from the *News* and on to better things. "I've got an interview next week with the local TV station, Northern Lights," she said. "Don't tell anyone that yet. I'm really hoping this story will help swing the job."

"You'll get it anyway," I said. I had to try hard to sound pleased for her.

Then we talked for a long time about my new role. The more Kim talked about it, the more excited I got about the whole idea, although part of me had been a bit put off by the meeting at the council. I admitted to Kim I'd found it all a bit scary. "If someone told me they were going to sue me, I think I might cry," I said, giggling.

"That's only because you haven't had your law training yet. When you go on your course, you'll study libel until you're sick of the word. And believe me, you'll come out knowing exactly what you can and can't say about someone and where you can say it. It's really not that complicated, Maura, you'll sail through all of that."

"Thanks," I said. Kim had more faith in me than I had in myself, but then I never did have a great deal of self-confidence anyway. Something told me, though, that this was the kind of job where you at least learned to bluff your way along. And that would be a start.

Once again, I think about skipping work, but I get there without a problem and I don't notice anything odd about any of the customers. I come out of the wine bar into a mild, damp, spring night, arms tight to my sides, glancing around. As if from nowhere a figure approaches, making me start and catch my breath. It's a male figure, not too tall, with his hands in his jacket pocket and a baseball cap low over his brow. Skin prickling, I take a couple of quick backward steps, towards the doorway of the wine bar. He walks fast, right up close to me, keeping his gaze pointed down towards his shoes so that I can't see his face. He smells strongly of cigarettes. I'm about to turn and run back inside the wine bar when he reaches me, deliberately bumps hard into my side so that I stumble, and then turns away and starts to run. I steady myself against the cold brick of the wall, and watch, trembling, my heart hammering, as the figure disappears into the dark.

Chapter Nine

I don't know how long I stand trembling and staring into the darkness at the quiet, rainy streets where the man ran off and turned into nothing. A sudden hand on my shoulder makes me shriek with fright, but it's just Cathy from the bar. "Didn't mean to scare you!" she says. "I just thought you'd gone ages ago. You alright, lovey?"

I try to explain, blinking away tears. It sounds so stupid and pointless. There was a man. He ran past and bumped into me. I think it was on purpose. Why? I don't really know. Did he try to take anything? No. Did he touch me anywhere else? No. What did he look like? I couldn't really see. He had a baseball cap. Like around eighty per cent of blokes in London. Did he say anything? No. Where did he go? I don't know.

I say I will be alright, but Cathy says I'm in shock and phones me a cab, she even comes back to the flat with me. We check around and there is nothing out of the norm. I apologise to her, again and again, until she cuffs me lightly on the shoulder and tells me to shut up.

"Better safe than sorry," she says. "Think of it this way. Nothing taken and you're not hurt. It was probably just some idiot who gets off on scaring young women. They're out there. Doesn't mean they'd actually do anything. Try to forget about it, eh?" Cathy glances at her watch and dashes back down the stairs. I carry out my usual locking-up routine and this time, again, I put the chair against the door. My head says Cathy is right. But something deep in the pit of my rolling stomach says that it was no coincidence.

The next day is Sunday. It's a day off and I would give anything to be somewhere around people, not on my own. Something makes me call Paul Hollings' mobile number and ask to see him. He turns up at the flat mid-afternoon.

"I'm sorry to bother you on a Sunday," I tell him.

He shrugs. "Wasn't busy. If there'd been a match on you'd have got short shrift, but I'm kicking my heels. You alright?"

"I just wanted to ask you a couple of things."

He opens his hands. "Fire away."

"Are you sure, I mean, absolutely sure, that you didn't let Nick know where I was?"

He frowns. "Of course I didn't. Why would I do that?"

"Not deliberately, but what I mean is, could he have found out somehow? Followed you, or… or… "

"Definitely not. He doesn't even know I've spoken to you." Paul is staring away from me, as if he's trying to work something out.

I tell him about the man. In daylight it sounds an even smaller, sillier incident than it did a few hours ago. He bites his lip for a minute. Then he just shrugs. "Just one of those things, I reckon. It's London. Half the people on the streets are lunatics and the other half are downright rude. But not all of them are out to get you, Maura."

I don't want him to go straight away, so I ask Paul how his story is going. "I think you know the answer to that," he says, shaking his head. "Very slowly. It's just a good job I've produced some other stories in the last couple of weeks, otherwise I'd be out on my ear. I don't usually spend this much time on a story like this one."

"I guess not. Sorry. Do you have a deadline for it?"

"Not exactly a deadline, but I need to get it finished in the next week or so. There are some legal things that need sorting out. We're talking to the lawyers about giving the tape over to the police or the Director of Public Prosecutions or someone, to ask for the case to be re-opened. And I need to front up a couple of the people that are on the tape, the ones who were clearly involved in what happened to Kim."

Thinking about this makes me feel anxious. "Paul, this tape."

"Yeah?"

"You've, had a good look at it, obviously."

"Yes, of course. Lots of looks. You don't want to see it, do you? I'm not sure if that would be a good idea, Maura. I think it would upset you."

"No," I say, quickly. "I couldn't bear to see it. I just wondered, can you see me on this tape, at all?"

I feel myself going red as I ask this. But Paul shakes his head. "Not at all. In fact, after I first spotted you in the street I made a point of getting the tape out and looking through it again, just to confirm you were who I thought you were. But there was no sign of you on film. Obviously, you were around, somewhere, so you must've been behind my man with the camera. Or well to one side of him."

"Oh. Okay." I wonder, later, if I looked visibly relieved when he said this.

Paul says he has written up his notes about me. He's provisionally written the entire story, but he does need to front up Nick and one or two others.

"One of them used to be a councillor," he says.

"Black," I say.

"That's the one. Andrew Black. Dressed up in some ridiculous costume on this tape, but identifiable, nevertheless. You know what it reminds me of? Those Venetian masked carnivals when people could do whatever they liked and get away with it, because they were in disguise."

I nod. "Yes, I know what you mean. It did have that unreal sort of atmosphere, that last day especially. So, you can see Nick and Black. Anyone else I know?"

Paul pauses for a moment. "I think you'll know this one. A woman in a great big flouncy black dress and hat. Huge tits. Sally Cooper. She's, er, she's the one Nick's been living with for a while."

I blink. "Yes, Sally. She's on the tape? Doing what, exactly?"

"You know, shouting, screaming, egging the guys on. It's pretty horrible. Don't you remember her there at the time? She's what you'd call noticeable."

I think about this. "Yes, she was around. I remember that now."

A small, bad part of me is secretly pleased that Sally, too, will not come out of this well.

I couldn't wait to get Tuesday's paper to see Kim's council story. But, to my surprise, the paper led with another story, a poor one about a city pensioner being mugged. I went all the way through the first edition and couldn't see the story at all. Eventually I called Kim's mobile. She answered, sounding snappy.

"Kim, it's Maura. I wondered what had happened to your council story."

"Hi, Maura. Bloody hell. Don't ask. Bray's getting cold feet again. He's had Black and Christopher on the phone and they've really been putting the screws on him. The whole thing's gone back to the lawyers. Again. I tell you what, Maura, if they don't print it, I'll be so pissed off."

"But you have enough evidence to run an entire criminal trial, never mind a news story! I don't understand why a local newspaper editor wouldn't want to publish this."

"Well," Kim said, gloomily. "Some people here have mentioned the F-word."

"What F-word?"

"Freemasons. Bray's one, of course, and if those two crooks in Dowerby aren't masons I'll eat my copy of *Essential Law for Journalists*."

"So, they might just… "

"My news editor is as hacked off as I am. But he reckons the editor might just keep putting it off until, well, until we all get sick of it and it quietly goes away. It's amazing what a funny handshake can still do, these days."

"Oh, Kim. I'm really sorry." As I spoke to her, the phone crooked between my ear and my shoulder, I was tearing my way through a huge pile of office post, most of it council agenda and other stuff to put in the diary. But as I glanced at the front of one envelope, I noticed it had a lawyer's stamp on the front. "Kim, there's a letter here addressed to you from a firm of solicitors in Dowerby. Do you want me to open it?"

"Guess you'd better."

I pulled out the letter. It was headed: Mr Stuart Christopher and Mr Andrew Black.

The letter stated that Kim had made slanderous allegations about the firm's two clients in the presence of a third party and that the clients were considering taking legal action and would clearly have a strong case if they were to choose this course. It went on to say that should the *News* print anything relating to these allegations, the clients would immediately sue the newspaper and Ms Carter for defamation of character. It warned that Kim and the newspaper's editor would be advised to think very seriously about publishing any of the allegations in any form.

Kim let out a deep sigh. "Thanks, Maura. Can you fax that to me here at head office?"

She gave me the fax number and I put it straight through.

"This will give Bray even more reason to stall," she grumbled. "All that work. I can't see how much more cast-iron he can want this story to be."

I felt sorry for Kim, after yesterday's excitement, and it seemed hugely unfair that the story could be covered up. Kim said I'd be surprised how many good stories don't see the light of day, thanks to a solicitor's letter. I looked out of the window to more rain and rows of sad-looking stalls in the market square with not many people wandering around them. I opened the paper again and this time checked out the photo of the fair that Ned had taken yesterday. Next to it were the few paragraphs I'd written. I was pleased to see it had quite a big show, a page five lead, and it even had my first byline. *Fair's Not Fair. Dowerby's A Washout. By Maura Wood.*

History could be rained off in a North market town as organisers of a popular fair struggle with their lowest ever visitor numbers.

Heavy rain and grey skies over the last two days have dampened the spirits of Dowerby's fair committee. The gloomy weather's put tourists off in their droves with stallholders reporting takings at a record low.

It could even spell the end of the traditional fair week, which has been held in Dowerby since medieval times, only taking a break during the two World Wars. Nick Wood from the fair committee said: "No-one can remember when the fair's done so badly, even in poor weather. Many of us are wondering whether we should carry on with the thing or just give it up as a bad job. It may be a tradition but perhaps it really has had its day."

Stallholder Aggie Martin of Country Glow Candles said: "I stood here in the rain all day on Sunday and I sold two little candles for £1.50. It's hardly worth aggravating my varicose veins for that."

And there's more bad news for the fair stalwarts. Weather forecasters say the rain and cloudy skies will be with us for the rest of the week.

I was thrilled to see my first legitimate piece of journalism. I felt proud of myself and cut it out of the paper. Something to keep and treasure. Kim had told me to buy a scrapbook and start pasting my cuttings into it. "Anything with a byline, at first. Then you can decide to stick to your best stories," she advised. "But you will need to show cuttings when you go for other jobs." This I couldn't imagine, but I'd begun to learn that Kim's advice was usually worth following.

I started tapping out another story about the fair. I'd been lucky, Kim said, when I'd told her about this new one, because it was a proper news story rather than just an ill-disguised advert for the fair.

The curse of this year's Dowerby Fair continued yesterday when four people were taken to hospital with suspected food poisoning.

Environmental health inspectors moved in to close down one of the fair's longest-standing traditions, the medieval-style hog roast. The hog roast's been part of the fair as long as anyone can remember and local butcher Chuck Charlton said he had never had any problems with it before.

"I'm sure there's nothing wrong with my meat," he told the News *today.*

"These environmental health rules are just bureaucracy gone mad."

But day-trippers Alan and Vera Hardman from Newcastle were two of those treated for suspected food poisoning at Dowerby Infirmary late on Monday night. A spokesman for the hospital confirmed two other cases were also being treated.

Mrs Hardman said: "We're staying for the week, as we always enjoy Dowerby Fair. But we couldn't get an evening meal in our guest house so we popped out for a slice of the hog roast. It was pretty expensive but there didn't seem to be many places to eat. Everything else was closed. My husband started suffering from stomach pains about an hour after we'd eaten then I started feeling very sick. I thought we were going to die. When we got to the Infirmary, I remember the doctor said 'Not another one.' The nurse said they were going to contact the council because they were being inundated with people being ill after they'd eaten the hog roast. It's ruined our visit to the fair. I'm not sure if we'll be back again next year."

The cases of food poisoning are a further blow to the organisers of historic Dowerby Fair, which is struggling this year with bad weather and low visitor numbers.

I finished the story, pressed Save and sent it over to the head office for the subeditors to look at.

When I picked Rosie up from nursery and went straight home, Nick was there. He'd been given flexible working hours from the factory this week because of his fair commitments, so I wasn't particularly surprised to see him. He walked towards me as I came through the front door. He had something in his hand. It all happened so quickly but just as I had walked Rosie through the door and bent to take off her coat, something hit me round the head, with force but without hurting too much. I jumped and gave a little shout, more with the shock than anything else, and looked up to see that Nick had hit me with a rolled-up newspaper.

"Hey," I said, and then he started hitting me again and again, round the head. "Stop it, Nick!" I yelled, trying to bat him away with my hands, not sure exactly whether this was some kind of strange joke. "What's going on?"

Nick dropped the newspaper and grabbed me by the hair, banging my head back against the front door. I heard Rosie start to cry. "You're asking me what's going on?" Nick spat. He banged my head backwards repeatedly. "I have spent the whole day trying to explain to people why my wife, my fucking stupid wife, has printed a load of confidential stuff about the fair in her fucking newspaper. And why I am quoted as saying something I never fucking said. That's what's going on for me. Now you tell me what the fuck is going on for you, Maura."

He'd stopped banging my head so I could answer. I was blinking back tears. My hair felt half wrenched out of my scalp. "Nick, stop it, you're scaring Rosie," I begged.

Nick turned round and told Rosie, who was wailing by now, to go to her bedroom. She turned and ran, still crying.

"Nick, stop this," I pleaded. "Can't we just, just talk calmly about this?"

Nick put his face close to mine and glared. Then he let go of my hair and took a step back. "Let's hear it then, Maura."

I swallowed hard. "Nick. I'm sorry. I didn't think anything you'd told me was confidential. You did say that stuff the other night and I... "

Nick punched me hard across the head, knocking me down to the floor. "That was private stuff. Nothing's been decided. You and your stupid paper have just quoted me as saying there won't be a fair next year. That the whole event is a pile of crap! How the hell do you think that looks for me? Didn't you think about me for one second or do you never stop thinking about yourself, your fucking great new job and that bitch who's your new best friend?"

"I'm sorry, I'm sorry," I said, still kneeling on the floor. The side of my head was throbbing from his punch. I felt dizzy, images blurring in front of me. "I should've asked you if it was okay to print. I'm sorry." I couldn't stand the sound of my own grovelling, but I had to calm him down, for Rosie.

"As far as anyone else is concerned, Maura, I never even fucking said all that, not even to you. You will print an apology in tomorrow's paper. Get it?"

I shook my head. "Well, I could ask the editor, but... "

Nick kicked me in the stomach, which knocked the wind out of me. I doubled up, trying to breathe, now sobbing with pain. And anger.

"If there isn't a complete apology in tomorrow's paper, you and I are finished, Maura. And I will fucking sue you and the paper. I'll make sure your fantastic new job doesn't last very long, don't you worry."

He turned away from me and picked up his jacket. I stood up, slowly, still holding my stomach. "Move," Nick hissed and he went out of the door, slamming it behind him.

I could still hear Rosie howling from her room. I ran upstairs and wrapped her in my arms.

"Why did Daddy hit you?" she sobbed.

I kissed her head, stroked her hair. "Daddy was just being

a bit silly. He was naughty because no-one should hit anyone, should they? But it's all over now. Mummy's just fine. Let's have a big cuddle and then we'll make our tea, yeah?"

Rosie looked up at me. "Is you okay, Mummy?"

This is what they mean when they say that children can break your heart. "Mummy is fine." I said, kissing the top of her head.

I was, of course, burning with anger. The humiliation I felt from the previous occasions had started to fade. Now I was afraid. Nick didn't come back for his dinner and I sat up until almost midnight, wondering where he could be. I couldn't decide whether to go to bed, or wait for him so that we could talk sensibly. It seemed impossible to do what he wanted, to get an apology in the newspaper. They rarely printed retractions unless they absolutely had to, I knew that much from Kim. I could hardly explain to Mr Bray that my husband had threatened me. Nor did I want it to look as if I'd got my facts wrong.

Then, with a sickening jolt I remembered the story I'd sent over today. The food poisoning outbreak. If Nick and the fair committee didn't like the first one, they wouldn't like that one either, even though again, every word and quote in it was entirely accurate. I wondered whether I should tell Nick tonight, whenever he came back, or wait until it turned up in the paper. I thought about how to tell him there would be another 'knocking' story, as Kim called them, in tomorrow's paper and I just couldn't find the right words in my head. I wondered about trying to get the story pulled. I tried calling the newspaper subs desk, keeping one eye on the door in case Nick came back, but there was no answer. The shift dealing with overnight stories must have finished. I could try again first thing in the morning.

It was now well past midnight and despite everything I started to worry about Nick. I suppose knowing that he was in the house gave me some reassurance, but when he was out, I couldn't tell what mood he would be in when he came home. I couldn't think where he could be until this time. I remembered Kim's claim that Nick was unfaithful, something I'd tried to push out of my head for Rosie's sake, but which kept creeping back at least a few times a day. Perhaps he was with some other woman right now. Or perhaps he and the other members of the committee were sitting round someone's kitchen table drinking some ghastly home brew and muttering about me, Kim and everyone else who seemed determined to bring down everything Dowerby held dear. I couldn't help smiling grimly at this idea. Thoughts ran through my head, scattered around like litter, taking no proper form or reason. Why had I thought it such a great idea to hold my marriage together at all costs? I didn't want Rosie seeing her parents fighting. I didn't want her to see her mother being beaten up, ever again. Once was too many times. Could I leave? But this was too big a thought. Could I really do it? My head was aching and I felt sore and scared.

Then, because I couldn't think straight, I started to imagine that something terrible had happened to Nick and this was why he hadn't come home. It wasn't like him, even when we'd had fights in the past, to stay away. I started to panic. I went to the door, opened it and stared down the street into the blue-blackness. I couldn't see anyone, so I started walking a few steps along the road. I saw a man coming towards me and realised it was Nick.

He saw me too. He had been drinking heavily because he was staggering. He kept walking, slowly, and when he got a little closer, he hissed, "Get in that fucking house, you stupid bitch."

I slowly followed him inside. "Nick," I said, trying to sound calm. "I was looking for you. I was worried about you because it had got so late."

He slapped me hard across the face. "I've been out and I can bloody well go out if I like. You do what you fucking well like, don't you?" he snarled.

I tried to force down the rising fear inside me. "Okay, okay. I just… "

Nick picked up a small wooden coffee table and smashed it against the living room wall. Its leg cracked. He started throwing pots and ornaments around, breaking them. He'll wake Rosie, I thought wildly, she'll see more of this. In a complete panic I ran out of the front door and into the street. Nick was yelling at me to get back inside and that he was going to kill me. I banged hard on my next door neighbours' door. They were an elderly couple and seemed to take ages to answer it, but when Nick saw what I was doing, he went straight back inside and slammed the front door.

Eventually, Mrs Blakelaw and her husband came to the door together and peered out, with their door chain still in place. "I'm sorry to wake you, I'm really sorry," I started to say. "It's Nick, he's going mad. He's smashing my house up. Please, please can you call the police?"

The old man just stared at me and shook his head. "We don't want to get involved in that sort of thing."

I couldn't believe it. "I'm not – I don't need you to be involved – I just need you to call the police. Please," I begged them. "My little girl's in there. Please. Or let me use the phone, please."

They said nothing for a few seconds and I started to sob. After what seemed like several minutes, they pulled the door chain and stood back. Mr Blakelaw pointed to the telephone, on a little embroidered cloth on a hall table.

I was shaking so much I could hardly press the numbers. I asked for the police and told them that my husband was being violent. They said they would send an officer along. I asked Mrs Blakelaw if I could wait in their house until the police arrived. "You can wait here," she said, indicating the hallway. I stood there, trembling. I was angry with them, too. "Why didn't you want to help me?" I asked between sobs. "You're looking at me as if I'm the one who's a criminal here."

Mrs Blakelaw just shook her head. "You should sort it out

between yourselves, this sort of thing." She looked at me as if I smelled. "We hear all the rows. We're sick of it. I feel sorry for that poor little lassie. Don't think you can drag us into your mess. You should just get back in that house and sort it out with your husband."

"If I go back in that house, he'll probably kill me," I said. I couldn't think of anything else to say. I just stood there, my arms wrapped around myself, trying to stop shaking. It seemed like a long time until the police arrived. There was one female officer and a man. I tried to explain what had happened. The woman officer asked Mrs Blakelaw if she could make me a cup of tea. The old woman looked very reluctant, but I was led into Mrs Blakelaw's kitchen, while the male officer knocked on our front door.

After about ten minutes, he came back in and beckoned to the female officer, who said her name was Sandra. They had a murmured conversation in the hallway, before coming back in.

The male officer looked at me carefully. "There's no evidence of any violence, Mrs Wood," he said. "There is a broken coffee table, but your husband says that happened earlier today when you stood on it to reach a shelf."

"He broke all my ornaments," I said. "What's happened to those? He... he hit me."

I could tell by the way they were looking at me that they didn't entirely believe me. What had Nick said to the policeman?

"I couldn't see any broken ornaments, Mrs Wood," the officer continued. He looked over at his colleague. Sandra sat down next to me at the table. "Do you have any evidence that Mr Wood was violent towards you? Any bruising? Anything like that?"

I put my hand up to my sore scalp where Nick had pulled my hair. I touched my face. "He pulled my hair and slapped me," I said. "He kicked me in the stomach. That was earlier on."

I pulled up my shirt. There was no sign of any bruises.

Pulling hair and hitting in the stomach rarely leaves any marks.

The police officers said nothing.

"Have you seen Rosie?" I said. "My little girl? Is she okay?"

The man nodded. "I've checked on your daughter, Mrs Wood. She's sleeping peacefully. Perfectly alright." He paused. "Mrs Wood. I'm sure you can appreciate how difficult it is for the police to get involved in this kind of domestic situation. You have called us out and said your husband was being violent to you. I've spoken to him and he denies this, although he says you became hysterical towards him this evening because he'd been for a drink and came home late.

"There is no sign of any violence in the house or on your… person. It's very hard for us to know what to do."

Sandra looked at me. "What would you like us to do, Mrs Wood?"

"I don't know, really. I'm sorry." I found myself adding, "I shouldn't have called you out. I was just scared. At the time."

Sandra frowned. "Do you feel able to go back in the house now?"

I looked down. "Erm… I might… I might go and stay with a friend. Just for the night."

"That sounds like a good idea. Just to cool things down a bit. Do you need to get anything from the house?"

"My bag," I said. Sandra came with me to my own house. I could hear Mrs Blakelaw telling the male police officer that I was always shouting and screaming and how sorry she felt for Rosie. Nick was sitting in the living room, which was completely tidy, apart from the skewed coffee table, which he seemed to be trying to fix. "Hi, Maura," he said, gently. "You okay now?"

"I just need my bag," I said. I went to get it. In it were the keys to Kim's flat. I moved in a state of shock. I could hear people talking around me, but it felt like it was happening to someone else.

I heard Sandra say to Nick that it was probably a good idea if we both cooled off. "Where will she go?" Nick asked. "Rosie will want her mum in the morning."

"She's just staying the night with a friend," Sandra replied. "Best just wait until the morning before you speak to her, eh?"

"I'll be back to take Rosie to nursery," I said to Nick. The mention of my daughter's name seemed to spark some life into me.

He looked at me mildly. "It's okay, Maura. Why don't you get a little extra sleep in the morning? I'll take Rosie to nursery myself."

I slowly walked out of the house. Out in the street, I turned to Sandra. "It's like a different person in there."

I couldn't tell anything from her expression.

"Why don't you do what Nick says, get some sleep now. Can I take you anywhere?"

I told her it was just a short walk to my friend's house. I walked down the street, past the small cottages and homes with people sleeping peacefully inside. How had it come to this, I thought. What do I do now? I let myself in and went up the stairs. Kim's flat was tidy, cold and un-lived in. I had a long drink of water, crawled into her chilly bed and sobbed with a mixture of fury and shame.

"That disgusts me," Paul shakes his head. "I can't stand that. Men who hit women. So you think no-one really believed you? Not even the police?"

"I'm sure of it," I tell him. "Looking back I don't know if he was conscious of this, but he always did things that didn't leave a mark, like hitting my stomach or across the top of my head. And the thing that also made me mad was that my neighbours knew what was going on. But they thought it was my fault, somehow more than Nick's."

Paul clicks his tongue. "It was Nick's fault. I promise you."

I tell Paul I'm thinking of getting a takeaway and ask if

he'd like to join me. He shakes his head, getting up. "I should be going."

I try to keep him talking. If nothing else, having a big bloke in the flat makes me feel a lot safer than I do on my own, even if Paul has probably never been in a fight in his life and is too overweight to even run very fast.

But eventually I'm out of fake casual conversation and Paul says he really has to dash. "But look, Maura, I can't think of any way Nick would be clever enough to know where you are. He'd have to have been following me, and he's not likely to go to those lengths, is he?"

I force myself to agree with what Paul is saying. Of course, it makes sense. Nick could never find me here. I want to believe him. I really do.

Chapter Ten

Paul comes into the café on Monday, round about lunchtime, and asks me to meet him when I finish to get something to eat. The other girls are winking and nudging in a none too subtle way. I just smile at them. I'm amazed they think any man would be interested in me.

Over a quick pub sandwich, Paul says, "Maura, I have to go to Dowerby again tomorrow. I'm going to front up Nick, Black and a couple of the others. I'm also going to tie up some other loose ends. I wondered, how would you feel about coming with me?"

I stare at him. "Paul, you're joking. Surely. I couldn't go anywhere near that place. What makes you think I'd even consider it?"

He looks down at his pint. "I wondered if you maybe wanted to go and see your little girl. How long is it since she's seen her mum?"

My stomach clenches. "Paul, don't, please. How can I just turn up after five years and knock on the door? Nick would send me packing, to say the least. In a way, he's got every right to. And poor Rosie, what would she make of it all?"

He looks at me, very directly. "Don't you want to see Rosie again?"

"Of course. I'd kill to see her again. You know that. It's just I don't think I should, now. Not like this at any rate. It would confuse her. She might get upset. And as for Nick

169

and that Sally, I'm sure they wouldn't let me anywhere near her."

"But you're Rosie's mum. You have rights. You walked out and left her for a reason. Because you didn't feel safe. And I'm beginning to realise how much Kim's death affected you. You haven't really been thinking straight ever since, I don't reckon.

"Why don't you at least have a think about it? Isn't there some way you could gradually get back into seeing Rosie regularly again? Maybe through a solicitor?"

I stare at him. Seeing Rosie again is something I surely do not deserve.

Paul fishes in his jacket pocket and pulls out a card. "This woman is a fantastic family lawyer. I know her because she's good for a quote, but she's also won some hopeless cases and some pretty good deals. Think about at least making an appointment and chatting things through. You don't have to go any further than that, if that's what you decide. The thing is, if this case goes back to the coppers and Nick gets arrested, Rosie may well be without a dad for a while, and Sally isn't even a relation. Rosie might need you, very soon. Just think about it, yeah?"

I turn the card around in my fingers. Paul holds out his mobile. "Want to make a call?"

I didn't sleep much during the night at Kim's. I kept going over and over it in my pounding head. Little details, like the way Mrs Blakelaw looked at me, the fact that the police seemed to believe Nick so entirely. It was after six in the morning when I fell asleep and what seemed like moments later there was a loud hammering at the door.

My first thought was that I could just ignore it, because this wasn't my flat and I wasn't really supposed to be here. Then Nick's voice shouted through the letter box. "Come on, open up, Maura, I know you're in there."

I stared at Kim's little bedside clock. Quarter past eight.

Rosie flashed into my head and I charged downstairs, still just wearing a silky pyjama top belonging to Kim. I threw open the door but Nick was alone. "Where's Rosie?" I demanded.

"Where do you think? I've taken her to nursery."

"It's a bit early, isn't it? I don't usually take her till almost nine."

Nick pushed past me and started walking up the stairs.

"Hey," I said, but not very forcefully, because it didn't seem like a good idea to aggravate him, now that I was alone with him again.

He threw himself onto Kim's sofa. "So," he said. "What was all that about last night?"

I stared at him. "Nick, you were smashing the place up. I was terrified."

"Don't be so pathetic." Nick wasn't looking at me. He was staring round the room, taking it in. "I was just pissed off with you wandering the streets looking for me. All I did was go for a drink. You're just determined to embarrass me at the moment, aren't you?"

I shook my head and said nothing.

"Of course the police realised that you're a bit, let's say, stressed at the moment, so I don't think they'll charge you with wasting their time. Oh, and I called round to Mr and Mrs Blakelaw and apologised. I explained to them that you're not feeling very well at the moment. In fact, I said you're taking medication for your nerves. They seemed okay with that.

"But this is the thing. Rosie was quite upset this morning when you weren't there. You've made her very clingy, you know. So I think you'd better be the one to bring her home from nursery tonight. And as long as that apology goes in the paper, we'll say no more about it."

Nick waited. For a few minutes I couldn't think of anything to say.

"You beat me up and you smash up my house. And you're the one offering to forgive me? That's nice."

"*Your* house?" Nick breathed out, hard. "You do your

utmost to ruin my entire reputation and social life. And then you try to, what? Get me arrested. And yes, I am offering to forgive you. Not many blokes would, Maura. Think about it. Think about Rosie. You don't want to break this marriage up and frankly, you'd never manage on your own. You can't even keep a simple budget and let's face it, this mad idea about being a reporter isn't really going to work, is it? So let's just try, if we can, to get back to normal. Whatever that was."

"Well, thanks for the vote of confidence," I said, feeling a lot braver than I did last night.

"Maura," he said, with a deep sigh, as if his patience was being tested. "Let's be honest, shall we? You'd like to think you're some gorgeous, go-getting career girl like Kim. Fact is, you're not. You're suited to staying at home and looking after your kid. You'll never look anything but ordinary. You'll never have a high-flying job. Get over it. You should be glad you've got a nice house and a decent marriage. And Rosie."

I felt my face go red. My body was prickling all the way through and it felt strangely light, as if I was only half there. "The thing is, Nick, I'm not sure if I do have a decent marriage. I'm scared of you. You lose your temper with me and you hit me. Even I know that's not right, not for me and not for Rosie."

Nick punched the sofa cushion and I flinched. "I've never touched Rosie and I never would," he shouted.

"You don't have to, you're hurting her by being violent in front of her."

"Crap," spat Nick. "I've never touched her."

"The other thing is, I'm not sure if I have a decent marriage when I hear that you have affairs all the time."

Nick stared at me. I noticed he didn't look shocked. "That's crap too," he said. "I don't know what you're talking about."

"Rhoda. She was one of them. And that fat Elaine?"

Nick shook his head and then laughed, in a really irritating, high-pitched sort of way. "Now I really think you've gone mad, Maura. You need help."

"Don't laugh at me, Nick. I know it's true."

He raised his eyebrows. "Really? Who told you? Wouldn't be Kim, by any chance?"

I hesitated. "It doesn't matter who it was."

"So, it was Kim. It must be, it's not as though you've got any other friends to gossip with, because no-one else can be bothered with you. This is just one of Kim's little tales." Nick sighed and drummed his fingers on the coffee table. Then he stood up. "Maura," he said. "I don't know how to convince you of this, but I have not been unfaithful to you. Not with Rhoda, not with Elaine, not with anyone. Kim, for some reason, is making trouble. She's been doing it all along.

"You know, at first, I thought she was after me. Now, I'm starting to think she's after you. Anything's possible with that little witch.

"Now that I think about it, you only started doing all these stupid things – that story in the paper and everything – because you thought I was seeing other women. Bloody hell, Maura, I understand it all now. I wish you'd just talked to me, I really do. We could've avoided all this nastiness."

He spread his hands out, in a gesture of innocence, or friendship, or something. I didn't know what to think.

"Well, look, Maura, I've got to go. I've got a stack of stuff to do for the fair. And I guess you're going into work, for now. So look, I'll see you tonight. Line in the sand, eh?"

I still couldn't find anything to say. I wish I had said something as he stood and walked out, instead of standing there, dumbstruck.

I forced myself to have a shower and make some coffee, although it had to be black because there was no milk in the fridge. Kim hadn't really lived there for some time. I sat down on the sofa to drink it, grimacing at the taste. Just then, I stiffened as I heard a sound at the door. It was a key turning. Footsteps came quickly up the stairs.

It was Kim. She gave a little shriek when she saw me. "Blimey, Maura, what a shock. I was expecting the flat to be empty. You okay? Silly question. What's up?"

I put down the mug of coffee and buried my head in my hands. Kim sat down and put an arm around me, shushing me and stroking my hair.

"Come on, Maura, tell me what's going on." Her voice was creamy-soft.

I started to tell her everything, although it was hard, and I kept breaking down in huge sobs. She listened the whole time, shaking her head and hugging me to her. When I'd got the whole story out, Kim made some more coffee and sat beside me again.

"First thing, Maura, you can't go into work."

"I have to," I began, but Kim put a finger to my lips.

"No way, not in this state. I'll ring head office now and tell them you're not well. It'll be fine. Then you are going to have some aspirin and go back to bed for a couple of hours.

"When you've had some more sleep then you might be able to think more sensibly about what to do next. In the meantime, give me your house keys and I'll go round there and get you and Rosie some clothes. You can settle in here for a few days to give yourself some breathing space. How's that?"

I shook my head. "Oh, Kim. I don't know."

But she put her hands on my shoulders and steered me back towards her bedroom. "Go, sleep. You will feel better. And if you decide you want to go home, then you can just take your clothes straight back again. But at least let me do something useful for you."

I took the aspirin and curled back up in Kim's bed. She shut the bedroom door quietly and I heard her, out in the living room, talking to someone in head office and telling them I was not well. Shortly after that, falling asleep seemed to happen easily. It was midday when I woke up, my head heavy, but my mind clearer. The flat was quiet. I wandered into the living room and found two bulging holdalls in the middle of the floor. There was a note from Kim. I hadn't even heard her come back.

Hi Maura, hope you slept. I went to your house and picked up some of your and Rosie's clothes, underwear etc. Hope it's what you need. No-one was in the house when I went.

I'd come back to pack up some of my stuff, as I've handed my notice in at the flat but here's the landlord's number if you need to keep it any longer than the next ten days. You can stay here until then as far as I'm concerned.

Might see you a bit later in the afternoon. Take care, Love Kim.

It had the telephone number of a Mr Heaton on the bottom of the note.

I dragged the holdalls into the bedroom. Then I had my second shower of the day and found some clothes to put on. I decided I'd probably feel a bit more like a normal person if I spent a couple of hours in the office before going for Rosie. I could bring her back to Kim's flat and tell her we were staying here for a few days. Just while I decided what to do.

I went into the office for about two o'clock. There was a huge pile of post waiting to be opened, as well as the first edition of the *News*, which I'd arranged to have delivered. I suddenly remembered about the food poisoning story. I'd forgotten all about trying to get it pulled. Sure enough, there it was, a huge show on Page 3. It didn't have a byline this time.

Kim's corruption story still hadn't made it.

I spent a quiet hour opening the post, checking email, filing and reading the paper. Then I heard footsteps coming up the stairs. At first I thought it might be Kim, but then I heard more, heavier footsteps and voices.

The office door was pushed open. A small group of people walked in. Among them was Sally, Jim, a woman who I thought might be Councillor Black's wife, and two or three other men, who I knew by sight but couldn't put a name to. I knew they were all involved with the Dowerby Fair committee.

I stood up. "Hello, can I help you?" I asked, as politely as I could, although I could see they'd come to make some sort of complaint. "We want to speak to Miss Carter," said Jim.

"She's not here," I said, gesturing round the office. "I'm sorry. I'm not sure when she's next coming in."

"Yes, you do," said Sally. "When is she coming back?"

"I really don't know, Sally. What is it about? Perhaps I can help you."

Sally just made a face.

"The *News* seems to be carrying out a campaign against Dowerby Fair. We feel this is largely the work of Miss Carter. We have written a letter to her editor but we feel it is important that local people make our feelings known to her in person," Jim said.

I paused. Then I decided to own up. "If you're talking about the last two stories – the one about the hog roast and the one about the visitor numbers – then you need to talk to me. I wrote them."

Sally shook her head. "For god's sake, Maura, stop protecting that bloody woman. We know she wrote the food poisoning one. And she probably egged you on with the other one."

"I wrote both of them, myself," I said. I was furious that they didn't think I was capable of it.

"We know you didn't write the hog roast one," said Sally. "I met the couple that the paper quoted. The man said the reporter who spoke to them was a good-looker, a bit of a dolly bird. It had to be Kim."

I couldn't help laughing. "Sorry, Sally. Obviously I've got an admirer. It really was me."

Jim started to say something else when suddenly Kim's voice cut through. She'd walked in behind them, unnoticed.

"What's going on, Maura?" she asked. "I've just come back. You know, you're really not well enough to be here."

The little crowd all turned to face Kim. Jim began again. "We have written to your editor complaining about the apparent campaign the *News* is running against Dowerby Fair. We feel that the negative coverage, which we've never had before, is largely down to you."

"I try to tell the truth, that's all," said Kim, clearly ready to take the blame for my work.

"Kim," I tried to interrupt.

"Told you it wouldn't be Maura, she's just not up to it," said Sally. She stepped towards Kim. "You've ruined this year's fair. You and your lies. I don't know what your problem is, but we all feel that you shouldn't be here any more. If you stay, no-one in Dowerby will tell you anything again. We'll make it impossible for you to do your job."

"I doubt that," said Kim. "Most people in this town have been downright obstructive ever since I got here. I've still managed to do my job."

"That's not true," said the woman who I thought was Mrs Black. "My husband never did anything but help you out. And you've been sneaking around behind his back making up lies about him. Trying to ruin his reputation. He's having to take tablets because of you. He's in a terrible state."

"That won't bother her," sneered Sally. "Think about poor Liz Thomas."

There was a murmur of agreement and Kim sighed.

"Where's this going?" she asked. "Maura is not terribly well and I have a lot of work do to, if you don't mind. I'm sure my editor will answer your concerns, when he gets your letter."

"Miss Carter, we have come here to speak to you in person," said Jim. "We want to let you know that we represent the views of a great many people in this town. We feel that, frankly, you are no longer welcome here." There was a general murmuring and nodding. "You have caused untold damage to this community by your immoral behaviour. This attempt to sabotage one of Dowerby's long-standing and important traditions is the final straw. We have asked your editor that you be removed from your post as the district reporter and we are telling you in person that, if you insist on staying here, you will find that very few people will be prepared to help you or work with you in any way."

There was a brief silence and then Sally started to clap, joined by the others in the little group.

Kim's face flushed but she didn't move. "In spite of what you all think," she said, with only a slight quiver in her voice, "I didn't cause Mrs Thomas' suicide. I'm also not responsible for the weather. But I don't expect any of you to be capable of rational thought. Just blind prejudice. Now this is still my office. I would like you all to leave now, if you don't mind."

"So, are you going?" demanded Sally.

Kim's face gave nothing away. "I'll discuss any decisions about my career with my editor, if you don't mind. I'm asking you again to leave this office. Please."

"We've said what we wanted to say," said Jim. He led the others out of the door. We could hear them muttering quietly on their way down the stairs.

When they seemed to have gone, Kim slammed the office door behind her and clicked the lock on. She looked at me. I came out from behind my desk and went over to hug her.

"Kim," I said, holding her tightly. "You were amazing. You were so, I don't know, so dignified. That bloody mob… "

Kim laughed and threw herself into the leather chair. "What a ridiculous scene! That ghastly Jim bloke. It was the speech of his life, wasn't it? He just loved every minute of that. And that horrible old cow Sally. What a bunch of throwbacks."

"But Kim," I said. "What's your editor going to say? Isn't he going to be furious about it all?"

Kim shrugged and grinned. "I really don't care. I handed in my notice at lunchtime. I've got a new job to go to."

My mouth fell open. I stared at her. "What, really? Where?"

"That local TV job I told you about. I had the interview

last week and actually they offered it to me on the spot. But I waited until I got it all in writing today, then I went straight to see Bray and told him. He's happy for me."

"Wow, Kim, talk about timing. Congratulations, it's brilliant."

"I wasn't going to give the lynch mob the satisfaction of letting them know, though," she said, laughing again. "Look, I came back to the flat this morning to pack up some of my stuff, only, well, you were there and sorting you out was more urgent.

"When you've picked Rosie up, why don't we go back and you can help me put my things together? I'll sort the office out tomorrow."

So that's what we did. I picked Rosie up from nursery – where her teacher commented she'd seemed a little upset during the day – and we went back to Kim's flat.

"Why are we going to Kimmy's?" Rosie asked.

"It's a little adventure," I told her. "We're going to stay the whole night. You can go to sleep there. That'll be fun, won't it?"

When we arrived, Kim had driven out to McDonald's and bought Rosie some sort of party box of food. "I know, I know," she said. "Don't look at me like that, Maura, I know it's not what you normally give her. I just thought Rosie would like it. Bet you do, eh, Rosie?"

Rosie was, of course, thrilled, particularly with the little plastic toy inside the box. She watched a bit of children's TV while Kim and I emptied her holdalls and threw her own clothes into them. I noticed Kim was carefully putting my and Rosie's things in the bedroom drawers. "There's no need to do that," I said. "You make it look as if we're moving in. I might not even stay another night."

Kim shrugged. "Well. We'll see. I wouldn't go rushing back home just yet. Don't give Nick the satisfaction."

Rosie loved having Kim bath her and wash her hair, while I ordered a takeway from the local Chinese restaurant. Kim let Rosie fall asleep in her bed.

"You two can bunk up in there. I can pull out this sofa bed."

"You're being really good," I said. "I don't know how I'm ever going to thank you."

Kim gave me a sad smile. "You can be the only person in Dowerby who doesn't hate my guts."

She went out to collect the takeaway and came back with two bottles of pink champagne. "For us," she said.

"What are we celebrating today?" I said, laughing.

"My new job, of course. And your emancipation."

Right on cue, there was a hammering at Kim's door. "Nick," we said together. Kim gave a long breath out. "Shall I just get rid of him?"

I nodded. "Do you mind? I just can't face another row just now. And I don't want him waking Rosie up."

Kim went down the stairs and I hovered in the living room, chewing my fingers and listening. She opened the door a little way and I could hear her speak, "Hi, Nick. We thought it would be you. Look, Maura's staying here tonight. Maybe she'll speak to you tomorrow, yeah? I should just leave her alone for a bit if I were you."

"Where's my daughter?" I heard Nick demand.

"She's upstairs, with her mum," Kim snapped back. "And she's already asleep, so I don't think a responsible dad would want to wake her up."

I stood behind the living room door, closing my eyes. "Christ, Kim," I muttered to myself. "You really know how to wind people up."

There was a short silence until Nick's voice came bellowing up the stairs, "I want to speak to Maura. Right now."

"Sorry, she's been a bit unwell today and on top of that, she's had a horrible time having to deal with some kind of a lynch mob storming the newspaper office. But you know what, there's nothing to be gained by having a row with her here and now, is there, Nick? After all, she's got me to stick up for her. You can bully her so much better when you've got her on your own. So go away, yeah?"

"Tell my wife," he shouted, walking away, "that I will be speaking to her. And tell her I've got plenty to say. You pair of fucking bitches."

"Bye," I heard Kim say, with a smile in her voice as she closed the door. I heard her click the door chain and latch into place.

"That's one pest dealt with," she said, running back up the stairs. Champagne and Chinese time, I reckon."

It sounds crazy, but we had a great night. We got mildly drunk on the champagne and some wine that Kim already had in the fridge. I kept pushing down the gnawing worries whenever they started to creep up.

"Seriously, Maura," said Kim, at one point. "You don't need that git of a husband. Why don't you and Rosie clear out?"

I thought about this. "But Kim, I'd need to keep my job, and that's in Dowerby. Can you imagine trying to live here with Nick round the corner and all that bad feeling left over from the fair? And Rosie, well, she adores Nick. I just don't think I can do it to her."

"Nothing's impossible," said Kim. "Just remember that. You can turn any situation round if you work hard enough."

Tuesday evening. I go back to the flat to change out of my greasy café clothes before heading to the wine bar. On the little table in the lobby of the flats, there's a letter for me, addressed to the name I'm using now. I open it and unfold a piece of paper with just three words. *FOUND YOU, MAURA*.

I turn the envelope over. There's no stamp on it. I crumple it up, staring around me, but of course this was probably delivered hours ago, as Mrs Yeadon's most likely picked it up from the floor and propped it up so that I'd see it.

On my way upstairs, I tap at her door and ask if she saw who brought the letter, but she says she didn't. "Was it a birthday card?" she asks. "I wish I'd known it was your birthday."

"It isn't," I say, blinking.

"But there was a delivery of flowers," she said. "I let the man into your flat, so that he could put them in water for you as a nice surprise when you got home. He really wanted to have them arranged in a vase."

I swallowed. "Did you see this man leave?"

"Of course, I waited on the landing for him and I saw him out. He wasn't in there long. Go and have a look."

I fumble as I put my key in the lock. There is a large bouquet sitting on the little table in the living room. There's no message or card with them and their strong smell catches my throat. I look around, unease creeping through my every pore. I walk through each room, as usual, checking every space. Deep down I know that whoever left the flowers is no longer there, but it's enough to know that they were here at all. That they could get to me, if they really wanted to.

At first, I think, apart from this unwanted bunch of lilies – and I never could stand the scent of those things – there is nothing else out of place. I sit down, my hands still shaking, with a glass of water. And that's when I notice that the photos of Rosie on the little mantelpiece have been moved. I jump up, thinking they've been taken, but in fact they are still there. They've just been placed face down.

I race around the flat, drawing all the curtains, checking everything is locked, ramming the sofa up against the door. I get into bed fully clothed and lie there for the rest of the night, unable to close my eyes.

Wednesday night. Paul drops round to the flat. Before I tell him anything else, I ask him how the trip to Dowerby went. "Did you see Rosie?"

"Did you phone that lawyer?" he asks me.

"Not yet. But I'm thinking about it, Paul, honestly. Please?"

"Sorry, I only saw her very briefly. Just a glance. She was playing in the street with a couple of other girls. They had bikes and things. I spoke to Nick for a few minutes at his front door and when I'd finished, the girls were further up the street. Sorry. But she looked fine, you know, from what I could see."

"What was she wearing?" I ask, I'm not sure why. Trying to get a picture in my head, I suppose.

"God, Maura. Er, trousers. Purpley colour. A top. I can't really remember."

Paul shrugs.

"Call yourself a trained observer," I joke.

I wonder if purple is Rosie's favourite colour these days. Could be. She was going through a pink stage when I last knew her. I don't know what my own daughter's favourite colour is. I know nothing at all about her now. And Paul's trying to convince me that she should be with me.

I force myself to think about Nick. "So you saw Nick," I say, carefully, to Paul. He looks at his fingers and I get that familiar hot, churning feeling deep inside.

"Look, Maura. He was pretty ice-cool. He said the whole accident – that was his word for it – the whole accident was looked into at the time and that he'd sue me if I so much as suggested it was anything other than a mistake."

"I guess you expected that," I said.

"Oh, yeah, sure. It's pretty much what Black said too. I didn't get to speak to Sally, she wouldn't come to the door. But Nick said something else, and I just think I probably should mention it to you."

"Go on."

Paul put a hand on mine. "He said he supposed this was all your doing. He asked me what you'd been saying. I made out I hadn't been in contact with you, that I didn't even know where you were. He obviously didn't believe me. I said, wasn't it the case that Mrs Wood had just disappeared, not long after the, um, accident?

"Then he said to me, 'That's what she wanted us to think. Tell her I'm on to her. And tell her to keep her stupid, mad mouth shut.' Those were his exact words. He's no charmer, is he? I just thought I should tell you. I mean, I guess if he really puts his mind to finding you, then he will. And I think you should just take extra care for a little while."

"How do you mean, take extra care? I'm in the middle of London, I have a false name, I don't have a bank account or a phone or anything... "

"I know. I know. But I'm telling you, Maura, seriously. It's an easy job to put a private detective on it, and if he gets a decent one then, they'll track you down somehow."

I push my hair out of my eyes, take a deep breath and tell him about the note, the flowers and the photos. Paul closes his eyes and groans.

"Any thoughts?" I ask.

"Someone must've been following me for a while. Maybe since I first went to Dowerby. Christ. They must be pretty good." He makes a fist with his hand, thumps himself on the forehead a few times. "Maybe now's the time for you to talk to the police."

I shake my head.

"Come on, Maura. You need to make someone aware that..."

I keep shaking my head. "Not the police, no."

Paul looks at me as if I'm an idiot. "Why the hell not?"

"They won't believe me, for one thing. What am I supposed to say? Someone left me some flowers and I think they moved my pictures. They'll just laugh, Paul. And what if they give my name away, you know, to Mrs Yeadon, to my bosses, that sort of thing? I might lose my job and my flat."

Paul sighs. "Look, at least get your workmates looking out for you. Make sure they don't give out any details about you. And just watch out, Maura. All the time. For christ's sake."

Chapter Eleven

After this, I wander round in a combination of dizziness and a sort of super-alertness. I can't sleep and I can barely eat, so my head feels light, almost separate to my body. Everything makes me jump and I respond to every sound and shadow as if I have a gun at the ready. I ask my workmates, at the café and the wine bar, to look out for anyone asking questions about me. They promise to do this. But I can tell from the way they glance at me, that they think I've lost it a bit. Cathy takes me aside at one point and tries to persuade me to take time off. I tell her that's the last thing I need. I never see anyone who looks like he might be a private detective, although I realise that my images of them might be entirely out of a movie. I buy a door chain that I can close from the outside when I leave the flat. I hope this will make someone think I am there when I am out, and that this might put them off. It will also stop Mrs Yeadon and her well-meaning interfering. No-one can be entirely trusted, right now.

Sunday comes and I am supposed to be telling Paul the end of my story. He's due to be coming to the flat, but he's late. Eventually I go down to the phone on the stairs and call his mobile.

"Hi," he says. He's very brusque. "I'll call you back. Don't go away from the phone." A few minutes later it rings again and I pick up the handset.

"Look," Paul says. "I'm using a mate's phone. I'm worried

that someone's listening to my calls. Don't panic, though, okay? Can you come out and meet me?"

He gives me the name of a pub near Covent Garden. It takes me more than an hour. I make my way through the crowds towards Paul, who's sitting reading the Sunday papers, a huge pile of them on a little table in front of him.

When he sees me, he gets up, takes my arm and steers me quickly out onto the street.

"Sorry about this. I'll explain things in a minute," he mutters, into my ear.

As we walk along, Paul glances behind him. He swears quietly. I glance up at him and say nothing. We keep walking. Eventually we find a café and he waves me inside towards a table. He keeps his eyes on the door and speaks from behind his laminated menu card.

"I'm sorry about this. I'm pretty sure I'm being followed right now. There's a guy who I spotted hanging around outside the newspaper offices this morning. Then I saw him at the tube station. I got a bad feeling about him, so I got on the next tube then got out at the next stop. So did he. I went to the other platform and got the tube back towards Covent Garden, and he did too. He went in the pub after me. So I thought it might be too risky to come to your flat."

"Where is he?" I ask.

Paul shrugs. "He could hardly come in here after us, the place is too small and he'd definitely be spotted. But he'll be outside somewhere close and he could follow you home. We need to shake him off, but I'm just working out how to do it."

He thinks for a moment as we order some coffee. "I'm going to go out there and if I spot him, ask him what he's playing at. But we still need to get you away safely. Tell you what, if I give you the fare, you could hop in a taxi while I have a gentle word with him and tell him I know what's going on. You could go to a hotel and I could catch you up. How's that?"

Somehow, I end up agreeing to this. We walk outside the

café and Paul looks around, eyes narrowed. Then he turns to me. "Right, go for it. Flag down the next taxi you see. I'm going to have a word with this creep." I start walking sharply in the other direction and I turn back briefly to see Paul speaking to a youngish man wearing jeans and a dark jacket. The young man's shrugging his shoulders and Paul's pointing a finger in his face.

I jump into a taxi and head for the hotel Paul suggested. I wait in reception until he arrives about quarter of an hour later. We check in and go to a room. Paul orders a bottle of wine.

"This is ridiculous," I say. "I almost can't take it seriously."

Paul shakes his head at me. "You have to take it seriously, Maura. That guy denied everything, which I expected, but he was following me, alright. And I haven't pissed off so many people lately that I can't guess who's paying him. It's got to be Nick. I think he wants to put me off and I think he wants to get to you."

"I don't see what I can do about it, then."

Paul sits on the bed, pouring the wine into two glasses. "I don't come to your flat or your work anymore. We wrap up the story and then we let the courts take their course. And we find you somewhere else to live, pretty quick."

"We?" I ask. "Look, Paul. Don't think you have to rescue me from this."

"I reckon I got you into this, in a big way," he says. "I'd hate to see anything happen to you. I don't trust your ex-husband as far as I could spit."

Paul sends for more room service, some sort of bar meal. As we're eating, or rather, as he is eating, because I can't touch any food right now, Paul says, "Tell you who else I spoke to when I went to Dowerby. Your old boss."

"Oh, you mean Bray. The editor of the *News*?"

"That's right. I needed to ask him for his memories of Kim, you know, but the subject of you came up, somehow."

I blush. I'd always felt guilty about the way I'd let Mr Bray down.

"What did he say about me?" I ask, not certain I really want to know.

Paul smiles at me. "He said he thought you showed a lot of promise. That you were picking up the job really well. That he was very sorry to lose you, but he guessed you had some sort of domestic crisis around the same time Kim died."

"Oh." It's silly how pleased that makes me feel. "Right. I thought he'd be angry with me for, you know, just disappearing like that."

"What he also said was that you could've been a very good reporter. And it got me thinking."

"Sounds dangerous."

Paul grins. "Could be. Look, you don't want to work in a café all your life, do you? You're far too bright for that. Why don't you think about going back into training? As a journalist, I mean?"

I shake my head. "Come on, Paul. You know why I can't go for a proper job. I'd have to give my real identity. I can't do that. Anyway, who'd take me on? I've been on the missing list for five years."

"I've thought about that. Listen, a mate of mine, he's the editor of a weekly paper in south London. It's not exactly *The Times* or *The Guardian*. It's not even anything like as big as the *News* was. And the money's bloody awful, if I'm honest. But it's the sort of place where people can start off. I was talking to him a couple of weeks ago and he really needs someone to work shifts for him. It's a great way to get back in the job because on a weekly there's not so much pressure. You know, you'd work Saturdays, for a start, and any other day you can. You basically type up non-urgent stories, for the paper and its website, to keep it updated.

"There might be a bit of keying in sports results and, obviously, if anything happened in the patch then you'd go out and cover it. The pay's crap, I mean, rock bottom, but if you do okay then he could eventually take you on full-time. What do you think?"

I just look at Paul as if he's stupid, and shake my head. "Paul, I can't. I can't, because he'd need my real name and everything."

"You can call yourself anything you like on a byline, you know. We could organise for some cash-in-hand payments for a few weeks to see how things go. He's desperate, he owes me a list of favours, and you could do with sorting your life out. This could be a start, couldn't it?"

I think about it. Working in a news room. It sounds interesting, but at the same time it leaves me terrified. I wish my brain would work properly, but I feel as if I can't think straight about anything right now. So I tell Paul I'll consider it. He tells me to spend the night here, where he's sure I'm safe, and that he'll get the bill paid on expenses somehow. Then he leaves to see if he's still being followed.

Thursday of Fair week. It was suddenly much warmer, but the skies were still very dark and overcast. The air felt heavy and threatening. Mid-morning, Nick came up to the office. I started when I saw him, but he spread his hands out again, his attempt at looking harmless. "Maura, Maura. Come on. I only want to talk. I know things got out of hand the other night. I'm sorry. I want to apologise, genuinely."

"You made me look like a lunatic," I said.

"Maura, I don't know what to say. It just all got out of control and I was thinking about my reputation, about what people were saying behind my back. I know, I should've been thinking about you and about our marriage. And Rosie. I'm sorry."

He paused and looked at me. I didn't say anything.

"Look, after this week, I'll quit the fair committee. I couldn't face another year of this grief anyway. And you've been pushed to the side by it, I know that now. Maybe we could book a little holiday and the three of us could spend some time together. We could try to patch things up. Properly."

I stared at him. I was waiting for him to mention how

I'd been at fault too, but he didn't. "Christ, Maura. Do you want me to beg?"

"No. Of course not, Nick. I'm just a bit… "

"You've had a lot to cope with lately," Nick said. His voice was soft. "New job and working with someone who's so difficult."

"Well, I don't think she… "

"Come on, Maura. I don't want the marriage to end. I'm happy with you. This has just been a blip. You don't want to be divorced, do you? You don't want Rosie to come from a broken home?"

The phrase made me feel slightly sick. He was right, I was very worried about the idea of divorce and how it would affect Rosie.

"You mean it?" I asked. "No more, you know. No more violence?"

Nick flinched. He couldn't bear to have his faults pointed out, even when he was in mid-apology for them. "No. No more. I know it's wrong. I've been stressed out. So, look, after this week, how about we all go off on a break? A holiday?"

The office phone rang. "Nick. Can we talk about this later? I've got stuff to finish. I can't think properly. I'll see you this evening, yeah?"

Nick raised his eyes. "Okay, fine, if you're busy." There was a sarcastic edge to his voice. I shook my head as he turned to go, but he caught the gesture and gave me a glare. Then he left.

Kim arrived, early afternoon. She'd been at head office, clearing up loose ends, she said. It looked like she'd come to do the same in Dowerby. "How're you feeling?" she asked. "I just left you sleeping this morning. You and Rosie looked so cute, cuddled up together."

"She's a menace to sleep with, actually. She never stops wriggling! Nick's been here, trying to patch things up. I said I'd go and talk to him later."

Kim shook her head at me. "You mean, you'll go back, make his dinner and get talked back into going home for good. Honestly, Maura. I think you're mad."

"I know you do," I replied. "But you haven't got kids, Kim. It'd be very hard on Rosie if we split up. Nick's talking about quitting the fair committee, so… "

"So he can spend more time with his family," she said, pulling a face.

"Yes, something like that," I grinned. "And he's talking about us going away for a break, maybe next week. I think he really means to try. I have to give it a go, don't I?"

"If you like," said Kim, mildly. It was a phrase she often used when she didn't agree with someone, but wasn't going to argue.

She opened her desk drawers and started piling notebooks and files into plastic bags. "I don't know how I've accumulated so much stuff, it's not as if I've been here all that long. It's the same at the flat. I don't know where I'm going to put it all. I've got a new place in the city centre but it's tiny."

"You've got a new flat?" I asked. That was fast, I thought.

"Well, I can hardly commute from Dowerby every day. And let's face it, there's not much to keep me here, even if I could. I've been staying at a friend's flat but that was always short-term. This new place, you'd love it, Maura. It looks over the quayside. Brilliant view. It's really nice inside but, like I say, pretty small."

"Wow. I'd love to see it."

Kim gave me an odd look. "Well. Yeah," she said. "You must come and see it sometime. If Nick ever lets you off the leash."

"He's not that bad."

Kim shook her head. "Yes, he is," she said. "Sorry, Maura. He is that bad."

I felt a hard lump in my throat but I said nothing.

"You know what," said Kim, looking at her bulging, splitting carrier bags. "I can't carry any more at the moment. I'm going to load these in the car and head off. I'm having a few drinks with some mates from head office tonight."

"Have fun," I said, hoping I didn't sound as choked as I felt.

"Yeah, should be good. I'll pop back tomorrow for the rest of my junk. God, Maura, you know what? I will be so glad when I can leave Dowerby and everyone in it far behind me. What a godawful place this is."

I tried really hard not to take this personally.

At three-thirty I went to Rosie's nursery to pick her up. Her teacher looked confused. "Oh," she said. "Rosie's daddy's already picked her up."

I stared at the teacher. "Her dad?"

"Yes. Did you forget he was coming for her today? She seemed very pleased to see him."

"Oh," I said, as calmly as I could. "I must've forgotten. Silly me."

I went home. I put my key in the door and could hear a murmur of voices, and I could smell cigarette smoke. I hated people smoking around Rosie.

The smoke belonged to Nick's father, who was sitting in my living room, along with his mother, who had Rosie on her knee. Nick wasn't there.

"Maura," they both cried, in far too friendly a way.

"Nick said you'd be back soon," said his mother, Jean. "He had to go off to a meeting about the fair. I hope you don't mind us being here. We were so keen to see little Rosie."

"You've come all the way from Spain?" I asked. "Nick never said you were coming."

"Well," began Jean. "We talked on the phone the other night and he said you were having a difficult time. We thought we could come and, you know, help out."

"Oh," I said. I could only get on with Nick's parents for a small amount of time. He knew this would put me in an impossible position. We couldn't talk properly with his parents breathing down my neck.

"We're more than happy for you to come and stay with us

next week," Jean went on. "It'll be lovely to spend some time with Rosie. And it'll give you a chance to spend a bit of time together. Sort things out."

"Nick asked you that?"

"Yes, dear, and we were more than happy to say yes," beamed Jean.

So, I thought. All that guff about sorting things out. He'd been on the phone to his mother and the whole holiday idea had been her idea. I breathed out hard.

Nick arrived home. He brimmed with false cheerfulness. I beckoned him into the kitchen. "I don't want to spend a week at your mother's," I hissed. "I didn't know that's what you meant by a break. And you could've warned me they were coming."

"Stop fussing," said Nick. "They've sorted their own bed sheets and things. You don't have to do anything. Also, I didn't mean the holiday would be at Mum's. Not at first. But when I looked at our bank accounts I realised you still haven't paid off that overdraft, so I thought I'd better come up with something cheaper."

I sighed. Somehow, he'd put me back in the wrong again.

"Rosie's having a great time," Nick added, nodding towards the living room where she could be heard giggling and singing with her grandparents.

I closed my eyes. "You didn't tell me you were picking Rosie up from nursery either. I looked a real idiot when I turned up and she'd gone."

Nick shrugged. "I only thought about it when my parents turned up. It seemed daft to have her stuck at nursery when they were dying to see her. It's ages since we visited them, you know."

"It also meant I had to come home," I pointed out. I felt like I'd been outmanoeuvred.

"God, Maura. You're so paranoid. None of this was planned. It's meant to help us out, anyway. Try to be pleasant, at least."

So I had to spend an evening making conversation with my in-laws. And cobbling together a meal for four adults. There wasn't much in the house and the kitchen was in a bit of a mess, enough for Nick's mother to make judgements about me, at any rate. And the living room smelled of their cigarettes and booze.

Nick talked a lot about the fair.

"This meeting we had today," he told them. "Some of the stallholders wanted to call it a day. It should go on till Saturday, but we just haven't been getting the crowds in. They're not making any money. But we've just had it confirmed that the local TV company is coming up tomorrow. They should've come up at the start of the week, if you ask me, and that might've brought a few more people into the town. But this is better than nothing. Any publicity's good publicity, eh, Maura, isn't that what the journalists tell us?"

"I don't think so," I said.

Nick took no notice. "Anyway, I had a long chat with the producer and they're going to put a little bit on the local news tomorrow night. They're also going to get some shots to use in a little documentary they're making to run in the New Year, all about interesting local traditions. So at least we might get a good head start on publicity for next year's fair."

"Which you're not involved with," I pointed out.

"No," said Nick. "Maura's not keen on me spending so much time on the fair," he explained to his parents. Jean gave me a tight little smile. "So I've said I might not get involved next year. But I can at least try and salvage what I can from this year's event."

The evening dragged. I had to bite my lip several times, particularly when Jean caught me in the kitchen and advised me, gently, not to be too hard on Nick.

"I know you girls like to be out at work these days," she said, shaking her head. "But I didn't go out to work until my Nick was at high school. I think they expect what they've grown up with, don't they?"

I stopped myself asking if Nick had grown up watching his father regularly hit his mother. But I was still furious with Nick for what felt like a huge, and very simple trap.

The next morning Nick got out of bed and said, "Halle-bloody-lujah!"

"What?" I asked, from under the duvet, still half asleep. There I was, back in the same bed again, as if nothing had happened. But with his parents in the spare room, I didn't have much choice. I realised I was living a lie, and wondered just how long I had been doing that.

"Look at this," said Nick, pulling the covers away from me. I sat up. He'd pulled the curtains aside and the sun was streaming into the room.

"Wow," I said, half-heartedly. "Sunshine. I'd almost forgotten what that looks like."

"Fantastic, bloody great," Nick was saying. "It means the TV shots will look that much better. We might even get a good turnout today. It could make up for the rest of the week. You've no idea what difference the weather makes."

I yawned.

"It's like a curse has been lifted," he said. I rubbed my eyes and tried to feel as enthusiastic as he sounded.

"You know what, it's because that bloody woman's finally gone. She's taken all the crap weather and all the bad stuff with her."

I shook my head. "What're you on about, Nick?"

"Bloody Kim, the witch of Dowerby. She packed up and left yesterday, didn't she? Sally saw her loading up her car. She's gone away and look, suddenly we've got sunshine, you're back home, our luck's turning."

"Well, nice theory, Nick," I said, getting out of bed. I could hear sounds that meant his parents were already up and about and I groaned inwardly. "But there's a flaw in it."

"What?"

"Kim hasn't quite gone yet," I said. "She's coming back to collect the rest of her stuff today."

"Oh?" Nick's eyes glinted. "Still time to give her a ducking, then. There's a queue of people waiting to do it. I think the sight would make up for the whole crap week."

"I suppose so, but I don't think you'll persuade her onto that ducking stool."

"Persuasion might not come into it. I think brute force would be quite understandable. In the circumstances."

After a night at the hotel I get a cab back home, all the time looking over my shoulder. I just have time for a quick shower and change of clothes before heading off to work. But as soon as I put my key in the door, loosening the new little chain, something makes my fingers shake. There is a smell, very faint, but just discernible. Something sweet and heavy. It's coming from inside the flat, not the stairway, because I only catch it as I open the door. I put my head in first and shout, "Hello?" There's the usual silence. I walk in, shivering, with a lump in my throat that I can't seem to swallow. I carry out my usual drill, walking all the way through each room. I open the wardrobe and look under the bed. There's no sign of anyone.

I sniff as I walk around again. Five years of living in a tiny flat, alone, means all the smells are your own. New ones – or should that be old ones? – jump out. I think I can smell something from the past. Nic's aftershave. He always was a bit too liberal with it. I wonder if my brain is making this up. If there is a smell, I can't pinpoint where it's coming from. My own head, more than likely, or so I try to tell myself. I check my watch and suddenly realise I need to get moving or I'll be late for work. Paul told me I should get cabs everywhere at the moment, but that would take even longer than walking. So I get myself cleaned up and ready, and dash out of the door.

After work, I go to visit the little newspaper office. Paul's persuaded me to do this, although I'm nervous at the thought of it. I'm introduced to someone called Vin, Paul's friend.

Vin explains pretty much what I know already, that I could work reporter shifts on a Saturday and he would agree, temporarily, to pay me cash in hand. He asks if I'd like to spend Saturday afternoon shadowing the duty reporter. I agree to this. The duty reporter's a woman about my age, called Lee. She's quite glamorous, I think, with very black hair, heavy eyeliner and matt red lips. But she's pleasant.

"Hey," she says. "Great to meet you. We'd all be delighted to have an extra hand, especially for the weekends. None of us are very struck on doing those shifts."

She has a wonderful voice, low and laid-back. Wasted in print, I think. Like Kim, who was made to be seen, Lee should be on the radio.

She shows me the newspaper's computer system, gives me a list of press telephone numbers for police, for fire and ambulance stations and another list of local sports stringers. She walks me round a shabby kitchen with a vending machine, kettle and microwave oven.

"That's pretty much it," she says. "No great shakes, I'm afraid."

I tell her I feel quite at home.

Then we spend the afternoon typing up what she calls 'overnights', but which are actually stories which will go in the paper the following Thursday. We put some stories onto the website. We make the calls every couple of hours. Men phone in towards the end of the afternoon with match results from local teams. The older ones who've been doing it for years prefer to do it this way and they're not proper journalists, just sports fans, so sometimes their words need knocking into shape. We take the scores down and tap them into the computer. The shift goes quickly. The only problem is that Lee asks me dozens of questions, as reporters tend to do, about where I'd worked before and my family life. It's harder to be vague with someone who asks questions for a living. But I get through it. I only tell her I've worked on the *News* when I've established she doesn't know anyone connected with it. And she doesn't query my name, just types it into the computer to create me a byline. I start to remember that I actually do like this kind of work, better than clearing tables or dealing with leering drunks in the wine bar.

Lee explains that the paper is understaffed during the week too. "We do have a union branch," she says, "although it's hardly very active. But we've been pressing the management to take on another reporter. Vin says if you can hack the weekend shifts, he might take you on full-time. Is that what he told you?"

"Not exactly. I haven't decided if I want to be full-time," I admit.

Lee says a few of the staff are meeting up tonight for a drink, if I'd like to go along. I say no. For now. But the thought of having a proper job, proper friends. I'm in serious danger of getting a life. Working the news shift also means that I keep forgetting, temporarily, about what else is going on. And I am beginning to wonder if things can change. For the better.

Chapter Twelve

It's 5.20 in the afternoon and I'm sitting, slightly out of breath, in a solicitor's waiting room. I can't afford to keep taking taxis as Paul suggests, and I convinced myself I was going to miss the appointment. My insides are bubbling like a pan of hot water. Paul's told me this woman is one of the best family lawyers in the business, or at least among those who take on low income clients like me, and it may be that she can arrange some contact with my daughter. But deep down, I'm sure I don't deserve to be allowed back into the life of this lovely, innocent little girl. Part of me thinks, almost without realising it, that this solicitor is going to tell me as much.

She doesn't look how I'd imagined, although now I can't tell you exactly what picture I'd made in my head. Someone more severe, certainly. This woman is called Susannah Bianchi and she is only as tall as I am. She's also a little on the plump side, which gives her, with her curly dark hair, a soft, motherly appearance. She smiles, shakes my hand and tells me to take a seat. "Well, you're going to have to tell me all about yourself," she says. "All I know is that you say your circumstances are... complicated."

"I'm afraid they are. Very complicated," I say, and I realise I'm shivering. "You might not be able to help at all, I understand that, so... "

"All my clients' circumstances are complicated," smiles

Susannah. "In fact I doubt if you can top some of the stories I've heard. Tell me from the beginning, if you can."

I manage a rather weak return smile and I make a start, glancing at some notes I've made. This was Paul's idea. He said it would help me to say everything I want to say, without rambling too much.

So I explain how I left my home after Kim's death. Susannah scribbles in huge, rounded script on loose sheets of paper. She stops me occasionally to ask questions. I tell her that when I left home, I didn't feel safe. I detail some of the worse violence and the threats. I explain how I've created a false identity for myself and am still working under this assumed name. But how, more than anything, I want to make contact with my daughter again.

She puts her pen down. "Phew. Well, Maura, you certainly have topped a lot of my cases. This is quite a tough one. But you know what, I might be able to help you. It just won't be a quick job."

Susannah tells me it will be her argument that, when I left Dowerby, I was suffering from a kind of post-traumatic disorder, after continued domestic violence and finally witnessing Kim's death. That I failed to contact Rosie because I feared a continued threat from Nick.

I think about this. "Well, I guess that's true. Now that you put it that way."

"I think the best way to begin to arrange contact with Rosie will be through the social services. You may have to agree to a psychological examination. It will just be to establish that you were suffering from a kind of post-trauma, which explains your effectively going into hiding, and also to confirm that you're a fit person to be spending time with your child."

I nod. "But then, will I... "

Susannah holds up a hand. "Like I say, Maura, this won't be a fast process. You still say you don't feel safe around Nick, especially now that this newspaper story is about to break, which could have all sorts of repercussions for him. So we'd want any contact to be at a social services centre, at least at first. So we'll have all contact done via social workers and myself. You won't have to give out your own address to Nick.

"What I will also do is write to Nick myself to tell him that I represent you and that you wish to establish regular contact with Rosie in the near future. And to tell him to expect to hear from us again. He might get his own lawyer, in fact I'd expect that he would."

My hands are still slippery and shaking. "Susannah," I ask, almost afraid to hear the reply. "Might the social services, might they say I can't see Rosie? You know, because I've been away so long?"

Susannah shakes her head firmly. "I'd say that's highly unlikely. If there's any objection it's likely to come from Nick. But we can get a court order. And unless you've had a history of neglecting your daughter when you were at home, or there's some other problem you haven't told me about, then no-one's going to stop you seeing your own child, even if that's under some sort of supervision for a while. Fact is, it's in Rosie's interests to have contact with her mother, and no court is going to disagree with that."

I blink back some tears. I can't really say why. Susannah nudges a box of tissues across her desk. "But, Maura. If you can, start thinking about using your own name again. Get on the books at work. We need to prove you're a functioning, law-abiding person again. Seriously."

I nod, still sniffling.

When I go back home, I do my walk-through of the flat, as usual. I'm alone, but of course I never really feel safe, these days. I take out the little album I have, with the photos of Rosie that Paul gave me. Since the visit a few days ago, I've carried it around in my bag. Soon, I think, it might stop hurting me to look at her face.

***

Later, Paul tells me the story is likely to be in the paper on Friday morning. Unless some other big story breaks, it will be on the front page and also across the centre pages.

"The Crown Prosecution Service says it'll consider reopening the case. That's the last bit we needed confirmed," he says. "It also means that we can still print what we want to print, because no-one's been charged with anything... yet. If they had, it'd scupper us.

"You know what, though, Maura, I'm gobsmacked at how important this two-bit fair is to Dowerby. Honestly, you'd think we were threatening national security. My editor's had Dowerby council's chief exec on the phone, saying the story could threaten the plans to restart the fair, and that this would have a serious impact on the local economy. He quoted a load of figures about how the tourism's suffered over the last five years. Suggested it would be really irresponsible of the paper to rake things up again, as he put it.

"I've also had a letter from Nick's solicitor saying any allegations about his involvement in Kim's death would be actionable. And another letter from Black's brief, saying the same sort of thing." He laughs. "They're all wetting themselves."

I wait. Paul has promised he'll help me find somewhere else to stay for a while. But I don't like to mention it. He's having his second cup of coffee when he brings the subject up. "I still think you ought to move out of here, until the story's in print and we've got a sense of the reaction."

"Where would I go?" I ask, not for the first time.

He clears his throat. "You know Lee?"

I nod.

"She could put you up for a couple of weeks. You'd be bunking on a sofa bed. But she'd make sure you're okay. I've asked her and she gave me the nod. You just have to say yes or no."

"Why would she do that? She hardly knows me."

Paul fiddles with the cuff buttons on his shift. "I went out with Lee, for a while. We're still good mates. She's doing it as a favour, and of course it is just for a very short time. I'll fiddle some expenses to give her some cash. Also, she got broken into a year ago so now her flat's like a fortress. I think it's a good idea, Maura."

"Does that mean she knows all about me?"

Paul gives me a sheepish look.

"Right." I swallow, hard. "You could have asked me first. You might trust her but I've only met her for five minutes. For god's sake, Paul."

I make him leave, although he's trying hard to persuade me to pack up right now. I almost push him out of the door.

Towards Friday lunchtime, I wandered out of the Dowerby office to buy a sandwich. The change in the weather took everyone by surprise. It was much better than the forecasts had predicted. The market square was packed, the stallholders busy and looking cheerful for the first time that week. A band had started to play on the makeshift stage and people had stopped to listen. I even saw a policewoman, in full uniform, dancing on the spot in time to the music, mouthing the song's words. The TV cameraman had his lens trained on her.

A burger stall had replaced the hog roast and the smell of frying food, mixed with the scent of the nearby fudge stall, was overpowering. I thought about buying Rosie a bag of the fudge, but just as I was wondering what particular ingredients had been used to turn the slabs their lurid shades of green and pink, I heard Kim's voice at my elbow. "I wouldn't, Maura. I took a bag of that for the photographers in head office the other day and even they felt poorly afterwards. And snappers eat anything, they're famous for it."

I turned and grinned. "Hello, you. Having a good last day?"

"Yes, so far, but that's because I've only just arrived." Kim gestured around her and grinned. "It's like I've wandered into a parallel Dowerby. It's just like the real Dowerby except the sun's shining and people are happy. Weird."

I laughed.

"I was about to go and clear out the rest of my stuff from the flat, then I'll pop into the office. Shall I bring us some champers?"

"Aren't you driving?"

"Yes, nothing's going to keep me here an extra night. You'll have to drink most of it, Maura, I'm sticking to one glass. Tough on you, eh?"

"Better not," I said, making a face. "Turns out my in-laws are staying with me. They already think badly enough of me, without me coming home squiffy."

Kim looked almost glowing, tanned and cool in her sleeveless white shirt and linen trousers. I watched, enviously, as she strolled off across the market square towards her flat. An old man caught her hands as she passed, told her she was beautiful, and started to dance with her. Kim took it in good spirits, jigged along for a few minutes and then gave the old chap a kiss before waving him goodbye.

I got down to some work. Mid-afternoon – just as Kim arrived at the office, as it happened – the sky went very dark. I glanced at the window and got up to put another light on. There was a rumble of thunder. I heard people outside laughing and giving mock screams. Another rumble, and suddenly the rain came down so hard and fast it felt as if the skies had split. Kim and I grinned at each other as we listened to people shrieking and running for shelter. The band stopped playing.

"Now that's more like the Dowerby I know and don't love," said Kim, opening a filing cabinet and peering inside. She sniffed. "Think I'll leave this stuff for you, it's just cuttings and old papers."

"I know that, I filed most of it," I said.

The phone rang and the news editor asked for Kim. "Hi," she said. "Yes, I'll be back in a couple of hours, just clearing up here." She paused. "When? Today? Really?" Another pause. "The last edition? I'm not sure if that even gets up here. I think we get the first and second runs. Oh, well. Okay, thanks for letting me know." Kim hung up. "That story about the council," she said. "There's going to be an investigation. Some kind of standards body that looks into local government, I think. So they're putting my story in tonight, but only in the final edition. Which of course we don't get in Dowerby. Still, at least it'll see the light of day, which is something, I suppose."

"Good for you, well done," I said.

"My final two-finger salute to Dowerby and its wonderful people," said Kim, with a grim smile.

"Kim, I'm one of those wonderful people. You know, the ones you can't wait to see the back of."

Kim tilted her head to one side. "Oh, Maura," she said. "You don't seriously think I lump you in with the rest of the idiots in this godforsaken dump, do you?"

"Well, you should," I said. "I live here. And I guess I'm stuck here, long after you've headed off for better things."

"Hey," she said, in a hurt tone of voice. "Stop it. I never meant to have a go at you. I think you're a brilliant woman. Yes, I do think you should get out of here too. Because, you know what, I think this stuffy old hole and that git of a husband are wearing you down to nothing. But when I complain about this place, it's not meant to be aimed at you. Honest."

She came over and hugged me. I felt my eyes prickle. "You've kept me sane over the last few weeks."

"Huh," I said, laughing. "I don't think many people would say I've done a great job of that!" Rain pounded on the windows and lightning flickered across the black sky.

There was a sudden, loud thumping noise at the bottom of the stairs. Several pairs of footsteps thudded up towards the office. The door was flung open and Nick, Sally and a few others from the fair committee stood there.

"Well, well," Sally said, with a nasty grin on her plump face. For a moment I was reminded of a time when I was about twelve and was caught on my own in the toilets by the scariest girls in the school. The smile on Sally's face was just the same.

"We've come just in time. We wanted to give you a proper send-off."

Kim blinked, but she didn't look worried. "What's going on?"

Nick and Sally took a step towards her. "Rule is, women not in costume get a ducking," said Nick. He was smiling too, but I could tell he was angry. There was a glint in his eyes that I recognised.

"Oh, no," said Kim, half-laughing and stepping back behind my desk. "You can't do that."

"I think we can," said a voice somewhere in the group. "I don't think you can stop us. Your ducking is by particular popular request."

Kim shook her head. She was trying to sound light-hearted but it didn't quite work. "No way. No. Look, I don't have a change of clothes, everything's packed up."

"You can unpack it again," snapped Sally.

"This shirt is… it cost a fortune. You can't soak it, it'll be ruined." Kim tried to sound convincing.

"Diddums," said Sally.

"Stop it," I interrupted, standing up next to Kim. "This isn't nice, stop it."

Nick strode across the office and gave me a little push. "Back off, Maura. This is nothing to do with you. We all feel we want to say goodbye to Kim properly. And guess what, the ducking pond's empty right now. The storm has seen to that. You won't even have much of an audience. Only us."

Sally was now next to Kim's side and took hold of one of her arms.

"Get off me," said Kim, trying to tug her arm away, but Sally held on. Nick gave me a warning look.

"Kim, just do it." Somehow, these words came out of my mouth. "Just get it over with. It'll only last a minute and then you can get changed and go. I'll help you get a change of clothes out of your bags."

Kim looked back at me as the group more or less frog-marched her towards the stairs. She was wide-eyed and shaking her head. I'd never seen her look genuinely scared before.

"Just go, Kim," I said, again. "It's only a bloody shirt. Let them have their five minutes. Then you'll be out of here."

This is the bit I keep re-playing in my head. Me, telling her to go and get on with it. The look on her face.

As they headed down the stairs, I heard her saying, loudly, "Okay, okay, I'll do it, just let go of my arms?"

I took a deep breath and followed. I was sure I'd done the right thing. The quicker she did what they wanted, the quicker she'd get away. They went out of the door into the square. It was still raining, very hard, and it looked as if a drain had overflowed again, pouring grimy water across cobbles. Puddles bubbled and the raindrops bounced off the ground. The thunder still growled overhead, which was also keeping people inside. I noticed that Jim's café was standing room only and people's eyes were on the small folk band that had moved there and was still trying to play.

I stood in the office doorway, watching as they pushed Kim up onto the wooden platform and towards the gruesome ducking stool, which looked a bit like a baby's swing with a bar across it, but with a seat on the end of a long pole. The sound the rain made, as it hammered on the stall canopies, was like a hailstorm. Kim, who was sticking her chin out and blinking against the rain, was strapped into the seat. The little group cheered as Nick operated the swinging mechanism that suspended it over the tank of water.

There was an even louder cheer as the chair was lowered, with a huge splash into the water. Nick brought it upwards again and Kim spluttered, made a loud scream and shook her head, her soaking hair flapping across her face. The rain gushed down. Sally shrieked with laughter.

"Again!" someone shouted and I heard Kim yelp as Nick swung the seat back down into the tank.

The rain pelted down and I struggled to have a clear view of Kim. This time, it seemed to take longer before he brought it back up again. I saw the councillor from Kim's news story, Black, helping Nick control the seat and push it back down for a third time.

Lightning flashed again, followed immediately by a thunder roll, so loud it had to be right overhead. I felt dizzy and blinked hard. I knew I should tell them to stop. I knew that they didn't usually duck people this many times, it wasn't fair. There was a kind of buzzing noise in my ears and I felt light-headed. My feet were rooted to the spot. My heart was hammering in my chest as I felt everything move in slow motion. My knees buckled and I slumped down hard on the soaking wet stone step and put my head down between my knees. The water was seeping straight through the seat of my skirt. I felt as though I was underwater myself, the sounds around me muted and pounding.

After what I thought was only a few seconds I looked up as the noise of people shouting started to filter, slowly, through to me. A man was asking me if I was alright. I blinked at the grey-white daylight, black shapes swimming in front of my eyes, and I looked towards the ducking pond. People were still shouting and the square seemed to suddenly be full of people. The man helped me to my feet and I muttered something about getting a drink of water. I walked slowly up the stairs, back to the office, locking the door behind me.

My back was to the wall and my head was turned, so I could just see out of the dusty window down on to the market square. Two paramedics lifted Kim's body out of the water tank. They carried her, covered up and on a stretcher, quickly and smoothly across to their ambulance. The window was so small I couldn't see what happened next. But I knew that

Kim was dead. And I knew this, too, I told her to go with them. And I was one of the reasons why Nick was so angry with her. I did nothing to stop them, in fact, I told her it would be alright. I played a part in all of this. I helped them kill her. Kim, my lovely, only, best friend.

There seemed to be a lot of noise in the square for a long time and at one point someone banged and banged on the downstairs door to the office. I didn't move. Eventually it got much quieter. I didn't move. I don't know how long I stood there, exactly.

Eventually, with aching, cramped legs, I walked slowly down the dark stairway and opened the heavy door. Outside the rain had stopped and the sun was back, the ground water turning to steam. I could see people dismantling their stalls, the metal tubes that formed the frames clanking, but there was almost no conversation going on. People were working with their heads down, trying not to look over towards the water tank, which was surrounded by a length of red and white police tape.

A young policeman was standing next to it, staring straight ahead. It was very warm now. Only a few puddles were left and stallholders splashed in them as they tried to pack up as quickly as possible. There was a strange, mixed-up smell, of hamburgers, pastry, wet plastic and something very sickly.

I spotted a huddle of men talking together, near to the tank. I recognised them immediately for reporters and photographers. One of them, a *News* photographer who I'd met before, just once, noticed me. He gave me a brief wave, said something to the others and then they all started heading in my direction.

"Hi," said the photographer, who I remembered was called Sean and who'd come up to Dowerby a few weeks earlier to take some pictures for one of Kim's stories. "Hey, it's Monica, isn't it?"

"Maura," I corrected him, shrugging when he apologised.

"Maura," said one of the others. He was writing down my

name. "You live here, right? We're having a hell of a time with this story. No-one will talk. You knew Kim Carter?"

"Yes, I did, I worked with her."

"You didn't see what happened, by any chance?"

"Yes." I could see their faces change, almost imperceptibly, and somehow at the same time I was aware of the police officer looking over towards me.

"That's the office where Kim worked." I said, pointing. "I work there too. Why don't you all come up and I'll help if I can."

I led the way. I could feel people's eyes burning into my back. I hadn't seen much, but I had to say something. Kim was dead for christ's sake, Kim, my best friend. I felt the fog in my mind start to slowly clear.

They all followed. About five of them, I think. One of them I now know was Paul, but he didn't register with me at the time. They all clustered around and one asked me to tell them what I saw. So I did. I also gave them the whole back story, about Kim's affair with Keith Thomas and about the council story.

I told them how the little group had come for her and forced her to be ducked. How from what I could see, she'd been deliberately held down. I noticed that they started to shuffle their feet and glance at each other. It sounded too incredible to be true. "And one of these was your husband?" one said to me. They looked at each other again. One or two of them stopped taking notes, put the notebooks back in their pockets.

"I don't suppose you can print most of that," I said. I don't remember getting a clear reply. One of them asked me what I'd thought about Kim. I told them I'd liked her a lot. That she was clever, funny, and ambitious. They asked if I had a picture. I thought about this for a moment, opened Kim's desk drawer and took out the box of photos she'd had taken for her interview with the TV station. They looked as if I'd given them all a hundred quid cash, each. "She was pretty fit, wasn't she?" said one of the photographers. There was a murmuring of agreement. It was like she was some woman walking down the street, not someone who'd just been killed.

Then the troupe left. As they were walking down the stairs I heard one of them say, "I know she was ambitious, but some people will do anything to get the splash." They all laughed.

I knew that eventually I'd have to go home. Talking to the reporters, actually telling the whole story, had completely lifted the weird muzziness that had settled in my head. I suddenly realised that Nick might be in a police station, that his parents would be sitting in my house with Rosie, wondering what on earth was going on. Slowly, I walked back to the house, put a key in the door and immediately heard voices, Nick's parents and Rosie. And Nick.

"Here she is! Thank goodness."

"Maura, you're alright. We didn't know what had happened to you."

I went to Rosie and gave her a hug, staring across her at Nick. The air was grey with cigarette smoke. "You're here," I said, confused. "I didn't think… you know… "

"What?" said Nick, raising his eyebrows at me. "I've told the police everything I can."

"But, aren't they going to charge you?"

Nick's mouth opened wide for a moment. "Why would they charge me? What with? Maura, I don't know what you think happened, but it was just a horrible accident. That stool wasn't working properly. It, I don't know, seized up or something. We've explained all that. There'll be an inquest, of course. But the police have assured me they don't think anyone is actually to blame."

Jean looked pale. "Well, Maura was very friendly with this girl, weren't you, dear? I'm sure you're in shock. Why don't you go and have a lie down?"

"Good idea," agreed Nick. He followed me to the bedroom, closing the door behind us. Then he stood just in front of me, his teeth gritted. "Listen to me, Maura. I don't know what you think you saw. But don't you dare go making things up. I've already had to tell a pack of reporters to piss off. They're like animals on a feeding frenzy. I don't know how you can want to do that job, Maura, it's disgusting.

"How do you think I feel about what happened? No, don't bother asking. It's only you who's entitled to any feelings around here, right? You think I'm capable of killing someone on purpose? Really, Maura?"

I stared at him. I couldn't answer honestly, because I didn't really know. I had seen first-hand how violent he could be, but murder? Kim was dead.

"Thanks very much, Maura. Very loyal of you. An accident. That's what it was, got it? And you know what? If you go round giving any other version to anyone, then I can't be held responsible, for you, for us, for anyone." He shut the bedroom door hard behind him.

The inquest was held the next morning, with Dowerby magistrates' court opened especially for it. I went, along with Nick. No press were there, probably because it was unusual to have this sort of hearing on a Saturday and I later realised that no-one would have tipped them off that it was happening.

The coroner was a local solicitor and from the same family firm of lawyers that sent Councillor Black's warning letter.

We all filed into a small, airless room. My mind was racing, still trying to make some sense of the last few hours.

"Because I am very aware of the extreme distress caused by yesterday's tragic events," began the coroner, "I have taken the unusual step of holding this hearing today. A great many people were involved in the incident, and to delay the hearing unnecessarily would only cause further suffering to them and to their families."

He read out some details such as Kim's name, age, address and that she was a journalist working for the *News*. He said there were no next of kin present. I realised Kim had never told me anything about her family. I wondered where they were and if they even knew what had happened. The coroner asked one of the paramedics to come to the witness stand. The man just said he'd been called out to the market square where he and his colleague had found the body of Miss Carter in the water tank. There were some attempts to resuscitate her, but she'd been declared dead at the scene.

A pathologist stepped up and said that Kim had died due to inhaling water into her lungs. It was asphyxiation due to drowning.

Then a police officer took the stand. He said he'd interviewed people at the scene and it was his understanding that 'the mechanical device known as the ducking stool' had become somehow stuck and that attempts to raise Miss Carter from the water hadn't been rapid enough.

"Officer. In an incident such as this," the coroner said, "there is bound to be some speculation as to whether the death could have been avoided or even that it could have been in any way brought about deliberately. What is your opinion of this?"

The officer shook his head, slowly and firmly. "No. The people involved made every attempt to rescue Miss Carter and it seems to be that the stool device was at fault. Any speculation that this was deliberate would be quite wrong. In my opinion."

It seemed to have taken only a few minutes, this so-called investigation into Kim's death.

Suddenly, the coroner was summing up. "Dowerby Fair and the tradition of the ducking stool have brought a great deal of pleasure to hundreds of people over the years. What happened yesterday, however, could not have been foreseen. There was what seems to have been a humorous attempt to bid Miss Carter farewell, on her last day as the district reporter. She was taken, as many young women have gone before her, to be ducked in the pond set up, as is tradition, in the market square.

"Tragically, the stool used in the event malfunctioned and it proved difficult to raise Miss Carter from the water tank.

Attempts to revive her then failed and Miss Carter died, the cause of death being asphyxiation due to drowning. Miss Carter's own panic in this situation may have contributed to the large amounts of water she inhaled.

"Miss Carter was a journalist and there may be those in her own profession who choose to speculate about these events. I wish to state that in my opinion, no individual or group of individuals is in any way to blame for this very tragic event. I record a verdict of accidental death."

I wanted to scream. I swallowed very hard, and made sure I didn't make a sound. Nick gripped my hand, very tightly. Outside the court, he let it go. He, Sally, the councillor and the others clapped each other on the back and hugged. They looked pale, tearful. Inside my head, there were sounds. Kim asking them not to ruin her shirt. Me, telling her to get it over with. Me, telling her it would only take a moment. Thunder and lightning. Kim's scream when they lifted her up from the water. Me, letting her go.

That afternoon, Nick took his parents to the station leaving me with Rosie. For a few moments, I sat, watching her playing with a favourite pop-up book. The same sounds were buzzing inside my head, as if someone was turning the volume up and down, playing the same words on a loop. Something made me stand up and look at the clock. I reckoned I had around forty minutes before Nick got back.

I packed Rosie a case of clothes, and took just a few things for myself. I walked into town and withdrew all the money from my bank account, which was only what the overdraft would allow. Then I went to Kim's flat and walked round to the back lane, where her car was still parked. I strapped Rosie into the back seat, put the bags in the boot and set off.

I didn't know what I was going to do. I just had one thought: to get as far away from Nick as possible.

It took several hours to get to my sister's house just outside Leicester. The traffic was heavy and slow, which was fine with me because I had never driven a car on my own before and my head didn't feel as if it was functioning properly. It felt as if someone had flicked a switch this morning, but I didn't know what it really meant. Rosie slept most of the way. When I got there, I parked Kim's car a little further along the street.

My sister, Veronica, didn't look overjoyed to see me, but fortunately she was very fond of Rosie and this took over everything. She made me tea, eyeing the big holdall I brought in with me, not asking any questions. I told her I'd found out Nick had been seeing another woman. I knew this would press a button with Veronica because my sister's husband had also had an affair, a few years earlier. She agreed I could stay the night and she even said that if Nick telephoned, she wouldn't tell him I was there. He did phone, twice, but she stuck to her word.

I didn't put Rosie to bed until almost ten o'clock, her long sleep in the car meant she wasn't ready to go to bed at her usual time. Then I went upstairs myself half an hour later, creeping around Rosie who was dozing lightly in the spare bed. I wrote a short note asking my sister to take care of her. I told her I didn't feel safe living with Nick any more. I sat, looking at my little girl, her cheeks flushed with sleep, a strand of her fine, still babyish hair across her face. I wanted to kiss her. But I knew that if I got that close, if I breathed her in, I wouldn't be able to leave.

At the time, I felt as though wherever I was going, whatever would happen to me, Rosie was best left out of it. She would be safe with Veronica. I knew that much. And I didn't have a choice. I still believe I did the best thing possible for my little girl, despite the gut-wrenching pain I had as I turned away from her and quietly closed the bedroom door. I didn't think about how that pain would be with me every day, from then on.

When I was sure Veronica was asleep, I crept out of the house and back to the car. I drove it for some miles, along back roads, with no idea where I was heading, until I came to some sort of river. I parked the car at an angle near the river bank. Then I started walking with only my light bag of clothes, back towards the city centre and the railway station. I sat huddled and shivering in a café, drinking coffee after coffee until shortly after seven in the morning, when I could board the first train for London.

"I'd withdrawn almost a whole month's wages," I tell Paul. "So I was able to get a bed and breakfast for a couple of days, then put a deposit down for rent on this flat. I got the café job pretty quickly. I honestly thought I'd pulled it off, especially after a few months went by. I wanted to make it look as if I'd killed myself, you see, and when no-one came looking for me I thought I'd done it. Now that five years have passed, I thought I'd be well forgotten."

"You wanted your sister to keep Rosie with her?" Paul asks.

"Well, I knew it was a long shot, but she never really liked Nick. So I just hoped she'd take her on. I just told myself that for once, she'd do something out of loyalty for me. I suppose if I'm honest, I knew Nick wouldn't stand for that and he'd insist on taking her back. But I tried."

"I don't think your sister put up a fight," Paul says. "I think she contacted Nick straight away when she realised you were missing and they agreed it was best for Rosie to be with her dad. I'm not sure how hard they even looked for you, Maura. I think they did imagine you'd done away with yourself. There was a missing person's appeal, but looking back over the cuttings, I think it was a bit half-hearted."

"Things sort of conspired against me," I say. "First they decide to revive Dowerby Fair after a few years without it. Your man comes forward with his video camera. Then you spot me in the street. I've been amazingly unlucky."

"Don't say it like that. Trust me, it's the best thing. You might get your life back, and Rosie might get her mum back, and we might even get to the bottom of what really happened to Kim. All the things that should've happened five years ago."

I know he's right. Paul has an early start in the morning so he leaves around eleven o'clock. Just after he's gone, I realise he's left his mobile phone on my kitchen table, and just as I'm shaking my head at it the buzzer goes.

I press it to release the lock. "Just come up, idiot," I say into the intercom. Then I open my door and step back into the flat. I hear the footsteps on the stairwell and my door pushed open. But when I turn it's not Paul standing in my doorway. It's Nick. And he's walking towards me.

Chapter Thirteen

Nick is pushing past me, into the flat before I can shut the door. He still wears the same aftershave and the scent of it makes me gag. There's also a slight cigarette smell around him. "Maura. Long time, no see."

I stand, rooted to the spot, trying to decide between running for the front door and staying put. Before I know it, the pointless words are out, "Nick. You found me."

"Easy, once I started looking. I didn't even need the detective in the end. Follow the chubby old hack, wait for him to drop his guard and hey, there you are. You always were a sort of journalist's groupie."

I take a few deep breaths. I mustn't let Nick see me panic. "So," I say. "What do you want?"

"I'll have a beer," Nick grins at me, sitting down on my sofa.

I can feel my body shaking with both fear and anger. Five years of looking over my shoulder, five years of trying to escape, and here he is. Laughing at me. "I haven't got any," I say, truthfully.

"Never mind. I really came for a little chat."

"Go on." My fingers are sweaty as I twist them together.

Nick sits forward. "Come on, Maura. You know what this is about. First you try to wheedle your way back into my daughter's life after running out and leaving her. And if that's not destructive enough, you start raking up all the crap about

Kim Carter. Can't you just let all that go? Some of us have got lives to lead."

"Wrong," I say, trying to keep my voice steady. "I didn't rake up the stuff about Kim. That was the newspaper. They've got some sort of tape of it happening. Paul just happened to recognise me, here in London. I just wanted to forget it all. Talking about it was his idea."

"How nice," Nick curls his lip.

"And I never wanted to leave Rosie. I wasn't thinking straight back then. All I want now is to see her. I don't want to take her away from you. I just want, I don't know, a weekend or something. Please, Nick. That's all."

"Stop thinking about your precious little self, for once, Maura. Christ, you haven't changed a bit, have you? Look. Rosie thinks you're dead. That was what you wanted us all to think, wasn't it? You can't walk back into her life as if nothing's happened. It'll freak her out."

I swallow. "So you're not going to let me see her?"

Nick half-laughs. "I'm bloody well going to put up a fight, if that's what you mean. So I suppose it'd be pretty handy for you if the police start sniffing around the Dowerby Fair incident. But I don't see what difference it's going to make, at the end of the day. It was all looked into at the time, and no-one was brought to blame. Fact is, Maura, you and your boyfriend are wasting your time."

"That's not true," I say. I know I shouldn't wind him up, but I can't seem to help myself. "I mean, it wasn't looked into at the time, not properly. There's a guy with a tape… "

"Have you seen it?" Nick spits. "My lawyer's trying to get it from the paper to see what's on it."

"I haven't actually seen it, Nick, no. But from what I gather, you can see what went on when you and your friends drowned Kim."

Nick stares at me. I can tell he's struggling to keep himself calm. He's breathing hard. "We didn't mean that to happen, Maura. That's the truth. We've all had a really hard time, living with what happened. And now I suppose you think you can get me put away for it. Then you can get your hands on Rosie again. Very clever."

I meet his eyes. The thought of fighting for Rosie instils in me what little strength I have left. No more bullying, no hiding away. "I've told you. It wasn't my idea, to reopen Kim's case, I mean. I don't even know this guy with the tape, all I did was tell Paul my side of the story."

"And a load of distorted lies that'll be."

I breathe deeply. "And," I go on, "I want to see Rosie again, yes. That's got nothing to do with the newspaper stuff. Of course I don't think she'll come and live with me. It never crossed my mind that might happen."

Nick shakes his head. "So if I get put into prison for this stupid accident that happened years ago, who do you think will look after Rosie? Let's hear it, Maura."

I hesitate. "Well. I hadn't really thought about you going to prison. I suppose, though, it would be your parents, wouldn't it? They'd take her, wouldn't they?"

Nick looks down at his hands. "They're dead, Maura. Thought your reporter pal would've told you that."

I close my eyes. "No, he didn't. I'm sor... ?"

Nick doesn't look up and interrupts me, "So, no, Maura, there are no grandparents around. There's only your sister and we both know she wouldn't want to take Rosie on. She sent her back to me like a shot the last time, remember?"

"Nick, I'm sorry about your mum and dad. I had no idea. But, you know, you wouldn't have to worry about me looking after Rosie full time, I'm not as irresponsible as you think... "

Nick jumps to his feet and grabs me by the shoulders. "How... fucking... dare... you?" he shouts, right in my face. "This is not going to happen, do you understand? I am going nowhere and you are not disrupting my daughter's life any more. She's better off without you. What a pathetic excuse for a mother you really are. You always were."

I stiffen and say nothing. He lets go and sits back down, raising his hands. "You really fucking know how to wind me up, Maura."

"Nick. Tell me what you've come to say."

"Listen to me. We both know what it will do to Rosie if this case gets reopened. Even if I don't get found guilty of something, manslaughter or, I don't know. Even if that doesn't happen, think about what she'll have to go through in Dowerby, with all the gossiping and stuff."

"She could move away," I said. "That would probably be a good thing. I don't think Dowerby's a great place to spend your life."

"And lose her friends as well as her family? Great. Listen, Maura, tell your reporter that you don't want the story to go in. You can stop it. The paper won't push the case to be reopened if they won't get a story out of it."

I shake my head. "Don't be stupid, Nick. I've got no say over whether the story gets in the paper or not."

"But you could ask for everything you've said to be taken out?"

"No, I can't," I tell him. "Not now I've spoken to him. I can't stop him printing anything. It's his story now. And anyway, even without my interview, they've still got the tape."

"Yes, but... " Nick sits forward and grasps my hands in his. I can see how hard he's trying to control his temper. "Why don't you ask him to give you the tape? Then there wouldn't be any evidence left at all."

"Why would I do that?" I ask, pulling my hands away.

"Because then you'd know Rosie would be safe. And we could come to some sort of arrangement, amicably, about you getting to see her. Come on, Maura. This is the best way."

I'd forgotten how persuasive Nick could be. No, not persuasive, manipulative. How he can be nice. I think about this for a moment, about whether it was too late to take everything back. But something inside me says it can't work. For one thing, I don't think Paul would hand over the tape to me. For another, I'm sure he wouldn't drop the story, not after all the work he's put into it. It probably wouldn't even be his own decision.

I can't trust Nick to let me see Rosie, once all the dirt's been swept back under the carpet. And also, I still wouldn't have lain Kim's ghost to rest. I don't think I can get my life back until I have. In fact, I don't think I deserve to get my life back until I've got some justice for her. I sent her off to her death. I told her to go and get it all over with, when somewhere, deep inside, I knew things would get nasty. I should've been sticking up for her. I should've helped her fight them off. I let her down and I need to set it right. I can't live with this guilt any longer. My mind races through all this in a matter of seconds. Suppose I tell Nick I agree, would he leave the flat? Then what would I do, keep running? No. It's time to stop.

"There are all sorts of reasons why I can't do this, Nick. Paul would never give me that tape and he wouldn't drop that story. And anyway, one of the reasons I ran away, it wasn't just because I was scared, it was because I always felt responsible for what happened to Kim. You and the others from the fair thought Kim had left that day. It was me who told you she'd be back. I told her to go with you and that it would be alright. I feel like I betrayed her. Delivered her to you. And I was too weak to put up a fight or help her out. So this is a way of getting justice for her, even though it's a few years too late. Sorry, Nick. I have to just go through with it all."

Nick stands up. He is talking through his gritted teeth and that old, all encompassing sense of pure fear runs through me.

"So, Maura. You make a damn fool out of me when we're married and now you stroll back into my life and wreck it all over again. I spend five years rebuilding mine and Rosie's life and you're just going to take everything away from me, out of some sense of justice? You worthless, stupid cow. This is you getting your revenge, isn't it, pure and simple. Just because we had a few rows and I lost my rag now and then. Just because I played away from home once or twice. This is you, quite happy to destroy me and countless other people, including your own daughter, just to get your nasty little own back."

In the films, someone being attacked often thinks on their feet, acts quickly. That's not real, though. Whenever Nick threatened or hurt me, it was like my brain and body closed down. I couldn't think. Couldn't move. Just wanted it all to end, and then I could come back to life.

There's a bleeping sound. It's Paul's mobile phone ringing. Nick whips round and glares at it like it's a person. "Switch that thing off," he says. "I'm still talking to you."

I hesitate, about to tell him it's not my phone, and he grabs my hair and hisses, "Switch that thing off." He walks me over to the kitchen table, still gripping my hair, and I pick up the mobile and switch it off.

Nick pushes me up against the wall and bangs my head back against it. "Okay, Maura," he whispers, his face right up against mine. "You have one minute to change your mind." He glances up above my head where there's a clock. "I'm timing," he says. "Fifty-five seconds."

I put my hands up and try to push them against his face, but I always was a hopeless fighter. He grips my hair even tighter, knees me in the stomach and pushes me down into a bundle on the floor. I'm clutching my body, trying to breathe through the deep internal pain.

"Forty seconds," he says, still in a whisper.

I'm sobbing quietly, trying to think of a way of buying some time. "Nick, please, Nick. Let's just talk again, please. Please. Hurting me won't help. If anything happens to me, you're the first person the police will come to."

"Oh, I've thought of that, Maura, don't you worry about me. I've got my alibi sorted out. Sally will be ringing the health centre's out of hours line and asking them for advice on my stomach bug right about now. And don't worry about leaving traces of me. They'll have nothing to go on when they've eventually found you. It'll look like the only person who was here tonight was your boyfriend, the ace reporter. What a shame. It's a terrible thing to be accused of something you didn't do."

I'm shivering all over now, ice-cold. "But Nick," I say, my teeth chattering. "Why risk it? Especially if I promise to try to get that tape for you."

Nick snorts. "Because no way am I going to go to jail over what happened to that poisonous little slag Kim Carter. And I don't trust you an inch. I know you won't help me, Maura, you'll go running straight to the police, or the press, or whoever will take you seriously. I might as well get done for getting rid of two bitches instead of one. It makes sense to me, Maura." He glances up at the clock. "And guess what? You've run out of time."

"No," I scream. "I said I'd changed my mind. I said I'd help you."

"Too fucking late," says Nick and he grips my neck and starts to squeeze.

There's a loud banging noise somewhere. The sound of something being broken. Shouting. I can't make out the words or who the voices belong to. I think I hear someone saying, Maura.

I try to say, "No. I'm not Maura." I try to force the words through his grip on my throat. There's a stinging, burning sensation before my vision goes blurry and I feel myself slipping. Further and further away.

The Northern News. May 15th

SEVEN YEARS FOR DOWERBY MAN IN "WITCH DUCKING" HORROR

A man from the small town of Dowerby was today jailed for a total of seven years for his part in the drowning of a former News *reporter during a bizarre 'witch ducking'.*

A Crown Court judge has today also slammed the Dowerby police and coroner for failing to properly investigate the death at the time.

The Old Bailey heard how 35 year old Nick Wood was part of a 'lynch mob' that dragged 28 year old Kim Carter to a makeshift ducking pond and repeatedly held her under the water until she lost consciousness. Although the judge agreed that the group did not intend to kill Miss Carter, he told the court their reckless actions nevertheless led to her death.

The incident took place six years ago at Dowerby Fair, a once annual traditional week-long event, celebrating old customs. The court heard how Wood, who worked at the SynTrekNorth paint factory, had taken the role of the fair's judge, allowing him to 'duck' women in the town. According to reports, members of the fair committee were angry with Miss Carter because of her adverse newspaper reports on the event and her exposé of council corruption.

The tragedy happened when Wood and several other members of the fair committee dragged Miss Carter from her office in Dowerby Square. She was taken to the recreated ducking pond and strapped into a stool, before being repeatedly lowered into the water and held under for long periods of time.

An inquest held at the time ruled Miss Carter's death as a tragic accident. The coroner accepted evidence that the ducking stool had malfunctioned, but this evidence and the equipment itself was no longer available.

The longstanding Dowerby Fair was scrapped. It was only when plans were announced to revive the event that amateur film-maker Brian Guy came forward with a video tape, taken on the day of the killing. Police then reopened the case.

The court also heard that father-of-one Wood repeatedly attacked his former wife, Maura Conway. Ms Conway, 34, now a journalist in London, left the marital home shortly after Ms Carter's death. Wood pleaded guilty to Miss Carter's manslaughter, conspiring to pervert the course of justice, and assaulting Ms Conway.

Jailing Wood, Judge Leonard Jobson said: 'It's clear that you and your fellow members of the Dowerby Fair committee held a grudge against Miss Carter and on that fateful afternoon you chose to punish her using the ducking stool, a device which had been used as part of the town's fair.

'But you allowed your feelings to get the better of you and this reckless repeated ducking resulted in Miss Carter's death.

'You had already been violent towards your wife. Five years later you sought her out and attacked her again because you believed she had implicated you in Miss Carter's death.

'I believe that you are a man who finds it impossible to control your temper and that you are a danger to women in particular. In the light of the seriousness of these incidents and your calculated attempts to cover up Miss Carter's death, I am sentencing you to seven years in prison.

'I am very disturbed to note that an inquest held just after this incident failed to ask the relevant questions. I would also urge Northern Police Force to carry out an *investigation as to why Mr Guy's video evidence was not looked into at the time.'*

Three other past members of the Dowerby Fair committee were also found guilty of charges ranging from assault to conspiring to pervert the course of justice. Former Dowerby councillor Andrew Black was fined £400. Café owner James Portland of the Market Square, Dowerby and Sally Maxwell, 34, of Oak Lane, Dowerby, were each fined £250.

KIM CARTER
When Kim joined the News *she was like a breath of fresh air, writes our features editor Nicky Moss.*

Kim was not only a beautiful person, she was an excellent reporter. Yes, us girls in the office were jealous, but Kim won everyone over with her hard work, talent and charm. It's no secret that Kim had a turbulent love life and was a constant subject of office gossip. But there was so much more to Kim than that.

Her exposé of corrupt practices at Dowerby council led to the resignation of several key councillors and officers, and won her a posthumous Mitchell Award for investigative journalism.

We at the News *have now agreed to set up a fund in Kim's name to help young women trainee journalists. Kim's talent was sadly lost to us all. But perhaps her name will continue to inspire other young hopefuls in our profession.*

Lee and I are getting things ready for Rosie's tenth birthday party. The living room in our flat is awash with pinks, purples and glitter. The woman from Princess Parties is setting up a table with brightly-coloured nail varnishes, blushers and lipsticks. "Oh my god," says Lee, in her slow, husky voice. "I'd have loved this when I was ten. I'd have killed for it. Having my nails and make-up done. Wow."

"I know," I grin, licking cupcake icing off my fingers. "I mean, part of me thinks it's ghastly, but Rosie's been through a lot in this last year. And making new friends is tough enough, so if this gives her a bit of extra street cred, then what the heck!"

I put my head around Rosie's bedroom door. "Alright?" She nods and smiles at me, then goes back to admiring herself in the mirror. She's created a party outfit out of shorts, tights, a sparkly top and about a hundred bracelets and necklaces. I look at how beautiful she is and my eyes go wet.

I can't believe this is really happening. This is something I'd fantasised and dreamed about, for five long, lonely years. My daughter, with me, and no-one to threaten or shout or tell us what to do.

In the end, it was Sally who'd brought Rosie to me, without a fight. Nick was arrested the night he'd tried to strangle me, after Paul kicked down my door and restrained Nick until the police arrived. He was never allowed bail. Sally had already been sent a letter asking that I should be allowed to see Rosie. She called my solicitor and offered to bring her to London. We met them at King's Cross station. Sally gave Rosie a hug and she spoke so kindly to her, part of me felt guilty for splitting them up. But there she was. My beautiful little girl, standing right in front of me. And that, for now, was all that mattered.

There were tears and sleepless nights, for weeks. It took a long time for Rosie to trust me, even to accept that I really was her mother. She barely remembers me from Dowerby. She had to have a lot of counselling, in fact we both did. If I'd thought she would just slip into my life, I was wrong. Rosie is still settling into her new school and her home, the new flat I share with Lee from the newspaper office. And she's so bright she scares me a bit, but I love that. I missed out on so much, I'm determined so soak up every last minute with her now.

I work full time at the weekly London paper and I've just passed its in-house training scheme. We're all permanently skint, but Lee has a plan to start sending freelance articles to magazines, get our names known, earn a bit of extra cash. Living with Lee worked out for the best. And I'm not looking over my shoulder any more. At least, not so much. Habits are hard to break.

It's taking a while for me to say goodbye to Kim and to realise I'm not as guilty as I thought. She's still there with me, whenever I write an intro I'm proud of, whenever I crack a dirty joke, whenever I eat something sweet, sickly and bad for me. But saying goodbye is a long job. And I'm glad I don't have a deadline.

Acknowledgements

This is a novel that's been a long time in the making. But thanks to everyone who's ever shown faith in it and in any of my writing.

Shelley Weiner and the late Alice Thomas Ellis affirmed the original idea at my first ever writing course, giving me the confidence to see it through. Very special thanks to Legend Press and all involved with the Luke Bitmead Bursary, in which the novel was a runner-up. Also thanks to everyone in the Creative Writing school at Newcastle University, where I was very proud to complete my PhD. The generous advice and input of staff and students has improved my writing enormously.

Finally and most important of all, I could never have done this without the unfailing love, support and patience of Mark, Naomi, Patrick and Mary, which has meant everything.

Exclusive
Additional
Material

Reflection

In my writing life, *In Too Deep* feels like a long time ago. But it's actually only five years since it had its first print run. I'll never forget the excitement when it was shortlisted for the Luke Bitmead Award and then, a little while later, when I got my first ever publishing contract with Legend Press.

In Too Deep had been a long time in the writing. People often ask authors how long it takes to write a book and of course, there is no single answer to that. I wrote the novel on and off while I was working full-time for the BBC, studying part-time for a Creative Writing PhD and bringing up two school-age children. So the writing was, let's just say, sporadic!

Once I had a full manuscript, it kept getting nibbles of success – it was shortlisted for one of the first Andrea Badenoch Awards run by New Writing North, for example, and occasionally I would show it to someone in the industry who would praise it very highly. But I was so scared of rejection that I never really pushed it out. That's a mistake I won't make again with any of my writing!

It was the Luke Bitmead entry that brought it to the attention of Legend Press and I'll always be grateful for their faith in the novel.

So – what was behind the story and why did I stick with it for so long?

The setting of Dowerby was inspired by the small town

of Alnwick, in Northumberland, where I used to have a base when I worked for the BBC. Alnwick is an odd little place: in many ways, very quaint and charming, but like most small towns, it's also very close-knit and old-fashioned. Up until the mid-2000s, it held an annual summer fair, where the high point was a re-enactment of the medieval ducking stool. Local women would queue up to be ducked into a tank of water by a man dressed in a judge's costume. It always struck me as quite an eccentric thing to do and so my dark journalistic mind wondered what would happen if that ducking stool was put to a very bad use.

(If anyone from Northumberland is reading this – hello, and let me assure you that all of the characters and main events are entirely fictional).

I had a strong, original plot on my hands and that's the prime reason why I kept at it, over the long time it took to complete a first draft. But there were other themes behind the novel, too.

I was a working journalist, as I've mentioned. It's one of those jobs that always sparks people's interest. Journalists are always being asked how they find their stories, for instance. They're mocked for using 'journalese' in their writing. They're often regarded with suspicion – more so, these days, than they were back in 2013, of course. And they're powerful. They can do a lot of good and cause a lot of trouble.

I wanted to use the novel to shed a little light on how local journalism works. Kim, one of the main characters, is a reporter on a local paper who is sent to cover the patch around Dowerby, a fictional small town (that looks a lot like Alnwick). Maura, the novel's narrator, is a wannabe journalist who learns about the job from Kim. A fellow reporter told me that he felt trainee journalists could learn a lot about newspaper reporting from reading the novel – which I took as a huge compliment.

But times move on. If *In Too Deep* was a defence of local journalism, then my second novel, *This Little Piggy*, takes a much harsher look at the industry. Set at the time of the miners' strike in the mid-eighties, that later novel is much more about what can go wrong when the press loses sight of its ethics and takes a political side when it ought to strive for balance.

Since *In Too Deep* was published, the news industry's been hit by phone hacking scandals and fake news. Trust in journalists is not high – only around twenty-five per cent of people in the UK expect journalists to tell the truth, according to Ipsos MORI. To put that in perspective, that's the same percentage of us who trust estate agents to be entirely honest.

Was *In Too Deep* too soft, then, on a problematic industry? I don't think it was. What the novel tried to champion was the vocation of being a journalist – the aspects of the work that brought me and many others into the job. These aspects include the urge to expose injustice, to hold authority to account, to inform and to amuse. Oh, and to tell a good story. Those ideals are still present in trainee journalists today – I know, because I teach journalism. No one goes into the industry planning to create fake news. And even Kim in *In Too Deep*, with her messy personal life, wanted to do the best she could as a journalist. With the right circumstances, I reckon she could have gone far.

There's another even darker issue at the heart of *In Too Deep* and that is domestic violence. I happen to know quite a bit about domestic violence against women. For several years I was a trustee of the charity Women's Aid in Newcastle. I can write now with the hindsight of readers' responses to the narrator Maura's plight when her marriage becomes increasingly controlling. There were many women readers who told me they recognised what Maura experienced and the lengths she went to escape it. That was very heartening. There were also a few – a very few – who said things like, "I don't believe Maura would leave her child." I think what they were really saying was, "I don't believe I could leave my child," which is a different thing and perhaps suggests a failure to truly put themselves in the mind of someone other than themselves. Because Maura's story is a composite of a whole host of real women's stories, some of whom did have to leave their homes and families, for similar reasons. Sometimes, in genuine fear for their lives, women have to make drastic, heartbreaking decisions and sometimes they're even led to believe their children are better off without them. According to the UK charity Living without Abuse, domestic violence affects one in four women, with an average of two women being murdered every week by their partners or ex-partners. Bear in mind too that this is a hidden crime and often goes unreported, so some of those figures may be an under-estimate. The reluctance of Maura's neighbours to help or even to believe her is based on something I witnessed first-hand. I'm afraid this is happening to a woman near you, right now. For real.

But also, women can survive this abuse and go on to build new and better lives. I'm glad that happened to Maura at the end of the novel. She was a bit of wimp and a pushover at the beginning, but I left her at the end in a position where she would be unlikely to fall for an abusive partner ever again and could concentrate on rebuilding her relationship with her daughter. Five years on, is Maura happy? I'm sure she is.

You may notice I talk about the characters as if they're real. Authors often do that. Even though we are responsible for inventing characters in the first place, the best writers relinquish control over them and allow them to take over the direction of the story. Kim was a case in point: she started off in my head as much more shallow and self-centred. But her good heart and intentions came to the fore as I wrote.

So how do I feel now about *In Too Deep*? I'm proud of it for its original plotline and the tough themes it tackled. Like all writers, I learn my craft as I go along, by writing more. So when I re-read *In Too Deep*, I do spot flaws in technique and style and things I feel I might do better, if I was writing this again. But it was a debut novel and I am not alone in that urge to constantly redraft – all writers have it and it's a good job that we have editors who can tell us when to stop.

If you're new to *In Too Deep*, then I hope you enjoyed it. I hope it kept you turning the pages and that you cared about the characters. And maybe, that you were sorry when it came to the end. Because that's how I feel when I read a really good novel – and if I inspired that response in anyone, then I'd be very happy.

Come and visit us at
www.legendpress.co.uk

Follow us
@legend_press